Jared ran a hand through .... ow whether to shake you or love you. What in the hell am I supposed to do with you, Cassie?"

"Love me?" She was certain she'd only thought the unexpected words, but one glance at his face, and she knew she'd said them aloud.

Her cheeks flamed at what she'd done. Where had that thought even come from? Much less the words? She couldn't want him to love her. She couldn't. He was a Yankee. And a thief. And . . .

And she was fast falling in love with the devastating Yankee sitting so proud and straight beside her. When had it happened?

Cassie moistened her lips. "Jared?" she whispered, longing in her voice.

He jerked the carriage to a sudden halt and pulled her into his embrace. "Oh, Cassie, my sweet."

He kissed her hard and long. Dragging his hands through her hair, he buried his fingers along her cheek, her chin, her throat. Cassie gripped his shoulders, hardly able to stay upright under his loving foray and the flurry of unknown emotions now coursing through her with every beat of her heart.

As if her action had drawn him to his senses, Jared eased away from her. Cassie moaned in mute protest.

"Come home with me, Cassie?" he asked in a husky voice.

She could no more have refused him than she could have refused her heart to beat. At that moment in time, nothing else mattered more than the look in his eyes and the beloved catch in his voice.

Her answer was no more than a whisper of sound on her lips.

"Yes," she said.

JOYCE ADAMS
MOONLIGHT MASQUERADE

ZEBRA BOOKS
KENSINGTON PUBLISHING CORP.

ZEBRA BOOKS are published by

Kensington Publishing Corp.
850 Third Avenue
New York, NY 10022

First Printing: August, 1994

Printed in the United States of America

To my sister, Sandra—the inspiration for Cassandra. Your strength, beauty, and love have always been an inspiration to me.

Thank you with love.

One

Thankfully the sprawling two-story house was ablaze with lights and music. That meant she was less likely to be missed from the Admiral's birthday celebration if she slipped away for a few minutes.

Cassie Van Dorn lifted the hem of her cream silk gown, stilled her crinoline from making any betraying rustle, and started up the wide staircase. Halfway to the top, the sound of voices alerted her to a couple entering from the veranda. Her heart dropped to her toes in a sudden lunge.

Taking a deep breath, she dashed up the remaining steps in a flash, knowing her dark hair and cream-colored gown would stand out like a beacon against the mahogany staircase. She took refuge in the first room she came to. A bedroom. Pressing herself against the wall, she strained to hear if the people were following her up the stairs.

If she were detected, she'd never be able

to explain what she, a guest, was doing upstairs, hiding in a bedroom like a common
thief. Heaven only knew what would happen.

It seemed all of Washington was on edge
since the sudden rash of robberies committed
by the man the papers had dubbed the
"Masked Marauder." Cassie hoped he didn't
mind that she was infringing on his work.
She stilled the nervous giggle that threatened
to bubble up and waited.

She tried to breathe evenly and slow her
racing heart. She was new at this business of
sneaking around a friend's house. Much less
at the act of thievery.

It seemed that she stood there motionless
for agonizing minutes. Finally, laughter
drifted up the stairs, and she heard the couple returning to the veranda.

Cassie held in the sigh of relief, not daring
to allow herself that luxury. Someone else
could walk up those stairs at any moment.
She had to do what she'd come here for. And
soon.

She had to steal those papers.

So much depended on her success. Will
Radford had impressed upon her the importance of this mission. She shivered at the
word "mission." No one had been more
caught off guard than she when quiet, unassuming Will had approached her for help.
She'd thought he was nothing more than another lobbyist and had been surprised to

learn that he was the head of the secession plot.

Of course, she'd known about the plot—who in the capital city hadn't heard of it, but she'd thought it had died three years ago. Only a few people knew it had been revived as a desperate attempt to save the Confederacy. And right now, people were depending on her.

Creeping to the edge of the doorway, she peered around. The amorous couple had disappeared, and now the path to the Admiral's bedroom appeared unhindered.

Her heart beat in uneven double time. She definitely was not cut out for this sort of thing. The remembrance of a war that had gone on too long prodded her onward. However, the temptation to simply walk back down those stairs and forget the packet of papers taunted her, daring her to give in.

She resisted the temptation. Just the thought of her parents separated for another three years was enough to make her go through with her reckless plan. Ever since Papa resigned his commission to become a field surgeon in Virginia, her mother had gotten into one scrape after another. Heaven only knew what trouble Mama would get into if Daddy didn't come home soon.

Gathering her courage about her like a shield, Cassie stepped out into the hallway and slipped along in the shadows to the Admiral's bedroom. She paused at the door, her hand outstretched. What if it was locked? What if someone was inside?

Questions and worries chased each other across her mind. Cassie caught her lower lip between her teeth and forced herself to continue with her plan. Clamping her hand over the doorknob, she turned the knob. Thankfully, the door opened easily under her hand. She pushed it open only far enough to allow for her wide skirts, slipped inside, then hastily shut the door behind her.

The only illumination came from a silvery beam of moonlight streaming in through the half-opened draperies of the wide window. On tiptoe, she crept across the floor to the armoire.

If the information from their informant was correct, the papers she needed were inside the Admiral's uniform pocket in the armoire. The Admiral had been seen tucking the papers into his front pocket at the office earlier that day.

So far, Cassie knew that the packet of papers wasn't in the dress uniform he was wearing at the party—that much she'd learned from dancing with him and surreptitiously checking his pocket when she'd purposely tripped and let her hand brush down his chest.

She opened the door, and as the hinges squeaked she squeezed her eyes tightly closed, as if the act would keep anyone else from hearing the betraying sound.

Feeling foolish, she snapped her eyes open and scanned the clothing inside. There it was. She felt the uniform pocket and heard the wonderful sound of crinkling paper. A smile tipped her mouth, her first true smile of the nerve-wracking evening.

Success! She drew the papers from the jacket and crossed to the window. These were the ones, right down to the tell-tale red ribbon holding the papers together that she'd been told to look for. Carefully, she untied the ribbon around the packet and unfolded the papers. Tilting them towards the moonlight, she scanned the contents.

Her mouth dropped open as comprehension dawned. In her hands she held the defense plans for the city of Washington. The thin red ribbon slipped from her numbed fingers and drifted to the floor.

Her hands trembled. Anyone caught with these papers in their possession would, without a doubt, be hanged. For a moment, fear bubbled up, threatening to choke her. But it was too late, her course had been chosen. She *had* to go through with this. In the right hands, these papers could force the secession of the capital city and end the war much sooner.

Cassie hurriedly folded the papers and tucked them away in the only place she could think of—the low decolletage of her gown's bodice. She intended to plead a headache as soon as she reached the safety of the party downstairs and could get her mother away. The last thing she needed was to be caught up by a partner for a dance. The papers would surely betray her.

Smoothing the lace-edged silk back into place, she hoped she wouldn't be required to take too deep a breath. The material was practically straining against the seams with the additional padding of the papers.

Jared Montgomery eased back, deeper into the shadows provided by the draperies and adjusted the black mask covering the upper half of his face. It was imperative that he keep his true identity secret. No one could know yet that the infamous thief the city was in an uproar over was, in fact, a Union officer.

The irony of the situation struck him, and he let a wry smile slip free. The daring little minx had beaten him to the prize. He had to admit that this was a first. Beaten at his own game, and by a woman at that.

She had intelligence and guile, he'd give her that. No gentleman would dare to search a lady in the place where she'd hidden the papers.

However, although the men under his com-

mand called him "Sir," he'd often been referred to as the opposite as well. The barest
curve of a smile creased his face—the dark-
haired beauty was in more danger than she
knew.

In the faint light, he studied her appreciatively. She wasn't tall; he doubted if the top of
her head would even reach his chin. The
moonlight turned her dark hair into deepest
black velvet, each curl shining in the moon's
beam of light. She had a heart-shaped face
and eyes of the deepest blue. Beneath the
creamy-colored evening gown she had the
body of a goddess. As if to taunt him, the lady
thief smoothed her hand across the cream silk
and lace of her bodice.

Jared jerked himself up, reminding himself of the packet of papers. He was here to
get the documents, not to allow himself to
be bewitched by a lady thief, no matter how
tempting the woman. She was likely as not
working for the head of the secession plot—
the man who'd murdered his brother.

Desire cooled within him to be replaced by
icy anger. He'd vowed revenge, and nothing
would stand in his way of killing the man
who'd taken Bryan's life, only days after his
eighteenth birthday.

Those papers in the wrong hands could
cause many more deaths. There was no way
on earth that he was going to stand by and
allow that to happen. The Admiral had been

a fool to bring the papers home to study them—where any amateur thief could steal them. Those plans should be locked up.

He needed those papers, and he intended to get them, one way or another. He had secret orders to report with the documents first thing in the morning.

He wasn't leaving the party until he had gained possession of those papers himself, and he knew the identity of the bewitching thief.

He watched her adjust the bodice of her gown again, and he could almost imagine that it were his fingers tracing the outline of the papers against her soft skin. Earlier she'd stopped close enough beside him to check the papers in the moonlight of the window for him to have reached out and done just that.

She cast a nervous glance about the room, skipping over the window coverings. Jared smiled beneath the black mask. She was definitely an amateur, that much he knew. He could practically feel her holding her breath, not daring to release it until after she'd made it safely out of the room—something he couldn't allow to happen. It was time to make his move.

If only he had been a few minutes earlier and beaten the lady thief to the papers, things would be a lot easier. Now he had to steal them back.

She turned away toward the door, providing him the perfect opportunity. As a seasoned soldier, Jared knew when to take what providence offered him. In one soundless move, he eased the window covering aside; the heavy draperies moved almost imperceptibly. Taking two long strides, he caught her, hauling her up against him and clamping a hand over her mouth.

Cassie opened her mouth to scream, but the wide calloused hand splayed over her mouth caught the sound. Panic welled up in her, and she tried to twist away. Her frantic movements did no good; the firm, muscular arms drew her back tighter against a broad male chest. It felt as if she were bound with bands of steel. She was well and truly caught!

Terror surged over her. Jail . . . prison . . . a hangman's noose loomed before her. Determined not to give up to her captor, she twisted, struggling against his hold, kicking and thrashing frantically. Within seconds she was breathless, her chest heaving beneath the stranger's strong hold.

Cassie fought back the panic that threatened to choke and overwhelm her. She wouldn't give in to it. She wouldn't. To give in now would . . .

Her mind caught the thought and held to it as tightly as the stranger holding her. Did she dare to simply do that? Right now, Cassie knew she'd dare anything to elude capture and what would surely follow.

Swallowing down the icy cold fear that ate at her from inside, she clamped down the compulsion to fight, and forced herself to suddenly, unexpectedly, make her body go limp. The man holding her stiffened in surprise, and the next instant she kicked back with all her strength, catching him full on the shin. Her heel throbbed from the contact, but she gritted her teeth against the pain, readying herself to escape.

Her captor swore and loosened his hold slightly, and she grabbed her chance. Jerking free, she spun around and raced for the door in a blur of cream silk and petticoats. Past the door, Cassie gulped in air and ran full speed down the stairs, not caring who might see her.

"Damn," Jared swore, shards of pain making him catch his breath.

She'd done the impossible—she'd escaped him.

Jared pulled off his mask and shoved it into his dark blue uniform pocket. Without the mask he became just another Union officer at the party. The black mask would do him more harm than good now. His mysterious lady thief was rejoining the party downstairs, and he had to stop her before she got away completely. No matter what, he intended to see that she didn't pass the papers on this night.

He spun around and headed for the door, precious seconds and painful steps behind her. When he reached the stairs, all he saw was the back of a raised hoop, cream-colored skirts, and a delicate ankle disappearing around the ground floor corner.

"Damn," he swore again, under his breath. She was like trying to catch quicksilver.

Once downstairs, he was forced to survey the ballroom to locate his lady thief. He hadn't imagined there would be this many dark-haired women of approximately the same height scattered around the room. He counted four at first glance, then dismissed two as obviously the wrong build.

Another flash of cream amongst the yellows, blues, and whites caught his attention. She was the right height; he ran his trained eyes from her dark hair to her satin-clad toes, pausing at the golden velvet sash encircling her small waist, and smiled. He'd recognize that shapely minx anywhere. A man didn't quickly forget a woman with the body of a goddess.

Jared quickly zeroed in on the only woman that met his remembered description of the lady thief. Besides her body, the slightly tousled dark curls, flushed cheeks, and a too-snug bodice gave her away.

Now to start his campaign.

* * *

Cassie scanned the dancers and wished for the umpteenth time that she could go home. She'd fled the upstairs bedroom nearly ten minutes ago and was becoming more nervous with every passing minute. The papers scratched against her breast, and she feared that any movement would give away the location of the plans.

However, she'd failed to convince Mama to leave yet. Her mother seemed determined to ignore her frantic signals to leave, blithely unaware of any problem. Alicia Van Dorn continued chatting away with the circle of women stationed near the veranda doors.

Cassie signalled again, but once again was ignored. How could Mama not realize something was wrong? Cassie narrowed her eyes in thought. Was her innocent-looking mama up to something again?

Cassie tapped her foot impatiently and flashed a quick survey of the room. It seemed calm, she assured herself, no cry of alarm yet. However, she had to get herself and her mother out of here before all hell broke loose over the missing documents. She could be placing Mama in danger, too. And she wouldn't allow that to happen.

The memory of her pretty, petite mother embroiled in the Baltimore riots still caused her to catch her breath in a shudder of fear.

They'd been visiting Aunt Vangie, and the next thing, before Cassie could intervene, her mother had joined the throng rioting against the incoming Yankee troops. It had taken ingenuity, the help of Secretary Cameron, and a hefty sum of money to get her mama safely out of that situation.

Next, Mama had befriended Widow Rose Greenhow only a month before the widow had been arrested and jailed as a Confederate spy. Cassie even suspected that her mama had carried a message or two for the wily spy. However, she'd never actually found proof, but her mama's vague answers still bothered her.

Bothered? Actually it had scared Cassie down to her toes. And now, she was sure that Mama's impulsiveness and boredom had gotten her involved in another wayward scheme of some sort or other. But what was it?

She sighed heavily. Sometimes Cassie felt as if she were the mother and her mama were the recalcitrant child. If only Daddy could come home from the Confederate field hospital, everything would return to normal. But that couldn't happen until this war was over.

Meanwhile, she'd do *anything* to help end it sooner. Anything.

She smoothed her bodice with one hand, checking that the papers still rested securely in their hiding place. The betraying crinkle of paper caused her to wince. She'd definitely have to get out of here. She couldn't dare risk dancing with anyone.

The sooner this evening was over, the better. That thought had scarcely left her mind when she felt a shiver of apprehension run down her spine. The fine hairs at the base of her neck prickled, and she stiffened at the sensation.

Immediately, Cassie sought out her mama, sure she had found trouble, but nothing seemed amiss there. Mama was still encircled by her cluster of friends, refusing to leave yet. In spite of this assurance, the uneasy feeling returned, even stronger this time.

Someone was watching her. Cassie knew it as surely as she breathed. She could feel a gaze upon her, so intense that it felt as if she were actually being touched by it.

As she turned, she could almost feel herself being pulled toward her watcher. Then, it seemed as if the crowd parted and left one man standing tall and proud in a Yankee blue uniform.

He'd stand out in any crowd. Tall, broad shouldered, and bronzed—this man didn't spend his days shut away indoors. His face was sculpted in strength and disturbingly handsome.

Dark blond hair brushed his collar. Not pale or reminiscent of a maiden, but dark, bold, and all male. It called to mind the deep, rich, golden hue of a mountain lion in winter. Lush, soft, and dangerous.

As a moth, drawn irresistibly toward the candle's flame, Cassie continued to meet him stare for stare. His gaze was unwavering, challenging, sensual without even trying. She could feel his eyes rove over her, taking in every detail from her dark curls that draped over one shoulder to her cream-colored slippers peeking out from beneath her wide skirt. His gaze searched, observed, caressed. And left her breathless as if she'd just dashed up a flight of stairs.

The skin beneath the papers heated, and she resisted the urge to adjust the papers hidden under her bodice. That act would surely give her away.

Suddenly, he smiled, and her heart doubled its beat. He had a generous, sensual mouth, softening a face hardened by too many years of war. And above his upper lip rested a dark blond mustache, trimmed to perfection. It drew her full attention to his smile. It tempted, daring her not to smile in return.

With the slightest of nods, he acknowledged her, then stepped forward. Cassie's heart skipped a full beat, she knew it. He strode across the ballroom, coming straight toward her with long, sure strides.

She didn't know whether to run away or, foolish thought, meet him halfway in the center of the room. Her brain told her one thing—flee—but something compelled her to stay.

He drew closer, seeming to grow taller and broader the closer he came. Oh my, she thought to herself, he was something to behold close up. Even more masculine than from across the room, and she wouldn't have believed that were possible if someone had told her so. He was most assuredly a striking figure.

More than one pair of feminine eyes followed his progress, but he would not be deterred. He came straight for Cassie with the single-minded determination of a seasoned soldier. Here was a man used to commanding and being obeyed.

Trouble was only a few feet away, Cassie knew it. Instinctively, she straightened to her full five foot and almost two inches in height and raised her chin. No one gave her orders—not if they expected them to be obeyed—she recalled. While she didn't search out confrontation, she'd never run from it a day in her life, and she wasn't about to start tonight.

As his eyes met hers, for an instant Jared had the sensation of two opposing armies readying to do battle. The lady had one hell of a determined chin, a definite sign that he was in for a real campaign if he planned to woo her and retrieve those papers.

His mother's admonition that "you draw more flies with honey" came to mind, and he widened his smile. There was more than one way to win a battle. He'd learned that in this war, and he tried to teach it to the troops he trained each day in his command. If ever there was a right time to put every bit of his offensive training into action, it was this moment.

Jared smiled and held her gaze as he came to a sharp halt directly in front of his lady thief.

"I'd ask for an introduction, ma'am, but I don't see any amenable matrons about, do you?" he challenged her, looking pointedly to either side of them.

In spite of herself, Cassie's lips twitched in suppressed laughter, and she smiled at his unusual approach. He was even more direct than she'd expected. Although his uniform rank proclaimed him an officer—a Captain, and his bearing confirmed that he was a gentleman, he reeked of impropriety. Why, she'd bet he could practically ruin a woman with just a smile.

She'd scarcely finished the thought before he caught up her right hand in his, drawing it up to his lips. His hands were calloused from the hold of reins and hard work. Cassie caught her breath as he placed a light, but burning kiss against her skin. It tingled where the soft hairs of his mustache brushed her wrist.

As he raised his head, Jared quickly surveyed her generous bodice. The cream-colored material strained, fitting too snugly from the obvious padding of the papers, he was sure. Suddenly, from between her breasts he caught the barest glimpse of the edge of a piece of paper. If he hadn't known it was there, he would have missed it. He averted his gaze before she could realize what he'd witnessed, and smiled into her eyes.

He continued to hold her hand in his, and Cassie eased her hand from his strong hold. The audacity, the sheer nerve of the man, Cassie thought to herself. That had been no simple kiss of a gentleman greeting a lady—it had singed her right down to her satin slippers. She stared back at him, admittedly intrigued and fascinated.

"Captain Jared Montgomery, ma'am," he introduced himself.

The words seemed to practically roll off his tongue. His voice held a deep resonance. It seemed to vibrate through her like the strains of a violin concerto. For a moment, she was left completely speechless. Not an easy feat for anyone to accomplish with her.

He raised his head, and his gaze met hers. Green-gray eyes twinkled back at her as if he knew they shared a secret. Cassie's breath caught in her throat and lodged there. He couldn't know about the papers, could he?

She shot a rapid glance down to the top of her gown, and his gaze followed hers. As she looked back at him, she felt her cheeks heat and redden in a blush. Damnation, now what was she to do with an attractive, curious Yankee officer and his damned interest?

"We could dance," he offered, as if reading her mind.

"No!" Cassie gulped back her instinctive denial. She hedged, "I'm sorry, but—"

"Now what would you have to be sorry for?" he queried with an all too knowing chuckle.

He knew! Cassie felt the shock of that realization all the way to her toes. She stared up at him, her mouth slightly open.

Laughter glimmered behind his steady gaze, as he waited for her answer. It reminded her of a cat's persistence, waiting outside a mouse's hole.

"Ma'am?"

Cassie tamped down her panic. He couldn't know. The papers were securely hidden away; she was merely feeling guilty. That had to be it.

She met his question. "Sorry, I . . . ah, I must plead a headache and—"

"And dance with me to rid yourself of the guilt . . ."

Guilt. The word echoed and re-echoed through her mind.

As he paused for what surely seemed an endless second, Cassie held her breath, waiting for what was to come.

"Over refusing me," he concluded.

He stepped back, then drew her forward to him. His reflexes were incredibly quick, and before she realized it she was pulled against his sure, steady, rock-hard body. She stared up at the lean, strong planes of his face and his square, firm jaw and knew she'd lost this battle. She'd been outmaneuvered. In another moment they were surrounded by dancing couples.

Conceding his victory, she nodded and let him catch up her other hand. Surprisingly, they seemed to move in unity, their steps matching perfectly in time to the music.

"Now I'm the one who is feeling guilty." Jared's deep-throated purr cut into her thoughts.

Cassie jerked her head up, missing a step. *Guilty.* Damnation, there was that blasted word again.

He sidestepped easily, missing her toes.

"Pardon?" She forced the question out, not sure she wanted to hear his answer. She was half afraid, and half tantalized beyond refusal. What was it about him that brought up such a disturbing feeling of guilt?

"Here I have the most beautiful woman at

the party in my arms, and I don't even know her name." He challenged her reticence.

"Cassie," she answered in quick relief, "Cassandra Van Dorn."

"Cassie," he said her name softly, letting it flow in the evening air.

Something about him stirred Cassie's memory. She didn't know whether it was his scent, a blend of the outdoors and pure male, or the now almost-familiar feel of his arms around her. And his calloused hand, like the man upstairs.

No, she was imagining things, she chided herself. This couldn't be her captor from upstairs. Could it? How she wished she'd had a chance to see his face upstairs, wished she could compare Jared's unusual green-gray eyes to those of her captor. She stared, studying him.

She missed another step, and Jared quickly sidestepped to avoid crushing her toes. Cassie saw a quick flash of pain cross his face.

"Is something wrong?"

He smiled. "A war wound," he stated.

In a pig's eye, she thought, biting her lower lip to hold the words in.

He was lying, she knew it. She'd be willing to bet his so-called war wound had come at her hands, or more precisely, her foot.

"I'm sorry," she mouthed the platitude, lying sweetly. "Is it recent?" she challenged.

"Very." His voice held a warning, like velvet with a hint of steel beneath it.

Cassie's breath caught in her throat. The game had suddenly, unexpectedly turned serious. The word "danger" blared before her, almost as if someone had called it aloud.

He was definitely a rogue, she thought, warning herself against his charm. A commanding, intriguing, dangerous rogue. And what more? Was he her captor from upstairs?

She was almost positive of it!

The music came to an end, and she acted instinctively. Slipping out of Jared's arms, she thanked him quickly, and before he could protest, she spun away out of his reach.

Forcing herself to walk, not run, Cassie told herself there was no shame in a tactful retreat. As she weaved her way through the couples on the dance floor, putting additional distance between herself and Jared, she wondered about that.

If that were true, and all she was doing was "retreating," then why did she feel as if she were fleeing for her life?

As Cassie eased past the last couple and joined the comparative safety of her mama's circle of chattering friends, she could swear she could feel Jared Montgomery's intense gaze on her right through the silk of her gown.

Something told her she'd be seeing him again.

Two

Safe at home, in her own bedroom at last, Cassie closed her eyes against the evening's disturbing memories and tried to concentrate on getting ready for bed. It didn't do a bit of good.

Remembering the feel of being in Jared Montgomery's arms, she tightened her fingers on the hair brush in her hand. *Go away*, she commanded him.

A pair of green-gray eyes taunted her, daring her to forget him. The memory of Captain Jared Montgomery even persisted in invading the sanctity of her own bedroom, leaving her thoughts as muddied as the Potomac.

"Damnation."

"Cassie, don't swear." Alicia Van Dorn smoothed back one of her own dark curls as she sauntered into Cassie's bedroom. She was an older version of Cassie, her hair still dark and glossy, not yet showing any sign of gray.

The hair brush slipped from Cassie's fingers, and with a guilty start she caught her hands to her chest, covering the papers still hidden in her bodice.

"Mama!" Cassie lowered her hands in relief and whirled around. "You startled me."

She tried to still the betraying tremble of her hand as she picked up the hair brush from her lap. She'd been so caught up in thinking about Jared Montgomery that she hadn't heard anyone come in.

"Oh, and don't kick your slippers under the bed as you usually do, dear," her mother added casually.

Too casually.

As her mother remained quiet, Cassie laid the brush down on the dressing table. Her mother's statement penetrated her thoughts.

"Why shouldn't I kick my slippers under the bed?" she asked in growing trepidation.

Silence greeted her question as her mama concentrated on smoothing out the bow of her own dressing gown.

"What now?" The words slipped out before she could catch them.

What new scheme had her mama gotten herself into this time? Cassie wondered with concern. Without Daddy around for Mama to concentrate her energies on, she seemed lost and constantly seeking some new adventure to occupy herself. The only problem was that each new venture got more dangerous than the last one. How could such a pretty, dainty woman find so much trouble so easily?

As the silence grew, Cassie watched her tiny, elegant mother pick up, then replace each item on the dressing table.

"Mother?" Cassie drew her attention, using the formal name she almost never used. "Why should I be careful about my bed? What's under the bed?"

Alicia Van Dorn replaced the perfume stopper in a pink bottle and looked up at her daughter, ignoring her apprehension.

"Oh, it's nothing for you to worry about." She waved her hand, brushing aside her daughter's concern like a pesky mosquito.

Cassie's stomach slowly tightened into a knot. The last time her mama had said, "don't worry," Cassie had barely kept her from being arrested and jailed.

When her mama took that oh-so-casual tone, it meant she was up to her bejeweled neck in trouble and needed Cassie to get her out of the latest problem her impulsiveness had catapulted her into.

Cassie felt *whatever* was hiding under her bed pulling her attention. She stared at the feather mattress, not knowing what to expect to crawl from beneath it. Her vivid imagination conjured up one thing after another, finally settling on the picture of a wounded Rebel soldier. She faced her mother, expecting the worst.

"Mother," she said sternly, "whatever have you done now?"

"Don't worry, dear." Alicia picked up the perfume bottle again and sniffed it appreciatively. "Um, I do like this scent."

"Mother, the last time you said 'don't worry,' I had to try and convince Mr. Pinkerton that you weren't a spy working for Mrs. Greenhow. And the time before that, I had to go to Secretary Cameron to keep you from being held in that jail in Baltimore."

"Don't worry—I haven't been with that group of rabble-rousers again," her mother answered casually, referring to her involvement in the outbreak of riots when the Northern troops passed through Baltimore on their way to the capital city three years before.

Cassie breathed a premature sigh of relief. Maybe she was worrying for nothing. However, her mother's next words tore the breath from her chest.

"If you must know, it's my latest shipment of morphine."

"Morphine!"

"Shh, dear. You don't want the servants to hear. One never knows whom one can trust nowadays."

"Mother," Cassie caught her mama's hands in hers, drawing her full attention. "What is morphine doing in our house?"

Comprehension dawned on Cassie, and she let her breath out in a silent whistle. Now her mother was smuggling pain-killing morphine to the wounded Confederates. A compassionate action for her soft-hearted mother, but considered treason by the Union.

"Mama," she asked in a low voice. "Do you know what the penalty is for smuggling supplies to the South?"

Silence greeted her question.

She tried again. "Surely you're not thinking about attempting to smuggle it South?"

For an instant, Cassie prayed the answer wasn't what she was thinking. It couldn't be.

"Oh, it's nothing for you to worry about, Cassie. I've done it several times. You know how badly the morphine is needed in the field hospitals."

"Several times?" Cassie asked with a squeak.

"Very badly needed," Alicia assured her daughter.

"Several!" Cassie repeated.

"Oh, yes, dear."

Her mother ran a hand down Cassie's long dark hair, in a soothing attempt, brushing a stray curl away from her cheek.

"Although at first I didn't know better, and I sewed it up in the hem of my petticoat. Well, I nearly attracted a sentry's attention what with the strange way my hoop insisted upon swaying. They watch for that, you know, dear. But, don't worry, I don't sew it in my petticoats anymore, I've learned a few tricks since then."

Every time her mother said, "don't worry," Cassie knew there was more bad news to come. She took a deep breath to calm herself and heard the papers hidden in her bodice crinkle. At the betraying sound, she closed her eyes. Stolen papers and smuggled morphine—it was almost too much to handle all at one time. She wanted to scream in frustration.

Instead, she opened her eyes and forced herself to speak quietly, lowering her voice to barely above a whisper. "Mama, when did you start smuggling morphine?" she asked.

"Dear, smuggling is such a nasty word. I prefer to think of it as sending packages of love and care to your father."

"Daddy's involved with this?" Cassie's voice raised in disbelief.

He wouldn't be a party to Mama's smuggling, would he? No, she was sure of it. After all, he'd been the one who'd asked her to take care of Mama while he was gone. He'd made her vow that she'd do everything in her power to keep Mama out of trouble.

"He doesn't know, does he?" Cassie confronted her mother's continued silence.

"Dear, your father is a very busy man." Alicia turned away, presenting Cassie with her back.

"Mother!"

Cassie took a deep breath, counted to ten,

and remembered her pledge to her father that she'd watch over her impetuous mama.

"And he does appreciate the supplies."

Her mother turned back to face her, with an earnestly innocent look on her face. Cassie had seen that look before. It always boded trouble. And tonight, more trouble was the last thing she needed.

"Exactly how much does Father know?" Cassie asked her mother in a low, soothing voice, afraid that if she raised her voice again her mother would simply stroll out of the room in silence, leaving Cassie to cope with only heaven knew what.

"Well . . ." her mother hedged.

"Exactly what?" Cassie demanded.

"Not now, Cassie. We've got more important things to talk about. Everything is about to come tumbling down all about us," she announced dramatically, catching Cassie's arm with both her hands. "Come here, and let's sit down and talk."

As her mother tugged insistently on her arm, Cassie followed her to the bed and sat down beside her. What could be more serious than her mama smuggling morphine south, she wondered? And did she really want to know the answer to that question?

"Cassie, I got a telegram from Vangie. She's coming for a visit."

"Aunt Vangie?" Cassie's voice filled with pleasure.

Her pretty aunt was always fun, and maybe she'd distract Mama from whatever new trouble she was intent on getting into.

Or get her into much more trouble, a little voice whispered in the back of Cassie's mind.

Evangeline Maitland was pretty, naturally drew everyone's attention, and never had a care in the world. However, she was also endowed with the curiosity of a whole litter of kittens—and likely as not was the nosiest person on this earth. Her aunt's overly inquisitive nature could catapult them all into prison!

"When?" Cassie asked.

"Tomorrow!"

"Oh, damn," Cassie whispered.

This time she noted that her mama didn't say a word about her swearing.

Instead, her mother nodded in agreement. "Now you know why I had to move the morphine out of my room. Vangie was sure to find it there. She can't seem to remember that we aren't still thirteen and always snitching each other's clothes like we used to." In spite of the words, she smiled in fond remembrance. "I declare, nothing's safe from Vangie."

Cassie failed to smile back at the comment. She shuddered to think what would happen if her curious aunt stumbled upon the morphine while looking for a new bonnet to borrow.

"I'll take care of it, Mama," she said, without the slightest idea of how she'd accomplish the task.

"Oh, thank you. I knew you'd take care of everything." Her mother released a long, deep sigh of relief. "You always do."

"Go on to bed, Mama." Cassie kissed her mother's cheek. "I'll see to your . . . shipment."

"Good night, dear." She waggled her fingers at Cassie in departure.

As she watched her mother close the door behind her, Cassie didn't have the faintest idea of what she was going to do with the illegal shipment hidden under her bed. However, she wasn't about to let her mama deliver it herself again. How she'd managed not to get herself arrested so far was a miracle.

Cassie nibbled on her lower lip, perplexed. Things were getting complicated. Tomorrow evening, under the guise of attending the Littleton's reception, she was supposed to deliver the packet of papers. She had to get them to Will Radford; he was counting on her, and she had no intention of letting the head of the secession movement or her country down.

So much depended on it. For now, she'd better make sure the papers were safe tonight—she couldn't very well sleep with them.

Throwing a nervous glance about the room, she retrieved the key from her bureau and crossed to the safe. It took only a moment to open it. Sighing, Cassie eased the papers from their hiding place down her dress and tried to smooth the wrinkles out of the edges, then placed the packet in the safe. Rubbing her tender skin, she winced. It felt like they'd scraped her skin nearly raw.

Closing the safe door, she removed the key and after another searching glance around the bedchamber, she slipped the key back into the top drawer of her bureau.

Relieved to have the papers secured, she crossed to the wardrobe and caught up a wispy pink nightgown of the softest silk and dyed lace. However, as she turned down the lamp, she knew that sleep would not come easy that night.

How could it? She had her mother's shipment of morphine hidden under her bed, stolen government papers locked in her safe, and her nosy aunt coming for a visit. What more could go wrong?

Jared slipped the spyglass back into his breast pocket and checked his pocket watch in the moonlight, then returned his gaze to the bedroom window. Cassie Van Dorn's bedroom had been dark now for nearly an hour.

He should know. He'd monitored her every move since she'd left the party after their single dance. As he'd hoped, she hadn't passed the packet of papers onto anyone else.

At least not yet. And she wouldn't be doing so if he had anything to do with it.

Right now those important papers were secured in her safe where he'd watched her place them. Secured and just waiting for him to retrieve them.

He adjusted his black half-mask and smiled. Soon, very soon, he'd have possession of the important papers concealed in the lady's safe. With the aid of the spyglass, he'd watched her retrieve the key and place the documents inside the compartment, then replace the key in the bureau.

Now all he had to do was use that same key and remove the papers. He dared not imagine the consequences if he failed. The defense plans of Washington in the hands of the damned secessionists—no, he couldn't allow that to happen.

Maybe, just maybe, if he kept an eye on Cassie, she'd lead him right to the man he sought.

Jared moved away from the base of the broad oak tree and its concealing shadows. It had served its purpose, providing a darkened place to tie his mount, while giving him a safe haven to observe Cassie's movements until the house became darkened inside.

He slipped like a shadow across the revealing moonlit lawn and flattened himself against the outside wall. Pausing to take stock, he glanced around him. All remained quiet. He turned and grasped the wooden lattice work of the trellis, careful to avoid the rose thorns sticking out. The fragrant scent of roses enveloped him, and he inhaled deeply.

On impulse he plucked a single rose and carefully tucked its stem into his waistband. The red petals stood out in sharp contrast to his black attire. He looked down and grimaced. The one part of his job that he could well do without was scrambling into his dark disguise in the shadows. But it was necessary if he was to keep his identity a secret.

Turning back to the job at hand, he grasped the trellis once more and began to climb. He scaled the side trellis with skill and expertise, garnered from many a night such as this.

The masked marauder, the city's newspapers called him, since they didn't have a clue to his true identity. Wouldn't they be surprised to learn that their infamous thief was a loyal Union officer?

He chuckled, a soft low sound below the black silk mask covering his features. Black—a fitting match to the rest of his attire of black shirt and equally black close-fitting pants tucked inside the same hue of supple leather boots.

At his next step, the wood creaked beneath his weight, and he froze still a moment, suspended in time and space. Then he flattened himself close against the side of the brownstone, awaiting any unwelcome reaction from inside to the all too betraying noise.

As he waited, a surge of excitement coursed through his veins. He'd be a fool to attempt to deny the thrill of danger he felt with each outing, or to give into it and chance missing the minute sounds that could foretell his demise. So far, luck had been with him.

Jared knew if he were caught, he'd likely face the hangman's noose. For the man he took his secret orders from could not acknowledge his actions, much less publicly sanction them. He couldn't even so much as lift a finger to save Jared's neck, not what with the election coming up. The price would be too high—this they'd both agreed on ahead of time.

Pushing the unpleasant thoughts aside, Jared resumed his climb. Time was ticking past, and with every second wasted, the chance of discovery grew greater, and he had no intention of being discovered.

It was a superbly simple plan. Climb up to the lady's bedroom, open the safe, and retrieve his papers. He'd already begun to think of the packet as belonging to him.

As he reached the balcony leading to her bedroom, he paused again and listened. All remained quiet. Deftly, he swung himself over the railing and onto the balcony without making a sound. Next, it was a simple thing to slip the door's lock and ease himself inside through the soft billowing curtains.

As the moon slid under a cloud, darkness enveloped him. He stood in silence a moment, giving his eyes time to adjust to the sudden dimness of the bedroom. To his right, he could make out the bed and a single figure asleep in it. Dark flowing hair draped over the sleeper's shoulder—Cassie Van Dorn.

The temptation to cross to her and scoop her up into his arms gnawed at him, shocking him with its suddenness and intensity. He resisted, reminding himself that his goal was straight across the room from him—the lady's safe.

After a few moments, the cloud passed over the moon, and rays of moonlight streamed through the window once again. Using its guidance, he surveyed the room to get his bearings, then crept across the bedchamber on silent footsteps.

As he reached the foot of the bed, he couldn't help himself and he paused, giving in to the temptation to observe her as she slept—without any defenses up between them.

He gazed down at her amongst the rumpled bedcovers. Cassie lay curled on her side sleeping, even more beautiful than she'd been earlier that evening. Her hair was unbound by any ribbons and spread across the pillow like a bolt of darkest velvet unfurled. It called to him like a siren's cry in the darkness, begging him to lose himself in its softness.

He longed to stroke her cheek where her silken skin had been turned almost translucent by the soft rays of moonlight streaming through the balcony doors. In the pale lighting, her high cheekbones set off to perfection the dark crescent of her lashes. His stomach coiled into a knot as he drank his fill of her.

Lower, he allowed his eyes to stray lower to where a pink lacy nightgown concealed her feminine charms, but barely. Although demure, the soft pink color accented her dark beauty, while the lace tempted him, nearly begging him to investigate what lay beneath it. The shadowed vee of her breasts taunted him, daring him to press a kiss against their softness. That was the same place where the lady thief had hidden the stolen papers earlier, he reminded himself.

It was all the reminder he needed, his blood cooling in his veins at the thought. Stiffening, he turned away and strode past the bed, crossing the room on silent footsteps to the bureau.

He eased the top drawer open and searched for the key. His fingers brushed cool metal, and he quickly withdrew the key. Turning away, he slipped the key into the

lock and with a deft flick of his wrist released the mechanism. As he turned the handle, a click resounded through the room.

Damn. He glanced behind him to Cassie,
but no sound came from the sleeping woman
across the room.

The remembrance of the only other time
his quarry had awakened while he was re-
claiming documents from an occupied room
still chilled him, making him ever cautious.
However, luck had been with him that unfortunate night, the startled woman had
taken one look at him clothed all in black,
and she'd promptly swooned. Likely as not
Cassie Van Dorn would do the same.

Nonetheless, he had no intention of sticking
around until she awoke. Quickly, he reached
inside the compartment and grabbed the papers laying on top. One glance assured him
that they were the documents he sought. Holding them in one hand, he carefully removed
the red rose and laid it in the safe in their
place. He couldn't resist smiling at the lady's
upcoming reaction to finding the single rose
instead of the papers in the morning.

Jared eased the safe closed, cautious not to
make a sound, and turned about. He took a
step toward the window, and then it happened. A board creaked, protesting beneath
his boot.

He shot a glance to the bed and knew his
luck had run out.

* * *

Cassie wasn't sure what wakened her, but something had. She tensed, listening and could feel that she wasn't alone any longer.

The papers. Her mind instantly thought of the important documents.

She sat upright, glanced around the room, and met the stare of a tall, muscular man dressed completely in black. And she screamed.

In the next instant, Cassie cut off her scream, hoping that her mama hadn't heard. Whatever had possessed her to do such a thing? She couldn't allow her mama to be involved in this.

For several endless seconds Cassie and her thief both stared at each other motionless. Instinctively, Cassie gripped the covers between her hands. He was dark as midnight, except for the burnished gold of his hair, which was only partially hidden by the black mask that covered his upper face. The eyes behind the slits in the mask captured and held her attention. In the darkened room she couldn't tell what color his eyes were, but she could feel the dangerous intensity of his gaze upon her.

With an effort she pulled her gaze from his. The mask covered to his lips, leaving her guessing as to his identity. A black shirt covered his broad chest and arms. Equally dark pants molded his lower body, fitting snugly and ending in dark boots. She forced her gaze back up and stopped at his hands.

Her papers. The thief had her packet of papers in his hands. The same papers she'd stolen fair and square earlier that night. And now *he* thought to steal them.

Oh, no, he wasn't!

Throwing back the covers, she bounded out of bed, oblivious to her state of undress.

"Put those down," she ordered.

She heard a sharply indrawn breath from the man staring at her. Then, instead of obeying her demands, the thief took a determined step toward the window. He wasn't getting away that easily, she thought.

Cassie dashed across the room determined to intercept him. Instead she landed right in Jared Montgomery's arms.

His breath rushed out in an "oof," and retaining his hold of the papers in one hand, he wrapped his free arm around Cassie, pulling her close.

Staring up at him, she repeated her demand, this time in a significantly lower voice, "Put those down."

From outside came the loud shout from a roving police patrol. Cassie stiffened. Oh no, what had she done? She prayed that her scream hadn't drawn the policemen's attention and investigation.

Her thief's only response to her demand

was to tighten his arm about her, drawing her closer. The faint woodsy scent of the outdoors, bourbon, and fresh roses drifted to her, tantalizing her senses.

Cassie could hear his breathing near her ear, could feel his firmly muscled body pressed against the length of hers. Suddenly, the realization of her state of dress and the thinness of her lace-trimmed nightgown came to her mind. She'd never paused to consider her clothing when she'd dashed after him. Her face reddened, and she was glad that the thief couldn't see the telltale blush in the darkened room. Just what did he plan to do now?

Cassie knew one cry of "Help! Robbers!" from her would surely bring the police charging into the house. She opened her mouth to cry out, then just as quickly shut her mouth in chagrin.

What could she do—ask them to arrest the man who was stealing the packet of papers she'd stolen herself earlier that same night? How would she explain that certain government papers had come to be in her possession in the first place? And what of her mama's morphine shipment tucked away under the bed?

A cry for help from the police now would likely as not land them all in Old Capitol Prison.

Cassie felt the hypnotic pull of the ruffle

on her bed. It seemed to shout to her and anyone that dared listen that something illegal was hidden underneath the bed, if only they'd peek beneath the pretty ruffled covering. She closed her eyes to keep from looking at the bed and took a deep breath.

There was absolutely no way she could explain away the refined white powder in the bottles of her mother's morphine shipment. And if questioned, her mama would likely readily admit to her latest endeavor without a qualm as to the possible consequences. Cassie could not allow that to happen.

A loud pounding on the downstairs door broke her out of her dilemma of questions. The man holding her started, jerking his head up at the sound.

The patrol. Cassie's eyes widened in dismay. The thief couldn't know that she wanted the patrol up here even *less* than he did at this moment.

In truth, the last thing she needed at this moment was a patrol investigating the goings on in her bedroom. Between the stolen papers, her mama's morphine, and her own involvement in the secession plot, her life could not bear the close scrutiny of anyone, much less the Yankee authorities.

But the man holding her couldn't know that.

With a sudden move, he wrapped his other arm about her, drawing her tight against him. She pressed her hands ineffectually against his wide chest, and she could feel the pounding of his heart beneath her palm. Her own heart beat in quick time to match his.

Oh, damnation, what had she gotten herself into this time? She stared up at her captor.

Jared stared down at Cassie's full lips. Why couldn't she just have swooned like any other woman?

Then, he did the only thing he could think to do. In a quick, unhesitating move, he lowered his head, his mouth covering hers, his firm lips taking hers in a kiss born out of desperation. He kissed her thoroughly, silencing any outcry she might make.

Three

Any protest Cassie had been thinking of making halted in her throat. Her thief's lips were cool against hers, but heated with each second the kiss went on.

"Ma'am!" a shouted call came from outside.

Cassie heard the policeman's call as if from a long distance.

Jared's arms tightened around her.

"Not a sound," he murmured against her mouth.

She had no intention of calling the police up to her bedroom, and their attention to the papers that crinkled in her thief's grip.

His voice was deep and husky and strangely familiar. Before Cassie had time to think anymore on this, his lips covered hers again. This time his kiss was gentler, softer, warmer against her lips, but every bit as demanding as the one that had preceded it.

Cassie caught his shirt in her hands, holding to him tightly, afraid that if he were to release her she would fall. He buried his free hand in her hair, rubbing his fingers back and forth across the nape of her neck.

The slow, sensual caress was in sharp contrast to the firm way he held her against his body. She could feel the full length of him pressing against her. He brushed his thumb against the lobe of her ear, the side of her neck, and back to her nape again. Her legs shook with the intensity of his loving onslaught.

She was like kissing warm velvet, Jared thought. Drawing in a cool breath of air to keep from drowning in her warmth, he paused, then brushed his lips over hers. Once, twice, and again.

He drew back only enough to gaze at her upturned face. Why did she have to be a secesh thief? Her lips, moist and slightly swollen from his kisses, beckoned to him, drawing him to her with a force all their own. He gave into their lure.

Unconsciously, Cassie traced the tip of her tongue across her lower lip. Her thief's eyes focused completely on the action. Cassie met his hungry green gaze, then froze.

She knew those green-gray eyes, had stared into their depths only hours before. With a gasp of recognition, she opened her mouth, but the name never made its way past her lips.

He captured her lips again, taking the sound a prisoner along with his loving. As his lips crushed hers beneath his, the name slipped from Cassie's lips, left unuttered in the room. "Jared Montgomery."

This time she felt the faint brush of his mustache against her soft skin. It was strangely pleasant, even more so than when he'd kissed her hand at the Admiral's birthday celebration.

The sound of running footsteps on the stairs jolted both Cassie and Jared back to reality at the same moment. They drew apart at the same instant.

Jared stepped back, and before she could stop him, he shoved the papers deep into his pocket. She threw out a hand, now desperate to regain the possession of the important papers.

"Until we meet again," he said softly.

The next instant, he spun around and sprinted for the balcony. Cassie dashed after him. This time she was the one who was too late.

Jared disappeared over the side of the railing, and she heard a dull thud as he landed safely below. And out of her reach.

"Damnation." Cassie clenched her fists to her sides in vexed frustration.

Whatever had possessed her to allow him to kiss her in that way and let him escape with the papers?

Now she had to get them back.

Suddenly the door swung inward. Cassie

whirled about to face the intrusion. She saw her mother standing in the doorway, her wrapper tied haphazardly about her, the bow askew.

"Cassie! Are you hurt?"

Cassie shook her head.

"Whatever is going on?"

Cassie opened her mouth, but before she could think of what to say, her mother rushed on.

"Whatever were you thinking of creating a commotion? I'll have you to know I had the devil's own time convincing the patrol that there was nothing in our house that needed their saving or investigating." She paused to fan herself with her hand. "I swear I thought I'd never get rid of those nosy men."

Cassie bit back her explanation. She couldn't involve her mother in the stolen papers! And there was no way that she could explain Jared Montgomery's visit, not to mention his kisses. Much less her own reaction to them.

"I must have been dreaming," she stated, taking a breath to stand up to the lie.

Her gaze slipped to the safe, and she felt her cheeks heat in embarrassment at the untruth she'd told her mother. The lie ate at her bruised conscience.

She wasn't accustomed to lying. Raised to be truthful and straightforward, she usually bordered on being too truthful. Now look at what was happening to her.

Not to mention that now she had to explain to Will Radford exactly what had gone so wrong with his simple plan for obtaining the packet of papers.

Precisely at seven o'clock the next morning, Jared sat in a tall-backed chair in front of a broad desk, waiting. The reassuring rustle of the packet of papers tucked in his uniform jacket relaxed him. He would be turning them over in minutes.

"How did it go?"

The door behind him clicked closed. Jared knew who the speaker was without looking.

The tension showed in the other man's voice. Jared could sense it even before he turned around to see the strain evident on the man's craggy face.

The high cheekbones looked more prominent than usual, the cheeks more gaunt. The pain of a nation divided by war had taken its toll on their president. The critics who doubted this leader's concern and pain should see him now, Jared thought to himself.

He stood to his feet and handed over the papers. President Abraham Lincoln took them with a sigh of relief.

"Any problems?"

Jared hesitated a moment, and the President picked up on it instantly. He pinned him with a piercing gaze.

Problems? Definitely so. However, the main problem facing him was that it seemed each time Jared met Cassie Van Dorn, he found that instead of talking to her and questioning her, all he wanted to do was take her in his arms and kiss her delectable lips. But he couldn't very well tell the President that, could he?

"They've been taken care of," Jared answered in a firm, confident voice.

"And the secession plot? Is it as we suspected?" President Lincoln asked, rubbing long fingers across his chin.

"Yes, sir." Jared sat forward in his chair. "Over the past week, I have learned that the plot to get Washington to secede and join the Confederacy has resurfaced. And the insidious plot is far from dead."

President Lincoln shook his head. "They have to be stopped."

"Yes, sir." Jared's voice tightened as he remembered how his brother had died attempting to do just that same thing.

Bryan, newly commissioned, had been here in Washington investigating Southern sympathizers behind the secession plot. Young, bright and handsome, Bryan had blended well into the Washington social scene. Until something went deadly wrong.

Rumors abounded that he'd been silenced by the man who secretly headed the secession plot. A secret that Jared intended to uncover no matter what it took.

"The repercussions should this group succeed," the President paused, drawing in a long breath. "The capital city, the War Department, the arsenals all would be in the hands of the Confederacy." Once again he shook his head. "Even the possibility must be stopped."

"I intend to stop it."

The unshakable belief that any success by the secession plot would lengthen an already too long war lay unspoken between them.

"Do you know how they had planned to acquire the papers?" President Lincoln asked.

"A woman stole them from the Admiral's bedroom," Jared told him with a wry smile.

The other man's eyebrows arched. "Indeed?"

Jared proceeded to fill him in about Cassie, leaving out a great deal of the details.

"She sounds like a very resourceful woman."

Remembering Cassie, Jared answered, "Very."

"Too bad she isn't on our side. But the plans are safe now."

"Perhaps we should let the secessionists have them," Jared said with a slow smile.

Once again, the President pinned him with his direct gaze. Unlike most men, Jared was not intimidated by it.

"The plans might lead us to the head of the plot. If their leader *thought* he had the defense plans to the city, he might act rashly. Rashly enough for us to catch him," Jared stated.

"What do you have in mind?" President Lincoln leaned forward in his chair and clasped his hands together.

"I think we should make a *special* set of the plans available again. A set that we make up."

"Ah, misinformation. It sounds like a good idea. Go ahead."

"Yes, sir."

Jared rose to leave, but the President stopped him.

"Do you really believe they will try for the plans again?"

"Without a doubt."

Jared knew that a very determined Cassie Van Dorn could not pass up the opportunity to possess the packet of papers once again. And he intended to see that she was provided with that opportunity.

A few words spoken within the hearing of a couple of specific Southern sympathizers would be all that was needed. By evening, it would be known that he still had the papers and where they were located as well.

* * *

The lilting strains of a waltz drifted through the foyer, confirming to Alicia Van Dorn's dismay that they were indeed late for Mrs. Littleton's reception. Cassie and her mother exchanged an I-knew-it look. Beside them, Aunt Vangie patted a curl into place and seemed blithely unaware of their tardiness.

Instead of a matronly hair style, Vangie wore her deep mahogany brown hair atop her head in a mass of curls, and in her hair she'd clipped a trio of dyed magenta ostrich plumes set in a gold coronet. She looked younger than her thirty-six years, her slim figure offset by the cinched waist and wide skirt of her magenta silk taffeta gown overlaid with lace flounces. Black embroidery edged the flounces and the low-cut shawl collar. She was sure to draw every eye in the room.

Cassie's lips twitched with a smile at the memory of the bantering between her aunt and her mama as Vangie had readied herself for the reception. Secretly, Cassie suspected that Aunt Vangie took so much time getting ready just to fluster her younger sister.

However, admittedly the time had fairly flown past since the moment Vangie Maitland had arrived amidst a flurry of baggage and hat boxes. The combination of one trunk and a portmanteau had contained gowns of every color imaginable—more than one person could even dream of wearing in a month's time. Satin bonnets, ostrich plumes, and headdresses were included to match each and every gown she'd brought.

Cassie frowned, well aware that several of those same colorful gowns would be tossed carelessly in a corner of the bedchamber when Vangie departed for Baltimore. Vangie always left behind the things she tired of. And it had taken over an hour to unpack everything, too.

Afterwards, Cassie and her mama had waited indulgently, while Vangie sorted through her wardrobe, chattering and changing her gown three times before they laughingly pulled her out the door, under much protest from Vangie. There was no such thing as hurrying Vangie Maitland—Cassie had learned that fact years ago. Try as one might, nothing worked.

Even with claiming to have hurried as best she could, Vangie managed to be over half an hour late to the reception for Mrs. Littleton's sister-in-law touting her return from Paris.

Now, in typical Aunt Vangie fashion, she ran her fingers down the flounced skirt of her bright magenta taffeta gown, and announced the results well worth the time and effort.

Beside her, Alicia wore a much more de-

mure gown of deep green silk muslin. Cassie
felt younger and almost carefree in her ivory
silk gown; her shoulders revealed by the
scoop neckline and set off with the wide lace
edging. She actually preferred the lighter colors, and it bothered her not in the slightest
that it had been deemed improper for young,
unmarried ladies to wear the bright colors of
Aunt Vangie.

As Cassie turned, her crinoline rustled
softly beneath the flounced gown. Each of
the three flounces to the skirt were caught
up and held with satin chevrons and satin
rosette bows. The light from the overhead
chandelier was captured and reflected in the
tiny agrafe of diamonds at the center of each
rosette. The ivory color and sparkle of the
gown highlighted her dark hair and creamy
skin. Cassie wore her hair cascading over one
shoulder, and not a single brightly dyed ostrich plume in sight.

As her aunt paused yet again, this time to
point out the bunting and banners draped
across the ballroom doorway for Sarah Littleton, Cassie caught her arm. She wasn't about
to be waylaid yet again. It had taken them
over ten minutes to maneuver Aunt Vangie
from the carriage to the ballroom doorway
as it was. Heaven only knew how much
longer it would be before she actually entered the party going on within.

Likely as not, Will Radford had already

been pacing the halls, waiting impatiently for Cassie to deliver the papers. She took a resolute breath. He wasn't going to like what she had to tell him.

There had to be a way to get those papers back. There had to be. And she was determined to find it.

"My gracious, I do declare the way you two have been rushing me about so, I'm not even for certain that my corset is laced straight—"

A startled gasp sounded to their left as Mrs. Warden raised her handkerchief to her mouth and fairly rushed away across the room as fast as she could.

Vangie shrugged her shoulders delicately at the woman's departure and sniffed. Undaunted, she glanced about the room and then caught Cassie's arm.

"Cassie, you rushed me so that I'd about decided that the last available man in the city was about to be scooped up," Vangie accused with gentle laughter.

"And would you look and see," she flung her arm out in a sweeping gesture, her black ostrich feather fan swinging from her wrist in an erratic movement. "Why there's plenty of handsome men left hereabouts."

Brown curls bouncing, Vangie looked the width of the decorated ballroom. She reminded Cassie of a heedless puppy, determined to take in everything in sight and to blazes with the consequences.

"Now, Cassie, show me which one is your young man," Vangie demanded.

"None at this moment," Cassie hedged, dreading the prying questions that she knew were sure to follow that admission.

"My gracious! What?" Vangie turned to stare wide-eyed at Cassie. "Why, when I was your age, I had more beaux than I could keep track of, I do swear. Didn't I, Alicia?"

Her aunt still held that same ability to attract men, Cassie noted as several gentlemen glanced their way. She often wondered why her pretty aunt remained unmarried. Surely she'd had offers. Of course, she'd professed to have been in love with Cassie's father before he'd married Mama, but that had been years ago.

"What with all these men here, Alicia, I can't believe that you haven't found Cassie even one suitable prospect for a betrothal." Vangie turned her attention to her sister. "As you should well remember, the longer a young lady waits, the more difficult it is to find a proper husband." She sniffed and blinked her eyes as if fighting back a sudden rush of tears.

"Vangie—"

"I can't believe you have been so negligent in that respect, Alicia. If you wait too long for Cassie to find a man, she'll sadly discover that all the men want younger women. After all, Cassie's future is at stake. Well now that

I'm here, we will have to change that unforgivable situation, and the sooner the better."

This time it was Cassie who gasped. Trust nosy Aunt Vangie to involve herself in every aspect of their lives before her visit had scarcely commenced.

"Ooh," Vangie squeezed Cassie's hand. "Would you look at Sarah Littleton's gown." Distracted from her earlier concern, she flitted onto the next thing to capture her attention.

Cassie closed her eyes a second in relief. It appeared that her "future," as Aunt Vangie had put it, was now safe from interference. At least for a while longer.

Beside her, Vangie sucked in her breath in a low whistle. "Fresh from Paris indeed." Leaning closer, she whispered, "I do swear that insipid shade of blue makes her look like a rung-out rag."

"Vangie!" Alicia scolded her sister.

In spite of herself, Cassie couldn't help smiling. The remark was typical for her aunt. One never knew what Aunt Vangie would say or when she'd say it. The evening ahead would be far from a usual evening spent at a boring reception.

"I never did like that Littleton woman." Vangie wrinkled her nose in a moue of distaste.

"Shh!" Alicia Van Dorn shushed her sister as Sarah Littleton approached their party.

"Alicia, Cassie." Sarah extended her hands in greeting. "I'm so delighted you could come tonight." She sent an icy stare in Vangie Maitland's direction. "And I see that you've brought a guest."

"Good evening, Sarah. I see your sojourn in Paris didn't improve your disposition any." Vangie extended her hand in an obvious gesture of reprimand.

Sarah ignored it. "If you'll excuse me, I have other guests to attend to."

"Excuse us, Sarah." Alicia caught Vangie's outstretched hand and pulled her to her side. "Come on, Vangie," Alicia Van Dorn prompted, "there are a couple of other women I'd like you to meet."

The announcement fell on deaf ears. Vangie scanned the room, eyes shining with laughter. "Alicia, I do declare I'd much rather meet a few men any day."

Alicia closed her eyes and groaned. "Vangie, would you at least try and behave yourself?"

"But it's so much more fun not to." She attempted to ease her hand from Alicia's hold.

The next instant, Vangie spotted an acquaintance.

"Ooh, there's Gideon Welles." She quickly jerked free of her sister's restraint. "I really must go pay my respects. He's such a dear man. It's too bad that he's much too old for Cassie."

This time it was Alicia who released a startled gasp of sound.

Vangie continued, unperturbed. "Although I swear he looks even more like old man Neptune than when I was here last spring. Tsk, tsk, that long gray beard and awful matching wig. But don't ever let him hear that I said that."

With that parting comment and a gay giggle, Vangie strolled away straight on an intercept path for the Secretary of the Navy, leaving Cassie and her mother behind. Bemused, Cassie watched her aunt cross the room, her skirts swishing amongst the multi-colored granules of sand sprinkled across the floor.

Mrs. Littleton had spared no expense in the reception for her sister-in-law, Cassie noted. She hadn't seen the beautiful patterns of sand used for a long time now. The practice of preparing the dance floor with intricate designs in multi-colored sands had all but been abandoned with the war going on.

"It's going to be a very long month, I fear," Alicia interrupted Cassie's thoughts.

Cassie grinned in acknowledgement. "She can be rather exasperating—"

Her mama raised an eyebrow. "Rather," she pronounced. "I don't know what comes over her sometimes. I swear, she's acting eighteen instead of her thirty-six years."

Cassie held back her smile. Her mama and Aunt Vangie couldn't be less alike, no matter whether either of them cared to admit it. Where Mama's concern for others took her into poorly-thought out schemes in which to assist them, which usually got her into trouble; Aunt Vangie tended to pry and snoop until she found out what she wanted to know, then promptly forgot why she'd wanted to know it.

"Remember, the last time Vangie was here for a visit?" Alicia continued. "She practically created a scandal with her untimely gossip about Mrs. Wiley. We must ensure that we keep those two as far apart as possible. I swear *she* has an opinion on everyone."

Cassie didn't need to ask who "she" was. One look at her mama's face and her frustrated sigh told all. Aunt Vangie.

"And her visit two years ago," Alicia shuddered. "She was even worse, creating one scandal after another. And so unpredictable, too."

Cassie remembered that visit by her aunt had made the holidays a very tense time, as if their first Christmas without her father needed to be made worse. Mama had spent the entire day in tears.

"Now I understand why she's never gotten married." Alicia clapped her hand over her mouth. "I shouldn't have said that. Sometimes I feel that I'm to blame for her being unmarried."

"Mama—"

"Thomas—your daddy—was calling on Vangie first. Then, we fell in love. It was years after our marriage before Vangie forgave me. By then, we had moved here to Washington. And, your father and I have been so happy. We do owe her something, dear."

"I'll help look after her," Cassie promised.

"Oh, thank heavens." Alicia sighed, the sound seeming to come all the way from the bottoms of her satin slippers. "I fear it's going to take both of us to keep her from causing trouble during this visit."

Cassie nodded her head in agreement. If Aunt Vangie discovered her involvement in the secession plot, there would be much at risk. Nervously, Cassie watched the small gathering of dancers moving across the wood floor. She wasn't here to dance tonight, or to find a beau as her wayward aunt intended. She had a job to do. She had to find a way to locate those papers again. But first, she had to confess her blunder and the loss of the packet of important papers to Will Radford.

"Oh, dear, I don't see Vangie," Alicia announced, dread in her voice.

Pretending to look for her aunt, Cassie glanced around the room. Where was Will?

She knew he'd be here. The guests consisted of a mixture of politicians, Yankees in blue uniforms, and the usual cluster of those whose sympathies lay with the Confederacy. The opulent reception was ripe with gossip and intrigue, if one but listened and watched.

It was the perfect foil for Will Radford and his secret workers.

"Cassie?"

She turned her attention to her mama. "Yes?"

"Now where did Vangie get herself off to?" Alicia raised on tiptoe. "Do you see her, dear? I'm half frightened out of my wits at what she might say to someone if we're not there to keep an eye on her."

Like an errant child who'd heard someone talking about her, Vangie sauntered up to Alicia's left side. "Don't worry so, Alicia. Goodness, I swear I don't know what you ever did to deserve that wonderful husband of yours."

Instantly, she clapped her fingers over her mouth. "Oh, I am sorry, Alicia. I didn't mean that. You know I love you, and Thomas, and Cassie as if you were my very own."

Silence greeted her pronouncement.

"You do forgive me, don't you?" Vangie turned suddenly teary eyes to first her sister, then to Cassie, begging their forgiveness.

"Of course, I do." Alicia hugged her close. Vangie wiggled out of the embrace.

"It's too bad that handsome husband of yours isn't here to dance with us, instead off tending to a field hospital. Remember how well he danced?" Vangie fluttered her fan between them, her earlier remark and apology already forgotten. "I guess I'll have to find someone else to dance with tonight. If any of the men here will even want to." She formed her lips into a pout.

"There are plenty of men who'd love to dance with you," Cassie rushed to assure her aunt. "It's too bad that you won't be dancing, Alicia. But it simply wouldn't be proper, would it?"

"No, Vangie. I spend my time talking with my friends. Cassie can assure you of that." Alicia seemed determined to set her sister straight on her subtly questioned fidelity to her husband.

"You go on and enjoy yourself, Alicia." Vangie smiled apologetically and rushed to make up for her cutting remark. "I'll chaperone our Cassie."

"But—" Alicia began to protest.

"Come, Cassie. If I remember correctly, the last time I visited, there was a young man by the name of William quite smitten with you." She put a finger to her pursed lips a moment. "Yes, William Radford was his name. I'm sure of it. But, I doubt his suitability for you."

Cassie raised her brows. Will Radford had never been "smitten" with her. They had merely spoken a few times in the past. Before she'd been asked to join his group to get the capital city to secede. Trust Aunt Vangie to make too much out of a few words.

"Aunt Vangie—"

Vangie flicked open her fan, the black feathers swaying back and forth with the sharp movement. Then she marched straight ahead, towing Cassie along in her wake.

Within minutes, Vangie had found a young man deemed suitable by her to dance with her charge. Cassie endured the dance with the overly-shy youth, a cousin of someone or other, with as much dignity as possible. They hadn't spoken ten words during the entire time the music played their dance. Mama had certainly been right—it was going to be a long month with Aunt Vangie in their home.

As her dance partner returned her to Vangie's side, Cassie politely thanked him. The second he turned away, Vangie caught her hands in hers.

"I've just learned in conversation that our Mr. Will Radford will not be attending tonight. Can you imagine? It seems that scoundrel is in some meeting at Willard's Hotel. If you ask me, they're probably playing cards."

Cassie started at the relayed news. *A meeting at Willard's Hotel.* She quickly hid her instant smile of relief. She recognized the scheduled code Will used whenever he'd been called South and was crossing enemy lines on a mission.

Vangie released her hands and waved her black ostrich feather fan back and forth in a show of disgust.

"And you two would look so good dancing together with your matching dark hair." She shrugged. "Although Will and I would look equally good dancing together, I dare say, and I wouldn't refuse him a dance myself."

Aunt Vangie giggled behind her fan. "You know, dear, he really is too old for you. Well, I guess I'll simply have to find you someone else to dance with tonight. Oh, that red-haired young man in uniform looks nice, doesn't he?"

Cassie let her aunt's matchmaking attempt drift past her. Right now, she was too happy to let Aunt Vangie's interference bother her.

Will Radford's unexpected trip meant she'd been given a reprieve. Her stomach fluttered, and she knew how a prisoner felt when his hanging sentence had been delayed.

She'd been granted another twenty-four hours in which to retrieve those papers. And she knew just who to see for information.

Cassie caught her aunt's now fluttering fan to still it. If she was going to be forced to endure another dance with a man of Aunt Vangie's choosing, just maybe she could help her in making her next choice of partner.

Scanning the room, Cassie spotted a slim,

bespectacled man with dark hair and a neatly clipped beard. Michael Jones, a clerk in the War Department, was the best source of information Will Radford employed. He'd been the one to alert them to the packet of papers to begin with. If anyone had fresh news of those papers, it would be Michael Jones.

Cassie tilted her head, catching his attention. In a barely noticeable motion, she nodded her head, signalling him that she wanted to speak with him.

Minutes later, he'd secured Vangie Maitland's permission to escort Cassie onto the dance floor. Cassie moved in time to the strains of a German, biding her time. If he had any information to impart, he would let her know.

"I've come upon some interesting news tonight." Michael held out the tidbit of information, then paused for her response.

Cassie waited for the next beat of the music before she spoke. "Umm, what would that be?"

Surreptitiously, she glanced around to be sure that no one else was close enough to overhear their discussion, then nodded ever so slightly to him.

"It seems that a certain Union Captain has come into possession of our package." His voice rose a level with excitement. "Rumor has it that he's perhaps waiting for the right amount of money from a certain source."

"That is good news."

Cassie smiled, eager to devise a plan to out-smart a certain Captain Jared Montgomery. The Confederacy could ill afford to pay for the papers she had already possessed once; the South needed every bit of money it had and then some. As the music drew to a close, she stepped back a step.

"Thank you," she assured her dance partner. "You've been most kind, and kindness is always rewarded."

Not a soul around them would guess that she'd just promised to see that the loyal clerk was paid upon Will's return. With a wide smile, he bowed and left Cassie's side.

It took only a moment to locate Aunt Vangie's vibrant-colored gown. She was fluttering her fan in a very flirtatious gesture at the man on her right, while winking at a senator on her left.

Like a honey bee who couldn't decide which flower to light on, Vangie flitted from man to man. A person could get tired just watching her. Cassie rejoined her as propriety demanded.

However, by the time another hour had passed, Cassie decided that being chaperoned by Aunt Vangie was exhausting. And a bit stifling. Cassie felt sorely in need of a breath of fresh air—and a moment alone without having to concern herself with what her unpredictable aunt might say next.

As Vangie flitted, then settled next to a smartly dressed and very married Union officer, Cassie took the opportunity and slipped away from her aunt's side. She knew it wasn't considered proper, but she was in desperate need of a breath of air.

She crossed to the garden doors. Ever so casually, she scanned the room. Mama was ensconced with her usual circle of lady friends, likely as not talking over what news any of them had heard from their husbands. No one would miss her for a few minutes.

Slipping through the open French doors, she quickly strolled down the walk and around the corner of the two-storied house. In another second she was safely out of view of anyone within the brightly lit house.

It was a beautiful evening, cool and crystal clear under the light of a full autumn moon. She sauntered, deep in thought, to a late-blooming rose bush set a few feet from a latticed trellis with its profusion of climbing vines. Fingering the velvety petals of a fragrant pink rose, she closed her eyes. Thankful of the quiet surrounding her and the cool, refreshing night air, she breathed in deeply.

A rustle of movement from above alerted Cassie, and she snapped her eyes open and glanced upward to see a dark clad figure descending the vine-covered trellis.

Four

Cassie stood frozen in place, her gaze fixed on the figure above. She could scarcely believe what her eyes saw.

Someone was robbing the Littletons' beautiful home. No, not just someone. The dark disguise was the mark of the Masked Marauder. At least that's what the newspapers proclaimed.

"Oh, no," Cassie murmured in a whisper of denial.

Just her luck. And she couldn't stand by and let the thief simply flee with his illegally gotten booty. Not without doing something.

She glanced around the deserted section of the grounds. Not another soul was in sight. If she raced back to the ballroom for help, the thief would be long gone before she could return with the men.

Although faint strains of music wafted into the surrounding grounds, Cassie knew she was too far from the ballroom's French doors for anyone to hear her over the music if she cried out. All that would accomplish was to send the thief scurrying away into the night.

It was up to her to stop him.

While she admitted in private to stealing that packet of papers from her friend, the Admiral, it had after all been for a good cause. That certainly didn't mean that she was about to idly stand by and let someone else burglarize her friends. Not if she could help it.

Cassie clenched her fists to her sides, readying to do battle, if need be. At the least, she might be able to force the thief to leave his stolen goods behind. Mrs. Littleton would be absolutely devastated to find the jewels that had been passed down to her from her grandmother missing. Gone. Stolen.

Gnawing on her lower lip in consternation, she watched the figure descend. Black leather boots, close-fitting black pants, her gaze continued upward to the dark shirt covering broad shoulders that flexed with each step of his downward climb. Dark blond hair brushed his shirt's collar beneath the black tie of a mask covering part of his face.

The sudden familiarity of the figure struck her, and Cassie gasped in stunned amazement.

Dear Lord! The city's most infamous thief, the Masked Marauder, was none other than Jared Montgomery.

Cassie stood spellbound for all of a minute. As she continued to stare upward in disbelief, she felt the sensation of cool air against her tongue and realized that her mouth was gaping open. She snapped it closed.

Stunned, shock held Cassie rooted firmly in place for all of another ten seconds. Then she bolted into action.

Grabbing up her full skirts, she took several quick steps closer to the trellis, then stopped. Just what did she think she was going to do to stop him?

The question arose without the slightest answer in her mind. All she knew was that when Captain Jared Montgomery's feet touched the ground, she'd be there waiting.

One, two, three—she mentally counted his descending footsteps. One more rung of the trellis to go, and he'd be down. Cassie drew in a breath for courage.

"Stop. Thief," she called out in a hoarse, choked voice. "Damnation," she whispered under her breath.

Jared spun around to face the cry and almost lost his hold on the trellis. One foot swung just inches above the ground as he scrambled to regain his hold and not tumble to the grass below in an undignified heap.

It took him only the space of a few seconds to survey the lone woman standing so defiantly below. Jared couldn't believe his eyes. The dark hair shimmering in the light of the

full moon, the heart-shaped face with its determined chin tilted up to him, and the
shapely body enclosed in the perfectly fitted
gown could belong to only one person. Cassie
Van Dorn.

He released his breath in a ragged sigh.
She looked fully prepared to try and stop
him. Luck had most assuredly abandoned
him the moment he first laid eyes on this
woman, he thought to himself.

There was nothing else to do but to continue his descent to the flat ground below
the trellis. With both booted feet on firm
ground, he released the wood structure and
turned to face his paragon of bravery.

As he faced her, Cassie threw out a hand
as if to ward him off.

"Stay where you are," she warned in a
voice that came out sounding much firmer
than she felt at the moment. She resisted the
temptation to retreat a step, instead biting
her lip and holding her ground.

In the short span that separated them she
could see his eyes glint with suppressed
amusement. The corners of his mouth
turned up in a semblance of a smile.

"And who is going to make me do that?"
he asked in low velvety tones. "Hum, Cassie?"

She felt a jolt all the way to her toes at the
utterance of her name coming from his soft
voice. Crossing her fingers against the lie she

was about to tell, she raised her chin in defiance.

"There are several men on their way here right now. They'll be here any moment."

"And I suppose you called them?"

Cassie kept the fingers of her right hand crossed. "Certainly."

Jared studied her upturned face for the flash of a few seconds. Unable to resist, he took a step nearer.

"Liar," he whispered to her.

A smile crept over his lips as he took another step closer. He watched the agitated rise and fall of her breasts beneath the shimmering fabric of her gown as Cassie's breath rushed out in a gulp, and his smile widened.

That smile meant trouble, Cassie knew it as sure as she breathed in the cool air around her. Almost as if in a daze, she watched him draw nearer, then raise his arms to reach out for her.

Oh no, he wasn't.

She quickly stepped back out of arm's reach. The glint in his eyes proclaimed his intentions louder than any words ever could. The scoundrel intended to kiss her into silence.

She wouldn't allow it this time, she vowed. She couldn't allow it. When he kissed her, she couldn't seem to think for herself. A quite unfamiliar and unsettling prospect.

She retreated another quick two steps, and

her heel caught in the hem of her gown. The tug of her skirt pulled her backwards, and she flailed her arms to remain upright. Her sudden movement only served to increase the downward tug of her gown.

"Damnation," she muttered under her breath.

As she was pulled steadily backwards, the scent of roses suddenly grew stronger, and she realized in the flash of a second that she was about to land amongst the blooms and protruding sharp thorns.

With a speed she hadn't known he was capable of, Jared surged forward and swept her up into his arms, saving her from the rose-bush.

His chest was firm and rock hard beneath her hands. Gulping, she caught hold of the fabric in a desperate attempt to avoid the thorns. His heart raced underneath her knuckles.

She stared up into his face, noticing that the smile that had tipped his lips before was now gone. Was that worry she saw creasing his mouth?

Unable to resist the impulse and without a thought as to the consequences, she raised one hand and ran a fingertip over the creases along his lips. His gaze darkened from between the slits in the dark silken mask covering the upper half of his face.

Enthralled, Cassie trailed her fingers upward to the edge of the silk covering. She eased a finger beneath the mask.

In a sharp movement, Jared jerked his head, and the mask fell loose into her hand. Cassie met his gaze and recognized the wanting in his green-gray eyes. She felt it throughout her body.

Giving in to that desire, Jared lowered his head, and his mouth covered hers in a breath-stealing kiss. It was like receiving a present, and watching a parade, and all the best of everything she could think of rolled into one thing at once.

Cassie clutched the satin mask tightly between her fingers and returned his kiss. Tentatively at first, then gathering more strength as a tide of warmth rolled over her in waves, she slid her arms up and wrapped them around his neck. She could have no more stopped the purely natural movement than she could have stopped drawing breath. In fact, holding tightly to Jared seemed as natural as breathing.

In response, his arms tightened around her, holding her ever closer. Cassie's heart raced, and a delicious wave of dizziness came over her. She felt as if she might swoon—for the first time in her life. Except that she wasn't standing, and a person really couldn't swoon if they were already being carried, could they? Having never swooned before she wasn't sure.

She really should make him set her down;
it was quite improper. And she would make
him, she truly would. In a minute.

He was a thief, after all, her conscience
told her. She ignored it. Somehow, when he
held her so close to his chest, that fact didn't
really seem to matter. No, not a whit.

But it should, her conscience nagged at
her, a niggling whisper in her ear. In the
next instant, Jared's mouth left hers. Cassie
felt bereft, wanting, needing his lips back
upon hers. Instead, he trailed kisses down
the column of her throat, bathing it in loving, silencing her conscience. A gasp of
sound escaped Cassie's lips.

Lower, he traced the curve of her collar
bone, and Cassie felt as if she might melt
into a pool of warmth in his arms if he continued. He did. The soft, satiny brush of his
mustache against her shoulder caused her
skin to tingle.

He ran his lips back and forth along the
deep lace neckline of her gown, dipping his
tongue between the exposed valley of her
breasts. Cassie squeezed her eyes tightly
closed at the sensations he caused. No one
had ever touched her there, much less did
what he was doing and causing the feelings
he was causing. Her breasts felt, oddly
enough, heavy. And wanting. A soft moan
slipped past her lips.

He retraced his path from the vee of her

breasts to the dip of her throat to her chin, then taking her lips at last. His kiss was warm and demanding.

Ever so slowly, he lowered her body, brushing the length of his until her feet touched the ground. Cassie leaned against him, unsure of rather her legs would hold her up. At this moment, she knew if he left her, she would surely fall.

Instead of releasing her, he shifted his hold, tightening his arms about her, enclosing her in his embrace. His lips took hers again, this time in a stamp of pure possession.

Unable to do otherwise, Cassie surrendered to his claim. She met him with a claim of her own, aware that she was in danger of losing her heart to this Yankee thief. And at the moment, not caring a whit about that fact.

Suddenly, the sound of loud voices penetrated Cassie's mind. The party, she thought, coming fully to her senses. If they caught Jared now, they would have him arrested. And possibly even hung. She couldn't allow that. Even if he was a thief.

The last thing she wanted to do was to yell for help and see him arrested. Instead, she pulled back from his embrace, pushing against his broad, unmoving chest with all her might.

"Go!"

Jared snapped his head up at the unexpected command.

"People. They're coming," she stammered. She waved her arm in a gesture to draw his attention to the approaching men. "Now, go!"

She shoved him away, biting down on her lower lip. Her heart and her mind erupted into war. She was protecting a criminal. She was protecting the man she was coming to love.

With a final, quick kiss pressed against her lips, Jared turned away. He ran for the concealment of a group of trees lining the drive.

Cassie stood where he left her, watching his dark figure until it disappeared from sight. She touched her kiss-swollen lips with the fingertips of one hand. What had she done?

The next instant, the previously quiet trysting place erupted into shouts, and questions, and people.

"Are you all right?" someone inquired.

"Was that a thief I saw?" a man shouted.

"What happened?" another voice demanded.

The voices blurred together.

Cassie felt surrounded by jarring noise and the crush of people. Defensively, she raised a hand to her throat. Whatever was she going to tell them?

"It was that thief," a man shouted. "That

Masked Marauder. Dressed in black, I'm certain of it."

Cassie's heart dove for her toes in a sudden plunge. Her breath rushed out in a gasp of instinctive denial. However, the people ignored her distress, intent on discovering the thief's identity. Accusing faces turned to her.

"Did you get a look at his face?" another voice asked in sharp demand.

"He . . . he wore a mask," she stated, avoiding answering their question.

How could she tell them that it had been Jared Montgomery, Union Captain, a thief in whose arms she'd found the closest thing to heaven possible. Oh, damnation, she'd certainly gotten herself into a fix this time.

"Leave the poor girl be." Mrs. Littleton rushed to her side. "Oh, you poor dear. Did he harm you?"

"No," Cassie hurried to assure her.

Everyone pressed around, all speaking at once. Suddenly the evening's calm, cool air became stifling. Cassie started to raise her hand, then realized that she still held Jared's dark mask in her grip. Quickly, before anyone could discern it, she lowered her hand, burying it in the voluminous material of her skirt.

Cassie curled her fingers around the bit of satin that Jared had left behind, hiding her hand and the mask in the concealing folds of her gown. A part of her wanted to protect him. Another part of her demanded that she turn him in. She didn't know which one to listen to. Except that she knew without a doubt that she could not speak the words that would condemn him.

"What was stolen?" one of the men asked.

"Oh, dear me, I don't know," Mrs. Littleton responded in a faint voice. She fanned her hand back and forth, waving a scented handkerchief in front of her face. "Oh, dear me. I do suppose we will have to search the house and—"

"Nothing is missing," Sarah Littleton pushed through the crowd and rushed up to her sister-in-law.

"What?"

"The house is fine," Sarah assured the distraught woman beside her. "I checked, and your jewels are safe. Nothing has even been disturbed."

"Are you sure?" The question slipped out before Cassie could stop it. She'd seen Jared coming down the trellis from the upstairs. Surely the Masked Marauder had stolen *something*.

"Nothing is missing," Sarah insisted in a loud voice.

Cassie frowned, watching the other woman closely. Something was going on. Sarah Littleton was too insistent. Too defensive.

What had she stumbled into?

"I'm sure that Cassie caught him as he was arriving," Sarah explained.

"But—" Cassie cut the denial off. Something strangely out of place was going on here. Surely Jared had stolen something.

Something the Littletons didn't want known.

"Cassie, dear, thank you for saving our home. We owe you a great deal." Mrs. Littleton caught Cassie's hands in hers.

A wave of shame rushed over Cassie. She had done nothing of the sort. Quite the opposite—she'd helped the thief to escape. Her conscience jabbed at her, and she longed to tell them the truth.

Whatever did she think she was doing? She couldn't very well tell them that she had, in fact, caught the thief coming down the trellis and then allowed him to kiss her practically senseless. If Sarah Littleton wanted everyone to believe that she'd scared him off before he'd entered the house, so be it.

Cassie met her mama's questioning gaze, and a blush stole up her cheeks. Alicia's eyes narrowed in thought, and she stared hard at Cassie.

Questions would surely be forthcoming, Cassie thought to herself. And her mama would not be easy to deceive. She had always been able to tell whenever Cassie had attempted to tell an untruth.

"Perhaps it was simply an old beau coming to pay his respects to Sarah," Vangie Maitland piped up with a tinkling laugh and a swish of her wide skirts.

Her comment was met with stunned silence and more than one shocked gasp.

"Vangie," Alicia rushed to fill in the gap. "Not everyone here shares your distinct sense of humor. Please forgive her?" She turned to the crowd that had formed. "I'm quite sure that Cassie is utterly worn out by her ordeal. If you will excuse us, I think we should take her home."

"Oh, Alicia—"

She cut off Vangie. "We're leaving."

With this, Alicia Van Dorn caught Cassie's hand in hers and led the way back through the house and out the front door. For the first time in her life, Vangie followed her sister's lead.

Jared slipped back into the shadows and observed the scene at the Littletons' house. It appeared that no one was going to pursue him.

He felt a twinge of guilt for the situation he'd left Cassie to face alone. Why had she allowed him to escape? The question rose again in his mind.

He slipped his hand into his breast pocket. The dispatches were still safely concealed there. He couldn't believe the audacity of the Littleton woman. She'd dared to carry back dispatches from certain French officials to the Confederacy. Well, these papers would not find their way South, he had seen to that. President Lincoln would be pleased. They were both doing everything in their power to put a stop to this secession plot and stop the bloodshed as soon as humanly possible.

There had already been too much blood shed in this war. Pain knifed through him at the memory of his younger brother. Bryan had held such a love of life, and it had been snuffed out. Too soon.

Bryan had just become engaged to a young lady, of a fine Washington family with Union sympathies, only days before his murder. His life had only been beginning.

Jared clenched his hand into a fist, crushing the dispatches. His brother had been shot at close range and obviously must have known his killer. He would find the person responsible for Bryan's death, and once he did, they would pay. The murderer had not only killed Bryan, but destroyed his family as well.

His proud father had seemed to shrink with the news of his youngest son's death. In truth, Robert Montgomery had never recovered from the loss, and his heart had given out a month later, leaving his wife to bury him. She'd had to face the ordeal alone, since Jared had been off fighting. Now, he owed it to her to track down his brother's killer—the man who'd destroyed their family.

Jared straightened and loosened his grip on the dispatches, shoving the cold memories back to the dark recesses of his mind. It was time he left here and got back to his work; he had to deliver the papers. As he turned away, the clamoring noise from the side of the Littletons' house brought back a mental picture of Cassie. One question haunted him.

Exactly what was Cassie Van Dorn's involvement in all of this?

He fully intended to find out.

As soon as they arrived home, Cassie pretended an exhaustion she was far from feeling to avoid her mama's questions. Within minutes, her mother brushed a kiss across her cheek and crossed to the bedchamber door, sending Cassie a "we'll discuss this later" look.

Content to have at least postponed the unwelcome discussion until the morrow, Cassie sighed and retrieved the black mask from under her pillow where she'd hidden it when no one was watching. Thoughtfully, she rubbed it between her fingers.

The movement brought forth a mental picture of Jared Montgomery. For the umpteenth time she asked herself how she could have allowed him to escape.

Allowed? She'd practically ordered him to flee. Whatever had happened to her sense of justice? What was happening to her?

That was twice she'd allowed him to escape. The first time with *her* papers, and the second time with heaven only knew what from the Littletons' home. There wouldn't be a third time, she thought with firm determination.

Or would there?

Just the same as last night, Jared's face filled her thoughts. Damnation.

Was her last waking thought each night destined to be of Jared Montgomery?

Next time they met it would be on her terms, Cassie vowed in the silence of the room. She fully intended to retrieve those papers that Michael Jones had informed her that a certain Union Captain still held. By this time tomorrow, those papers would be hers.

With this thought and a mental picture of Jared firmly entrenched in her mind, she punched her pillow and turned over.

Cassie awoke to the sound of women's voices raised in anger. It took her only the space of half a minute to recognize the voices as belonging to her mother and Aunt Vangie.

"We are not going!" her mama shouted, disbelief and shock coloring her usually calm voice.

"Oh, Alicia. Don't carry on so." Aunt Vangie drawled in a bored tone, in spite of its elevated volume. "It's only a party, for gracious sakes."

Cassie had a mental picture of her aunt tossing her head in a typical Vangie Maitland gesture of vexation, her brown curls bouncing.

Her aunt loved a good argument, and Cassie suspected that she started most of the arguments on purpose and not out of the innocence she pretended.

"We are most assuredly not going. And that is the end of it," her mother announced.

Cassie could almost hear her mama stomp her dainty foot in defiance to Vangie's attempt at maneuvering her into agreement.

"Alicia, don't be such a fool."

"Me, a fool!"

"Yes, you, sister dear."

"I can't believe that even you would actually accept an invitation to a soiree celebrating the *Union* victories over our Confederacy."

"Oh, Alicia." Vangie's tone dismissed her sister's comment.

"Whatever were you thinking of? To attend a Union celebration while my Thomas is fighting for the Confederacy and what he believes in—"

"Oh, posh."

"Vangie, you never cared for anybody but yourself in your entire life."

"What?" A shriek cut the morning air.

Cassie sighed. The argument below was worsening. She would have to intervene. Unlike some of their arguments, this one was not going to wind down to a quiet end.

"You know I care for Thomas," Vangie yelled aloud. "And Cassie and you, too," she added quickly.

The spat between the sisters filled the house.

Cassie closed her eyes, wishing she could shut them out. She wanted to play peacemaker between her mama and Aunt Vangie about as much as a snowball wished for a sojourn in a hot oven.

Last night's long hours of self-incrimination regarding her actions toward Jared Montgomery had left her poorly prepared to face a rising battle between her mother and Aunt Vangie first thing this morning, much less to be called upon to make peace between the two of them.

It would be like trying to separate two spitting, battling kittens and a bowl of cream. Somebody was bound to get scratched.

As the angry voices below the stairs continued to raise in volume, Cassie threw back the bedcovers. She might as well go downstairs and put a stop to the bickering. It wasn't going to get any better without her interference.

Cassie recalled her mama's prediction. It was going to be a long month.

These arguments happened as regular as the sunrise every time Aunt Vangie visited. It was almost as if she enjoyed starting the arguments and baiting her sister. Sometimes Cassie wondered why the two sisters didn't keep their distance from each other.

However, at least once a year Aunt Vangie would contact Alicia, and her mama would usually invite her for a visit. Mama lived under the impression that her sister spent too much time alone, which she considered unhealthy, and that Vangie needed family around her. Cassie suspected it was more out of a sense of misplaced guilt, which Aunt Vangie played up in the fullest.

Personally, Cassie found it hard to believe that her father had ever been truly interested in Aunt Vangie. Perhaps he'd been attracted to her at first, but that would have been as far as it had gone. Sure her aunt was pretty, but he and Mama were so happy together, and had always seemed perfect for each other. He would never be able to put up with Aunt Vangie's tantrums and machinations.

As Cassie grabbed up her soft pink wrapper, a sudden recollection of the night she'd worn this same pink nightgown and wrapper, and confronted Jared in her bedchamber sprang to mind. As a heated blush stole up her cheeks, a crash sounded from below. She grimaced and reluctantly pushed aside all thoughts of Jared. It sounded as if the skirmish below had erupted into a full-scale battle.

Hurriedly, she tied her sash and dashed out of her room and down the stairs. Halfway to the bottom, she skidded to a halt.

Broken shards of a blue and white china vase, one of her mama's favorites, littered the polished wood floor of the foyer. A sprinkling of flower petals lay in bright array amongst the destruction.

"Don't you dare ever say that to me again!" Vangie screeched.

Another crash from the next room signalled the demise of a second vase at Aunt Vangie's hands.

Cassie took the remaining stairs at a run, stopping on the bottom one to carefully skirt the broken china. She reached the sitting room in time to see Aunt Vangie grab up a bowl.

"No!" Cassie called out.

Not that. The blue bowl in her aunt's hands happened to be the one that her father had given her mama shortly before he'd departed for Virginia. If Aunt Vangie shattered that particular item, all hell would break loose.

Dashing across the room, Cassie snatched the bowl out of her aunt's hands before she could send it crashing to the floor in a shattered heap. She cradled the precious bowl in her arms, unwilling to put it down within her aunt's reach just yet.

"What is this all about?" Cassie hugged the bowl to her chest and looked from one woman to the other.

The two sisters couldn't look more opposite this morning. Alicia wore a plain wrapper of palest ivory, while Aunt Vangie was decked out in a bright cerise wrapper with satin trim and a wide bow at her waist. She reminded Cassie of a bowl of fresh cherries on display.

"She accepted an invitation to a Union celebration soiree. For all of us," Alicia announced with a dramatic sweep of her arms.

"Oh, posh. Your mother is behaving like a fool," Vangie accused.

The two sisters fell silent and glared at each other. Alicia was the first to look away. A smug smile of victory lit Vangie's face for the barest of an instant, before she formed her lips into a pout.

"I was only doing it for Cassie's sake."

"Me?" Cassie squeaked, wondering how she'd gotten pulled into the argument.

Trust Aunt Vangie to accomplish the impossible.

"Why, of course, dear." Vangie lowered her gaze and sauntered up to Cassie's side.

As Alicia glared her distrust, Vangie slipped an arm around Cassie's shoulders.

"Last night was sorely lacking in available

men, and I simply will not stand by and let you be placed on a shelf. You're not getting any younger, my dear."

Cassie's gasp passed unnoticed by her insistent Aunt Vangie.

"We must find you a promising beau, or marriage will elude you," Vangie stated in a matter of fact tone that brooked no argument.

In a swirl of skirts, Vangie turned to confront Alicia. "Let's be realistic, sister dear. The only ones left with any money to speak of will be the Yankees. No matter how this war ends, that's the way it's going to be." She waved her hand in a dismissive gesture. "The sooner we all accept that, the better things will be."

"Vangie—"

"Alicia, don't be a fool! I'm being sensible, not disloyal. If you entertain any hopes of finding Cassie a suitable match, we must look to the Yankees. And at that party, there will be plenty of Yankees—wealthy Yankees at that."

Head held high, Vangie turned away and headed for the stairs. She had casually dismissed both Cassie and her mama along with the argument with a presumption that only Vangie Maitland was capable of, Cassie thought. A twinge of admiration for her surfaced.

"Now, I'm going up to pick out my gown

for tonight. I suggest you two do the same. It will take positively hours to ready ourselves. It is imperative that we be at our very best."

Aunt Vangie caught up her skirts and with a delicate sniff, flounced up the stairs to her bedchamber. The loud slam of the door punctuated her mandate.

Cassie and her mama were left to survey the wreckage left behind. Gingerly, Cassie sat the bowl she'd protected down on the window table.

"That woman is going to be the death of me," Alicia proclaimed dramatically.

Cassie bit her lip to restrain the smile that threatened to tip her lips upward. Mama would not take to that gesture kindly at the moment. She turned away and began clearing away the broken china.

By late afternoon the house was a flurry of activity in preparation for attending the Union soiree that evening. Aunt Vangie had won the altercation, as Cassie knew she would.

Shaking her head at the turn of events, Cassie caught up the freshly pressed gown and crossed to the foyer. Aunt Vangie had every one of the servants occupied with fetching her one thing or another. She wasn't sure just how her aunt had accomplished that feat.

As Cassie rounded the corner of the stairs, she glanced up in time to see a figure slipping into *her* bedchamber. She almost dropped the gown spilling across her arms.

She had no doubt to the person's identity. She'd recognize that overly bright cerise dressing gown anywhere. Aunt Vangie! And she was going into *Cassie's* room.

Mama's morphine! The thought jolted Cassie down to her toes.

She couldn't allow Aunt Vangie to discover it. No matter what it took to stop her.

Cassie let out a yelp and dashed up the stairs.

Five

Mere steps from her bedroom door, Cassie skidded to a halt, her slipper-clad feet sliding on the highly polished wood floor of the stair landing. Her senses returned with a rush of reason, blocking out her earlier near panic. It wouldn't do to go bursting into her room in such a haphazard manner.

The action would only serve to raise Aunt Vangie's suspicions. And like a tenacious terrier, once Evangeline Maitland thought she had something to sink her teeth into, she would do it with a vengeance. Aunt Vangie would never rest until she knew *exactly* what was going on in the Van Dorn house.

Damnation! There was no way on this earth that Cassie could allow that to happen. She tightened her fingers on the skirt of the gown draped across her arms.

She forced herself to draw in a deep, calming breath and tried to steady her galloping heart. With a hand to her chest, she set her face in the most sedate expression possible. Satisfied she'd at least succeeded in part, she reached out a hand that refused to remain steady and opened the bedroom door.

At first Cassie didn't see anyone in the room, and she looked around in disbelief. She *knew* she'd seen Aunt Vangie slip inside and close the door. Then she spotted her aunt bent down, pawing through the top drawer of the bureau. She was so intent on her search, for only heaven knew what, that she didn't immediately hear Cassie enter the room.

Recalling that she'd already removed the key to the safe from the bureau drawer, Cassie swallowed down a sigh of relief. Luckily, she had found a new hiding place for that key. After Jared's night-time foray, she had moved the key to the back of her armoire, hidden away, high on a tiny ledge of wood. She couldn't picture even Aunt Vangie looking for it there.

"Aunt Vangie, can I help you find something?" Cassie asked in a deceptively calm, helpful tone that hid her inner nervousness.

Beside her, Vangie jerked upright and slammed the bureau drawer in a quick movement. A guilty flush stained her fair cheeks.

"Oh Cassie, you like to scared the life right out of me." She fanned her face with her hand. "I swear, for the rest of the night I'm going to be as nervous as a long-tailed cat in a room full of rocking chairs."

In spite of herself, Cassie giggled. She

must have truly surprised her aunt for her to have said something like that.

"My gracious, you really shouldn't sneak up on someone that way, dear," Aunt Vangie gently reprimanded. "I couldn't find you about, so I was looking to see if you had a coronet I could borrow tonight. It wouldn't do to wear the same one I wore last night."

Cassie bit back her smile. It appeared that she had well and truly spiked her aunt's plans for now—if indeed she had been searching the room out of pure curiosity and not simply looking for a coronet.

"I'm sorry, Aunt Vangie, but I don't own a single coronet."

"What? How Alicia could have been so remiss, I swear I don't know. Oh, excuse me, dear, I truly shouldn't say anything like that. She is your mother, after all."

Aunt Vangie turned away, her gaze quickly skimming the room. She reverted her attention back to Cassie—and the bed.

Cassie's heart leaped for her throat, then tumbled to her toes. Not the bed, please, not the bed. She had to get her aunt out of the room. Now! Before she could stumble onto the morphine hidden beneath the bed and its ruffled coverlet.

Crossing to the bed, she quickly laid the gown across the coverlet. In an attempt to hide the slight tremble of her hands and draw her aunt's attention away from other things to the gown, she smoothed out the folds of the voluminous skirt. The gown shimmered iridescent blue in the light.

"Oh, dear girl, is that the gown you plan on wearing tonight? Oh, do say yes," Aunt Vangie insisted. "I won't hear of any other answer from you."

Vangie ran her hands over the silver threads edging the gown's bodice.

"Cassie, my dear girl, you will most certainly draw the Yankees' attention in this." She patted one of her own mahogany curls into place. "I will have to find something equally dazzling to wear."

Aunt Vangie stepped back a step and surveyed the gown, then Cassie. Tapping a fingertip against the tip of her chin, she stared hard at her, until Cassie began to know how that long-tailed cat that her aunt spoke about would be feeling.

"It is *almost* perfect. Humm." Vangie snapped her fingers. "I know. All it needs is a silver coronet and just a smattering of those peacock blue ostrich plumes I brought with me—"

"Aunt Vangie," Cassie cut in hurriedly, hiding her shudder of dismay. She wasn't about to attend a party with peacock blue ostrich feathers sprouting in her hair. "Remember, I told you that I don't have any coronets. And you were looking for that silver one for yourself. I'll be happy to make do with the satin ribbons I'd planned on wearing."

"I swear that I don't know what Alicia is thinking. Tsk, tsk," Vangie clicked her tongue. "You don't own even a single coronet."

"Aunt Vangie—" Cassie stepped forward, hoping to encourage her aunt to leave. It was beginning to look like an impossible task.

"Of course, you know, Cassie, that I never meant to imply that your mother . . ."

Her mother . . . Cassie ignored the rest of what her aunt was saying as an idea began to take shape and form in her mind. She grabbed onto it like a drowning man would clasp a lifeline.

"Speaking of Mama—I think I remember that she had a silver coronet. It would look stunning in your hair," Cassie announced with a gleeful clap of her hands "Why don't we go see?"

"Well," Vangie drew the word out into two long syllables.

Cassie quickly linked her arm with her aunt's and before Vangie had any chance to come up with an excuse to stay in Cassie's room any longer, she led her to the open door.

"Let's go and check with Mama."

Without pausing, or giving her aunt an opportunity to change her mind, Cassie pulled her along behind her to her mother's bedchamber.

"Mama?" Cassie called out in warning, wanting to ensure that her mother knew they were approaching her room.

While she was sure that her mother had secreted all of the morphine shipment under her bed, she couldn't be for certain that Mama wasn't up to something else as well. And she couldn't take the risk of being wrong.

Cassie came to a halt outside her mother's doorway, trying to give her the extra moments of warning if she needed them.

"Mama," she called out. "It's Aunt Vangie and Cassie."

Unprepared for Cassie's sudden stop, Aunt Vangie plowed into her back, pushing her forward through the open doorway and into the room.

"Oh, Cassie." Alicia shut a drawer to her dressing table and turned around. "Vangie."

Cassie eyed the drawer and then her mother suspiciously. Please, don't let her be up to anything else, she silently mouthed the prayer.

"Aunt Vangie and I were searching my room for a coronet for her to borrow for tonight's soiree, and we couldn't find one in my room. I thought I remembered that you had a beautiful silver one," Cassie rushed to explain, hoping that her mama would understand the near crisis that had been averted, and still hung over them, threatening should her aunt continue her searching.

One glance at her mother's stricken face confirmed to Cassie that her mama had indeed understood her message.

"Your room?" Alicia quickly attempted to cover her blunder with a fit of coughing.

"Whatever is wrong with you, Alicia?" Vangie queried, crossing to her sister's side to administer a slap on the back.

"I could use a . . . glass of water . . . Cassie, dear?" Alicia asked, sending her a pleading look.

A frown crinkled Cassie's forehead for a moment. Her mother had never been prone to coughing spells . . . and if she wanted something, she would usually ring for a maid.

Unless she was signalling her to do something. Such as move the morphine?

"Yes," Cassie answered quickly. "I'll, ah," she paused, trying to think of a way to relay her upcoming actions to her mama. "I'll *move*, ah, and get you some water."

"Yes, do that, dear." Alicia nodded her head and coughed again.

As she turned to leave, Cassie saw her mother catch Vangie's arm and draw her close. "Oh, Vangie, please stay with me. I may need you."

Cassie slipped out the door, then forced herself to walk to the stairs in case her aunt was watching. Once she was sure she was out of sight of the two women, she dashed to her room, careful to shut the door silently behind her.

It took all of two minutes to scramble under the bed and pull out the box from beneath. Thank goodness that only one dozen small bottles of white powder greeted her. She didn't know if she could have managed many more in a single trip. Quickly, she snatched up a petticoat and threw it over the box of bottles to hide the contents, just in case she met anyone on the stairs. Especially Aunt Vangie.

Hefting the small box, Cassie tiptoed back to the door. Hardly daring to breathe, she opened the wooden panel a crack and peered out, then jumped as she heard Aunt Vangie's raised voice.

"My gracious, Alicia. The way you were carrying on, one would think you had taken ill. I certainly hope you aren't acting up just to get out of going to that party tonight."

Her mother responded with another fit of coughing.

Cassie grinned. She hoped her mother's ploy to keep Vangie at her side worked. She eased the door open, all the while praying that Aunt Vangie wouldn't take this moment to flounce out of her mama's room in a fit of exasperation. That's all she needed.

Gripping the box securely, Cassie slipped

back out into the hall and made a calculated
dash for the stairs. She took the steps as fast
as possible with the box held tightly in her
arms. She skidded when she reached the bottom and precariously balanced the small box
of bottles, scarcely preventing them from
tumbling out of the box to the wood floor.

She glanced about her, at a loss as to
where to hide the shipment. It had to be
someplace where neither Aunt Vangie or the
servants were likely to look. And it had to
be quick.

"My gracious, Alicia," Aunt Vangie's voice
trailed down the stairs, causing Cassie to
jump. "The way you're carrying on, a person
would think you'd never had a fit of the va-
pors before."

Cassie ducked back behind the staircase. It
seemed she was just in time, for a second
later a door slammed upstairs.

Oh, my gracious is right. Cassie bit her lower
lip, waiting for her aunt to come flouncing
down the stairs. Now what was she to do?

She hugged the box of morphine to her
chest protectively and desperately looked
around for a suitable hiding place, all the
while keeping her ear attuned for any giveaway noise that would signal Aunt Vangie's
descent down the stairs.

As she held her breath, it remained quiet
upstairs for several moments, and Cassie took
advantage of the silence. She quickly bent

down and shoved the box securely beneath the last step, then stepped back and brushed any dust from her hands. Mama's morphine would just have to stay there for the time being. She dared not chance moving it again right now.

"Cassie!" Aunt Vangie yelled out.

Mama's water! Cassie remembered her earlier pretense to sidetrack her aunt. There wasn't time to get to the kitchen and back now. Instead, she dashed for the study.

Grabbing up the crystal decanter, she poured a splash of sherry into a glass. The amber liquid was a far cry from water, but it would have to do.

Cassie spun around and hurried back up the stairs again as fast as she could without spilling the liquid over the side of the glass. At her mother's door, she paused to tuck a stray tendril of hair behind her ear. It wouldn't do to look like she'd just been crawling under beds and hiding behind staircases, would it?

"Mama? Are you better now?" she asked, entering the room and holding out the glass to her mother. "I brought you a sherry."

"Thank heavens," her mother responded with a heartfelt sigh.

Alicia took the glass from Cassie and swallowed the contents in one gulp. "Bless you, dear." She gave the now empty glass back to Cassie.

"Mama—"

"Where is it?" her mother whispered.

Suddenly looking up over Cassie's shoulder, Alicia said in a louder voice, "Why, Vangie. I'm feeling much better now."

Vangie glanced from the tell-tale empty sherry glass to her sister and back to the glass. "My gracious, Alicia! Sherry at this early hour of the day? Whatever has come over you?"

Cassie bit back a gurgle of laughter. She met her mama's questioning gaze and mouthed the words, "Behind the stairs."

Across from Cassie, her mother's eyes widened. She shook her head back and forth slowly as if to say that would never do.

"Yes," Cassie mouthed the word with finality.

Her mother turned to Vangie and sent her an apologetic smile. "Thank you, Vangie, for your concern. I'm fine now. Cassie's little drop of sherry truly helped me. And now that I'm feeling better, I think it's time that we all started readying for the Yankee soiree you are so set on attending."

"Well!" Vangie flounced to the door. "I don't know whatever has made you so changeable."

"Vangie?" Alicia stopped her. "Would you and Cassie mind searching my bureau drawers for that silver coronet? I fear that I don't recall which one I put it in. I'd help, but I do need to go downstairs for . . . that glass of water. I feel my cough coming back."

As she passed Cassie, her mama winked at her and whispered, "I know where to hide it."

For the next five minutes Cassie attempted to fully occupy her aunt's attention with their search for the missing coronet, all the while wondering where on earth her mother was hiding the morphine. She shuddered to think of the possibilities.

After searching the drawers, Vangie turned to the dressing table. She shoved aside item after item, until a small drawer to the side of the dressing table revealed the coronet they'd been searching for.

"Well, at last." Vangie held it up in triumph.

"Oh, good, I see you found it," Alicia walked into the bedroom at that moment, jostling Cassie on her way past.

Cassie gasped as she felt her mama slip a cool metal object into her hand, then close her hand around it. As her fingers felt the metal she recognized it as a key.

"Your father's desk. Bottom drawer," she bent close, whispering the words, then dropping a kiss on Cassie's cheek.

"I do believe it's time that we all started readying ourselves for tonight," her mama announced.

"Yes, Mama," Cassie answered, knowing

that now was not the time to ask questions with Aunt Vangie standing there with them.

Things most assuredly seemed to be going from bad to worse, she thought. Now, it appeared that she had two keys to keep hidden.

An hour later, Cassie smoothed the voluminous full skirt of her gown over her hoop. The pale blue skirts shimmered in the light, catching and reflecting each glimmer of lamplight.

A sudden thought occurred to her. The iridescent quality of the gown would be a definite disadvantage if she had to sneak about outside at all. If she were to follow her plan to retrieve the papers, that would most assuredly require skulking about in the dark.

She knew without a doubt that her mama would insist that she wear her pale blue velvet pelisse with the gown. One problem—the cloak was trimmed with white fur and ermine tails—surely guaranteed to catch anyone's attention in the dark of night. No, she'd need a dark cloak.

She had to find a way to leave the beautiful pale blue cloak behind.

Cassie shot a glance around the room, searching for an answer to her dilemma. As her gaze landed on the bed, she had her answer. The area under the bed could most assuredly hold her pelisse, now that Mama's morphine shipment was secreted elsewhere. No one would consider looking there for the misplaced garment.

Quickly, she caught up the beautiful velvet and fur pelisse and crossed to the bed. It took a good deal of effort and exertion, what with her hoop and petticoats in the way, to lay the wrap out and slide it under the bed. Checking to ensure that not a corner peeked out, she sat back on her heels and surveyed the floor. Then, certain that all was fine, she smoothed the ruffled coverlet back into place.

She had scarcely had time to stand up and adjust her hoop when the bedroom door swung open. In truth, her skirts were still swaying in what Mama would refer to as "a strange way." Her heart raced into double time, and she barely stopped herself from jumping in agitation.

"I was right. That gown is absolutely stunning on you." Vangie Maitland waved a hand at Cassie and breezed into the room. Uninvited.

Her citrine gown stood out like a beacon, commanding attention from anyone within viewing range. Once again, the tightly cinched waist set off her figure, and a set of matching dyed ostrich plumes waved amongst her dark curls atop her head.

Cassie's first thought was that the particular hue of her aunt's bright gown would clash with anyone else's mahogany-colored hair, but on Aunt Vangie it didn't. Instead, the shade of reddish-yellow performed the impossible, turning her hair the fine patina of a rich sable stole.

"Aunt Vangie, you look beautiful," she complimented with sincerity.

Her aunt blushed becomingly at her praise.

"Are you ready? Alicia is determined that we not be late tonight." Vangie threw up her hands and shook her head. "Although why it matters a whit is beyond me."

"I'll only be a moment."

Cassie crossed to the dressing table and picked up a silver heart-shaped locket extended on a blue velvet ribbon. She clasped it around her neck, adjusted the silver heart, and turned back to face her aunt.

"Ready," she announced.

"Oh, my gracious." Vangie covered her neck with the fingertips of one hand. "I've forgotten my jewels. Tell Alicia that I'll be right along."

Aunt Vangie fled the room as quickly as she'd entered, much to Cassie's amazement. And relief. Now there was no one about to notice that she wasn't carrying her pelisse draped over her arm.

Gathering her skirt carefully, Cassie left the bedroom and descended the stairs, hoping to reach the sitting room before either

her mama or Aunt Vangie. She needed a few precious moments alone to plan her night.

She succeeded in being the first one downstairs and sighed with relief. So far so good, she thought, crossing her fingers for continued good fortune.

Nervously, she gnawed on the tip of one fingernail. Jared would surely be at the soiree tonight. She paced the width of the sitting room and back again.

It was, after all, a Union party scheduled to celebrate Union victories that they were attending. Her stomach rolled, rebelling at the thought. There was nothing to do but close her mind to her conscience and attend the soiree. Perhaps some good could come out of the event. In fact, Jared Montgomery was sure to be present.

She couldn't unmask him, her heart told her. Couldn't reveal him as the Masked Marauder. But she could devise a way to retrieve those papers. Perhaps that would act as a salve to her wounded pride.

Suddenly, the way was as clear as crystal to her. She would connive to get close to Jared, so she could retrieve the papers. But . . . she brushed aside the niggling start of a warning.

There was no real danger—not if she was careful.

She knew what she must do.

At the sound of voices, Cassie counted to

three and strolled out of the sitting room to join her mama and Aunt Vangie.

"Oh, there you are," her mama exclaimed. "For a moment I thought we were surely going to be late. Shall we?"

"Oh, I've misplaced my pelisse," Cassie said as if she'd only this moment noticed it was missing.

She'd waited until the last possible second to make her announcement, ensuring that there wasn't enough time to find the garment that was at this very moment secreted under her bed.

"Oh, Cassie," her mama responded in dismay, glancing to the door.

"I'll only be a minute." Cassie lifted her skirt, careful so not to wrinkle it. She turned for the stairway, but her mama stopped her.

"Cassie, dear. We don't have time for you to go look for it now. I do hate to be late. And I absolutely *refuse* to walk in noticeably late to a Yankee soiree."

"Oh, posh," Aunt Vangie admonished. "She can't very well go without one, Alicia. Besides, if we're the last to arrive, we will receive more attention."

Aunt Vangie waved her on.

"That's what I'm afraid of," Alicia muttered.

"I'm sure I have one that she could borrow," Aunt Vangie offered. "I'll help her find it."

Cassie bit back her instant denial. She

could well imagine the bright color of any garment owned by her aunt. The purpose tonight was not to attract attention.

"We haven't time," Alicia prompted.

"You two stay here, I'll only be a second," Cassie spoke up before her aunt could make a move for the stairs.

Catching up her skirts, Cassie ran up the stairs. It only took her a moment to retrieve the dark blue cloak she'd readied for this moment. She couldn't very well wear her lighter one when she stole the papers back from Jared, could she?

A mental picture of him standing in her room that night came back to haunt her. As she pushed it aside, it was just as quickly replaced by a second picture of him after he'd kissed her practically senseless at the Littleton's last night. As much as she tried this image remained with her all the way back down the stairs.

Cassie's last thought as she left the house with her mother and aunt was that she must try and protect her heart from the charming Yankee.

Light shone brightly from every window of the two-story house on Pennsylvania Avenue. Music and laughter from the Union soiree flowed from the house, issuing its own invitation. Cassie swallowed down her trepidation. Into the lion's den, she told herself as she entered the foyer with her mother and Aunt Vangie.

Candlelight glimmered in the entry, and the sounds of voices and laughter filled the air. Beside her, she could feel her mother stiffen in her deep blue gown. Cassie ached to tell her that everything would be fine. Instead, she reached out and gave her hand a quick squeeze of reassurance.

At the gesture, Alicia returned the pressure, flashing a smile to Cassie. Then, her mama raised her head in contempt of all the celebrations around her and entered the ballroom with a proud tilt to her head that practically asked for trouble.

Cassie sighed under her breath. It was going to be a very long night.

As she glanced around the gaily decorated room, Cassie recognized several faces. Gideon Welles with his long gray beard was here. Beside him, deep in conversation was Secretary William Seward. President Lincoln's Secretary of State stood with his large head thrust forward, listening intently to the other man.

Chief Justice Salmon Chase held court in one corner of the room with a small crowd surrounding him. It appeared that the elite of Washington had attended tonight. To the left she also spotted a couple of generals whose names eluded her. Not that it mattered, she told herself. She was here to find one man. Jared Montgomery.

Her gaze passed over Michael Jones, and this time it was the government clerk who signalled Cassie of their need to talk. For an instant Cassie's breath caught in her throat. What had gone wrong? Had Will Radford returned early? Had she ran out of time before she'd even been given a second chance to retrieve the papers?

Forcing herself to remain calm, she reminded herself that a message from their informant didn't have to relay bad news. It was only her guilty conscience prodding her that had caused the troubled thoughts.

Slipping away from her mama and Aunt Vangie, who were beginning to argue quietly over the extravagance of the soiree, Cassie sauntered to the refreshment table where he met her. To any attentive eyes it appeared to be a chance meeting. The young clerk dipped his head in a modest bow and then motioned to the table.

"May I get you a refreshment?"

"Why, yes. Thank you," she responded demurely, all the while wishing she could voice the sudden trepidation she felt.

But it wouldn't do to appear nervous or frightened. No matter how she felt inside, she had to appear calm and self-assured.

"Ma'am." He turned and gathered up two cups.

"It's a nice evening, isn't it?" she asked, an unwanted hesitant note to her voice.

She waited, holding her breath, for him to respond to her query. It was his chance to tell her that all was not well, to tell her that a problem had arisen. Or to assure her that all was well.

"Message received for you to meet Will at eleven. At Bodie's."

"I'll be there," she promised.

She knew the location well, she'd met Will there twice before in the past. Mrs. Bodie's shop was renowned for displaying the latest fashion in bonnets, and it was a mere two blocks from Willard's Hotel.

She only had until eleven o'clock tomorrow morning to retrieve the papers. Cassie could almost feel the sands of the hourglass slipping away through her fingers.

As Michael Jones extended the refreshment to her, he leaned closer and whispered, "The papers are stuck to the back of the captain's headboard."

He recited off an address situated a mere few blocks away, and she recognized the area, but it took the space of a full minute for the import of the seemingly meaningless words to reach her brain. The papers!

Relief swamped over her in waves. Mr. Jones had managed to learn the location of the papers that they sought. And that location happened to be tucked behind Captain Jared Montgomery's bed!

Cassie swallowed the sudden lump that rose to the back of her throat. How was she to retrieve the papers from his bed?

As if the thought had conjured him up, Cassie glanced up to meet Jared Montgomery's gaze from across the room. Her heart did a sudden flip-flop, then sunk to the pit of her stomach.

son appeared to be locked in way Cassie
Jared triumphantly clutch... ...
Cassie settled into the sudden, intoxicant...
...of the risks of her career. It was sud...
...to survive the consequences, the lack...
...As the tempting treasure proved too alluring...
...felt tempting to the spirit that could stop...
...dare him as her heart. Her heart told...
...indeed perilous, and Jared...be all in far...
...mission...

Six

Cassie held her breath, waiting.

Jared strode across the room, coming straight for her. All thoughts of Will Radford, as well as her mother and her aunt fled, to be replaced by only thoughts of the man approaching her.

The dark blue of Jared's uniform set off his burnished hair. It seemed that the thick, dark blond pelt absorbed the very light from the chandelier above, then reflected it back. Cassie gulped in a breath for her suddenly air-starved lungs.

This was the man she was supposed to steal from?

She wasn't certain that she could do it.

Run, a little voice in her head warned her. *Don't,* her heart ordered back.

Confusion clouded her thinking for the time it took for Jared to reach her side. Before she knew it, he was smiling down at her. And it was too late to escape.

"May I have the pleasure of this dance, Cassie?" Jared's voice held a note of command wrapped up in a harmless request, much like hard steel wrapped in deceptively soft black velvet.

She couldn't have refused even if she'd wanted to do so.

The soft lilting music around them penetrated her thoughts. A waltz. A slow, romantic, enticing waltz was being played.

Why couldn't it have been a nice, lively polka? she thought for an instant. It would be so much safer and easier to deal with, and she could keep him at an arm's length or more. Then Jared drew her into his arms, and the time for thinking was past.

Her skin tingled where his hand rested on her waist, and she felt her skin warm beneath his possessive touch. As she attempted to ease away, putting the semblance of a respectable distance between them, he drew her closer. Once more, Cassie moved back a step, but Jared was having none of it. He stepped closer, and his arm tightened about her. It nearly took her breath away.

You're supposed to be finding a way to get closer to him, to belay his suspicions, Cassie reminded herself. It would hardly do to keep up their tug of war. This time, she didn't pull away from him. She told herself she did it only because it was necessary.

As Jared looked down at her, a questioning arch to his brow, she merely smiled up at him. They engaged in a silent, wordless battle of wills—his questioning, hers smilingly refusing to answer.

The music ebbed and flowed around them, and they moved in perfect time together in spite of, or perhaps because of, their intent concentration on each other.

As Cassie continued to stare up at Jared, meeting his gaze, once again the thought that *this* was the man she was expected to steal from wavered in her mind.

For the space of a heartbeat she knew she couldn't go through with her plan.

"We've got those Rebels on the run now. I heard that the casualties in that battle . . ." The speaker danced past them, leaving behind him the images his words brought forth.

The overheard words hit Cassie with the shock of a douse of icy cold water. Rebels . . . casualties . . . her father . . . in danger.

No—the plot to force Washington to secede had to be successful. The war had to end soon. Before anything happened to her father. Or to her impetuous mother. And it was up to her to ensure that.

She had to go through with her plan to steal back those documents from Jared. Too much depended on her actions tonight.

A sense of regret tugged at her. Anything that might have been between her and Jared would surely die when he learned that she had deceived him. And he'd learn that the moment he found out she had sneaked into his house and stolen the papers back from him. No man's pride would allow him to forgive that action.

The music came to an end, and Cassie fought back the sudden sting of tears at the back of her eyes. Clearing her now tight throat, she forced out a polite "thank you" to Jared, then spun away quickly out of his reach. She weaved between the dancers leaving the dance floor and sought out her mama and Aunt Vangie.

The sisters were quarrelling again. She shut out their hushed argument and watched Jared walk to the veranda doors and lean against a door post. His eyes followed her every move.

Cassie knew that her escape from Jared had been only temporary. Her heart fluttered like the wings of a butterfly at the thought, and she wasn't sure if it was from trepidation of their next encounter or anticipation of the feel of his touch again.

She should be getting close to him, she told herself, not attempting to elude him. But, try as she might she could not force herself to be so conniving as to use their budding relationship to betray him. It just wasn't in her. She would have to devise another way. Meanwhile, she would have to stay out of his reach.

It took Jared less than twenty minutes to maneuver Cassie into another waltz. This time being held close in his arms was a bit of heaven and hell combined. After her second dance with him, she knew she had to do her darndest to stay out of his arms. If he held her close again, she would never be able to go ahead with her plan to steal from him.

When the music came to a close, Cassie hastily retreated to the questionable safety of Aunt Vangie's side. She knew instinctively that her aunt would likely as not refuse to allow her to dance another dance with a mere captain. Vangie had her sites set much higher for Cassie's future. Cassie well knew this and used it to her advantage. Allowing her aunt to proceed with her matchmaking attempts, she successfully kept Jared at bay.

Cassie endured the next hour and a quarter by thoroughly planning and replanning her retrieval of the papers from Jared's bedroom. She refused to use the word "steal." She wasn't really stealing; she was merely retrieving what Jared had already stolen from her. And what about the Admiral, her conscience insisted upon asking her.

Brushing aside the niggling voice of her conscience, she danced with the assortment of Union officers presented to her by Aunt Vangie. A waltz followed a lively polka, then came a quadrille, another waltz . . . Cassie lost count of the number of dances foisted on her by her matchmaking aunt.

Conversations around her were filled with speculations on the upcoming presidential election or the upcoming battles. Cassie had little desire to listen to news of either. She only wanted the war over and done with; she wanted the senseless killing from a war that had gone on far too long to stop—before it swept away her father or her mama. If it lasted much longer, she feared she might lose them both.

She didn't know how long she could keep up with her mama's wayward schemes in time to stop them from endangering her or worse. And this visit by Aunt Vangie only complicated everything, increasing the danger with each passing day.

It was time to put her plan to retrieve the packet of papers into action.

This time when her smartly uniformed dance partner proceeded to escort her back to her aunt, she instead steered their course to her mother.

Alicia met Cassie's approach with a smile. "Are you enjoying yourself, dear?"

Cassie sent her mama a quelling look. "I swear if Aunt Vangie presents me with one more *prospect*, I may well scream."

Her mother laughed behind her fan.

"Please, Mama." Cassie caught her mother's arm and leaned close, lowering her voice. "Aunt Vangie has gotten absolutely intolerable. And I have developed a terrible headache. I truly don't think I can dance with one more available Yankee."

She forced out the lie, crossing the fingers of one hand and hiding the gesture in the wide folds of her gown's full hoop skirt.

"May I ask our hostess to arrange for a carriage to take me home?"

"I'll get my cloak and—"

"No, Mama," Cassie rushed to stop her. "If you come, Aunt Vangie will feel that she has to leave, too. And she'll be furious with me for dragging her away from the soiree."

Her mother sighed in agreement and glanced across the room to where Vangie stood amongst a circle of male admirers.

"Please?" Cassie pressed.

She could tell that her mother was weakening, so before she could possibly think it over or change her mind, Cassie gave her a hug and spun away.

It was a simple feat to seek out her hostess and say a few polite words, neglecting to mention her need of a coach. She didn't need one just yet. Cassie then retrieved her dark cloak and slipped out a side door.

Jared's house lay to the right. It was only a short distance, and she didn't want to draw anyone's attention by calling for a carriage. Instead, she started off at a quick-paced walk.

The walk to Jared's residence was short, a few mere blocks, but Cassie was nervously out of breath when she reached the oak tree situated about twenty-five yards from his house. Her heart pounded so loud that she was sure someone would hear it echoing through the night. She sought out the concealing shadows of the broad tree trunk and leaned against it a moment.

She'd done this before, she assured herself, trying to calm her racing heart and jangled nerves. The assurance did not a whit of good.

She'd never stolen from Jared Montgomery, a little niggling voice in the back of her mind warned her. But she wasn't really stealing, was she? She was doing important work for the Confederacy.

A tremor of unease stroked her spine. Stealing from Jared was a far sight different than retrieving the packet of papers from the Admiral's uniform pocket.

Cassie fingered the silver locket at her throat, a further sign of her inner trepidation. Her conscience and her loyalty to the Cause warred within her. The reality of the act of stealing yet again tore at her; yet she knew that the retrieval of the papers detailing the defenses of Washington were essential to the success of the secession plot.

And the success of Washington seceding from the Union was essential to ending the war and keeping her parents safe, she reminded herself.

Her resolve strengthened, she drew her

dark blue cloak tightly about her to hide any tell-tale glimmer or reflection from her light-colored gown and stepped away from the shelter of the broad tree trunk and its concealing shadows.

As moonlight streamed down, bathing the ground in a pale silvery light, she wondered how she'd ever thought it romantic and enticing. Right now, the moonlight offered a threat to her very safety.

Holding her cloak tightly closed, she dashed across the wide open area to the side of the brownstone. Once there, she pressed herself against the building, praying that her dark hair and dark cloak blended in sufficiently enough to avert any suspicions if anyone were to glance this way.

She inched along the outside wall until she came to a window. It was tightly locked, and she stifled her groan of frustration. Ironic that the city's famed Masked Marauder kept his windows locked against burglars. Glancing about to make sure that no one was in sight, she proceeded to the next window. The second one was also tightly secured. This time, the groan slipped out.

Damnation. She'd just have to keep trying until she found a way in.

Creeping along the outside wall, she reached the third window. This time luck was with her. The window was not securely locked, and Cassie wanted to cry out with joy. It took several minutes of jiggling the window and pushing before it loosened, and she was able to push it up. Biting her lip down on her silent shout of victory, she leaned in through the opening.

Darkness greeted her, and this time she was glad for the faint lighting from the moon outside as it filtered through the room. All she had to do now, was to climb in through the open window.

Her dark, heavy cloak was cumbersome, and she quickly shed it, draping it over the edge of a bushy shrub next to the window. She caught up her skirt in one hand and attempted to climb through the opening.

However, climbing through the window in a hoop skirt was no simple feat as Cassie soon learned. Try as she might, the wide hoop refused to cooperate. First, her hoop lodged sideways, wedging itself within the window frame. It was impossible to go any farther. Pushing backwards, she managed to maneuver the unwieldy hoop back outside.

The next time she tried to climb through the window, the edge of the hoop caught on the side of the brownstone, holding her firmly in place. It took her almost five minutes to set it free without ripping her gown in the process. Her mama was sure to notice a tear in her gown and ask questions that she couldn't answer.

Refusing to give up, Cassie rolled her

gown's skirt up around her waist to keep the fine material undamaged. It wasn't exactly proper or befitting a lady, but she didn't care one whit. Clamping the hoop downward as tightly as possible, she forced it through the window opening and clambered after it. She landed with a soft thud on the floor in a heap of ruffled petticoats and a now slightly askew hoop.

Biting her tongue on the laughter that threatened to bubble up at her ridiculous position, she climbed to her feet, using the wall as a brace. Then she proceeded to straighten her hoop and half-twisted corset.

Please, don't let Jared come in now, she prayed. Then, she added, please, don't let anyone come in.

She unrolled her skirt and spread it over the petticoat and hoop. She wasn't about to go walking around in anyone's house with her petticoat showing. Ready and determined to succeed in her quest, she set off in search of Jared Montgomery's bedroom.

It took her a scant few minutes to find the room. The house was not overly large or imposing, but held a sense of comfort all the same, she noticed.

However, once she entered Jared's bedroom, all sense of comfort or calmness left her with a vengeance. There was no doubt this was his room. Dark masculine furnishings filled the room. A faint hint of his scent hung in the room, a definite reminder to her of the man it belonged to. A dark blue uniform jacket hung draped over a heavy wooden chair.

Her stomach tightened at the thought of the broad muscular chest of the jacket's owner. Stop it, she ordered herself.

Forcing her gaze away from the jacket and thoughts of Jared without the garment, she approached the bed. Unable to resist the sudden inclination, she ran her hand over the coverlet, coming to rest on the pillow.

Her mouth went dry at the sudden mental picture of Jared stretched out in the bed that sprang unbidden to her mind. His long legs, wide muscled chest and shoulders filled the feather mattress, leaving little room for another person in the bed.

Horror at the path her thoughts were taking made her breath catch in her suddenly parched throat. She nervously moistened her lips and could imagine Jared's lips pressed against hers in a kiss that she knew would steal her very breath completely away.

Cassie pulled herself up. Shame at her wayward thoughts and the desires they raised caused her cheeks to heat. She put cold hands to her warmed cheeks. What on earth was she thinking of?

Here she was, standing in the man's bedroom, dreaming of his kisses. What she should be doing was retrieving the papers and fleeing before anyone, especially Jared, returned home and caught her.

She doubted if he'd welcome her uninvited presence with kisses. Not once he realized why she was here.

The thought spurred her onward, and she crossed the few remaining steps to the head-board. Bending down, she peered between the carved wood and the wall.

There it was. The papers.

She could see the folded pouch sticking out from the wood it was attached to. Easing her hand between the slab of wood and the wall, she inched her hand along the wood until her fingertips could clasp the paper. She pulled cautiously, but steadily, until the fastening gave way.

It released with a suddenness that sent her reeling backwards and almost landed her on the floor on her derriere. She staggered back and regained her balance. Breathing rapidly with nerves, she crossed to a window and quickly gave the papers a cursory glance in the beam of moonlight that shined in. The drawings appeared to be the same ones she'd gotten from the Admiral's bedroom.

Cassie folded the papers and tucked them away in the only secure place she could think of—the very same place she'd used before— her gown's bodice.

Success! She'd attained possession of the papers in time for her meeting with Will

Radford tomorrow. He need never know that she'd ever lost them and had to retrieve the packet a second time.

Smiling, Cassie retraced her steps back to the open window. Using the same tactic as before, she clambered her way through the window opening. It took her only a moment to right her clothing, close the window, and pull her cloak tightly about her. Then, she crossed to the safety of the oak tree.

It was a simple thing to walk back to the house where the soiree was being held and hail a carriage at the drive, without anyone being the wiser. The short ride home was completed without mishap or discovery. And if anyone inquired, she'd been nowhere near Jared Montgomery's house.

Once home, Cassie tiptoed up the stairs, hardly daring to breathe. As far as her mother and aunt knew she'd returned home nearly an hour ago with a complaint of a headache. She had no intention of either of them learning otherwise.

As she took each step, she paused, praying that the floor boards wouldn't creak and give away her presence to any of the servants who might be up and about. At long last, after what had seemed nearly an eternity to her, she reached the stair landing and her bed-chamber door. She slipped in through the open door, easing it closed behind her.

Not daring to light a lamp, she stole cautiously across the room to her armoire. Thankfully, the same moonlight that she'd cursed at Jared's house obliged her by helping to light the way for her now. Opening the door of the armoire, she reached up and felt along the tiny ledge for the metal key. Her fingers found it without mishap, and she dared to breathe a sigh of relief. One hurdle down.

She stepped back and removed the dark cloak from about her shoulders. Quickly, she hung it inside the armoire and closed the door. Mentally, she counted the tasks off one by one, making sure she left nothing to chance. All she needed to do now was to secure the packet of papers. She clutched the key tightly in her hand.

Crossing on tiptoes, afraid to make a single sound, she crossed to the safe. Once there, she fitted the key into the lock, turned it, and pulled open the door. A faint stream of moonlight illuminated the compartment for her.

As she stepped closer, the faint scent of roses wafted out to her. That's odd, she thought to herself.

She withdrew the papers from her bodice and started to place the packet of papers in the compartment when she saw the single red rose laying inside. Her hand froze in mid-air.

How had a red rose gotten into her safe?

The instant she'd voiced the question, she knew.

Jared Montgomery. He must have placed the rose inside the night she'd surprised him as he was stealing the papers from her. Red roses grew in profusion on the trellis outside her bedroom window.

The barest of smiles touched her lips. She laid the papers to one side of the safe and gently picked up the dried flower.

"Jared," she whispered his name.

One petal crumbled beneath her finger, and a single tear slipped from her eyes to run unchecked down her cheek.

Seven

The golden glow of the sunrise colored the morning sky as Jared Montgomery slipped into his dark blue uniform jacket and fastened the gold eagle buttons. Once again, he checked his pocket watch. It was almost time. And, it wouldn't do to keep the President waiting.

In spite of the upcoming meeting's importance, Jared was eager to have the conference over and done with. As soon afterwards as possible, he intended to stop and pay a visit to Cassie. Concern over her illness and early departure from last night's soiree had disturbed his sleep all night.

He strode across the room and bending down reached behind the headboard to retrieve the packet of papers. His fingers met only wood. He stretched his arm, reaching further along the headboard, searching with his fingertips for the packet fastened against the board. But they found nothing.

Unable to believe what his brain told him, he yanked the bed out from the wall. The bed posts scraped along the wood floor with a protesting screech. Leaning forward, he checked the back of the headboard. There was nothing there except wood.

Gone! The papers were gone!

He stared at the plank of wood. He couldn't believe what he was seeing. Someone had managed to steal the papers without his knowledge—a next to impossible feat. Who had done it?

Cassie Van Dorn.

He knew with rock solid certainty that it had been her. But how? When?

Jared wracked his brain for the answers. He had kept her in sight from the instant she'd entered the soiree last night. He'd known the second she stepped into the room, felt an almost undeniable pull at her presence.

Even now, he remembered the way her gown had shimmered in the light, turning her into a vision in pale silvery blue. Her hair turned even darker, an even richer black velvet where it had draped across a creamy— nearly bare—shoulder, offset by the gown's paleness.

He couldn't have taken his eyes from her if he'd tried. But he hadn't tried. He had stayed within reach of her all evening.

In fact, he'd been close enough to hear, at least in part, her complaint to her mother of a bad headache. He'd even heard her promise to call for the carriage to take her home.

Damn, he swore. That was it. The little minx had gone home alright, but only after she'd visited his house first and made off with the papers. How could he have fallen for her ploy of a faked illness? Much less worried about her?

He called himself every kind of a fool. Cassie might be an amateur at this, but she was a damn good one.

Well, the trap had been sprung. He should be happy, not deriding himself for letting her walk into it, shouldn't he? Wasn't this what he and President Lincoln had wanted to happen?

However, what had earlier seemed like such a skillful plan between him and the President now seemed foolhardy and dangerous.

Dangerous for Cassie Van Dorn.

Jared's stomach knotted into a tight coil of fear for her. Did she have any comprehension of the reality and danger of the game she was playing?

She was involved in the very secession plot he was sworn to destroy. An association with her could very well destroy him as well, his mind counseled him, but he ignored the warning. It was Cassie he was worried about.

For the first time in two years, something else took precedence over his relentless thoughts of revenge. Until he'd met Cassie, he'd worked with only one goal in mind—to uncover the plot and extract revenge for his younger brother's murder, which had surely been at the hands of the head of the secession plot whose identity he'd been so close to revealing.

However, Jared never counted on the attraction he'd feel for an intelligent, gutsy secesh beauty named Cassie Van Dorn. His emotions warred within him, presenting a jumble of confusion. Vengeance . . . attraction . . . love? Damn her, now what was he supposed to do?

He was due to report to the President in half an hour. It was not a meeting he looked forward to with any enjoyment or anticipation. He had to tell the President of the theft of the papers, and that meant involving Cassie.

As it turned out, Jared's meeting with the President was shortened. A pre-dawn missive from General Grant had prompted the calling of an immediate meeting of Lincoln's Cabinet, thus he'd been late for the prearranged meeting with Jared.

The conference lasted merely long enough for President Lincoln to issue special orders for Jared to visit a Union encampment that was situated on enemy lines. He was scheduled to leave at dawn the next day. Jared only had time to inform the President that the bait to their trap had been taken.

However, he'd casually neglected to relay

his certainty that the papers had been stolen by Cassie. There would be time enough later to tell that piece of information. Much later. Hopefully only after the head of the secession plot had been captured and sentenced would he have to involve Cassie. He felt a strange, almost overwhelming urge to protect her.

Deep in thought as he strode down the long hall of the White House, Jared nearly ran into a tall, dark-haired man dressed in Union blue. He glanced over at the man to offer his apology, and he halted instantly, a wide smile creasing his face.

"Trevor Caldwell. When did you get back?"

The other man glanced at him, his eyes lighting in equal pleasure and surprise. He reached out and clasped Jared's hand.

"Two days ago. Haven't seen you in over a month though. What are you up to?"

"I just left a meeting with the President," Jared answered.

"Oh," Trevor raised an eyebrow. "Still stealing whenever you can?"

Jared smiled in return. Trevor was one of the only other people besides President Lincoln who knew of his true mission, and the one person he'd trust with his life if need be. They had been friends since their days at West Point together. Jared's only regret was that he had been away from the city, fighting in the western theater, when Trevor could have used his help last year.

His friend's marriage to a Rebel spy could not have been easy, and their union had a tumultuous beginning. It had taken more love than Jared believed possible to heal the breech between Trevor Caldwell and Brianna Devland. But it had not only been possible— love had succeeded. Now Trevor and Brianna were the happy and proud parents of twins. A boy and a girl.

Shrugging off Trevor's question, he fired one of his own. "How's our favorite former Rebel spy?"

Trevor flinched. "Don't remind me. Thankfully little Mary and Jefferson are keeping Brianna busy and out of trouble whenever I'm called away." He slapped Jared on the shoulder and chuckled. "When are you going to try marriage?"

Jared colored visibly at the challenge as a picture of Cassie wearing the same pink nightgown the night he'd broken into her bedroom filled his mind. His chest tightened at the image.

When Jared didn't respond immediately with his usual teasing jibe of "when Brianna leaves you," Trevor sobered and stared at him with a penetrating stare.

"So, who is the lady?"

It would do no good to deny it, Jared knew

that. They knew each other too well for subterfuge.

"Cassie Van Dorn," he paused. "A Rebel secessionist," he forced the words out past clenched teeth. It was the first time he'd admitted Cassie's hold over him, even to himself. It seemed only fitting that he admit it to his closest friend.

"Oh," Trevor stretched the word out slowly. "Good luck, you'll need it. At least she isn't a spy."

"For what good that's doing me right now. I fear she's involved in certain things up to her pretty neck."

"I haven't heard of her, so at least she's discreet, unlike the unfortunate Mrs. Rose Greenhow." Trevor assured his friend. "Say, why don't you bring her over for dinner one night this week?"

"It's too soon," Jared answered with a tinge of regret to his voice.

"So the lady hasn't been conquered yet by your thieving charm?"

"It seems so," Jared grinned at his friend.

"Well, why don't you come on over one night, and we'll talk strategies. And Rebel women," Trevor added with a chuckle.

"Thanks, I just might do that."

After saying their goodbyes, Jared once again headed for the exit. He intended to stop by Willard's Hotel with the excuse of wanting breakfast, but in truth, to see what information he could pick up. The hotel was a Washington melting pot for gossip and intrigue, and he intended to use it to his full advantage. He'd need every bit of information before his special visit to the Union camp on the lines tomorrow. Who knew what he might encounter the next day? He wanted to be as prepared as possible.

Cassie left Aunt Vangie decked out in a bright fuchsia gown sitting comfortably in a wing chair in the sitting room and crossed to the foyer. Impatiently, she stared up at the wide empty staircase, running her hands down the skirt of her dusky rose day dress. What was taking her mother so long to get ready?

"Alicia!" Vangie called from the sitting room doorway. "We're waiting."

A smile tugged at Cassie's lips. Her suggestion of a shopping trip that morning had been met with a smile from her mother and exuberance from Aunt Vangie. This time, amazingly, Aunt Vangie had been the first one downstairs, and she now stood tapping her foot, impatient to be off. Shopping was the one thing Aunt Vangie could be counted on to never be late for.

Cassie checked the time. They still had plenty of time for her to make her meeting with Will Radford at Mrs. Bodie's shop as scheduled. She tightened her hold on her reticule, where she'd safely tucked the packet of papers to give to Will.

She'd hated the deception the suggested shopping trip entailed—she didn't really need anything like she'd claimed—so she'd best figure out something to buy before the morning was over, or Mama would be sure to ask questions about her sudden desire to go to the shops.

As if her guilty thoughts had prompted her appearance, Alicia strolled to the top of the stairs. Cassie stared at her mother in her pretty robin's egg blue gown, and a wave of guilt swamped her. She hated deceiving her mama most of all, but she absolutely refused to involve her in all this.

"Oh, don't get cross-legged, Vangie. I'm ready." Alicia called out from the top step. "I swear, Vangie, shopping is the only thing you ever have gotten in a hurry for in your entire life."

As Alicia tied the ribbons to her bonnet, Cassie couldn't help but compare the two women. Mama's simple, but elegant blue bonnet contrasted with Aunt Vangie's feather and lace confection of bright fuchsia. In direct opposite to Aunt Vangie, Mama disliked shopping in the mornings instead preferring a leisurely afternoon, while her sister loved to frequent the shops at any and every opportunity. Cassie didn't think it was possible for the two women to be more unalike.

They left the house, and the next hour was filled with strolling from shop to shop. As Aunt Vangie's purchases grew, Cassie carefully steered them in the general direction of Mrs. Bodie's shop.

"Oh, Alicia, do look at this." Vangie paused and pointed to the window display of a prominent modiste shop. "Isn't that the prettiest thing you ever saw? I simply must have it."

Cassie turned to look at where her aunt gestured to a gown of deep russet on display.

Her mama groaned, "Not another gown."

Vangie ignored her remark and caught her arm and pulled her toward the door.

"Oh, come on, Alicia. I simply must have that dress."

"Vangie, you just bought two gowns, and you brought along more dresses than—"

"My gracious, none are that color."

"Vangie—"

Cassie knew her mother would end up giving in and following Aunt Vangie into the shop. Meanwhile, she took the opportunity the distraction provided.

"Mama, why don't you go on and help Aunt Vangie with the dress? I need something from Mrs. Bodie's shop. I'll be back in a minute."

Her mother sighed, and Aunt Vangie

pushed open the door to the dress shop, her attention fully fixed on the desired gown. Before they could object to her departure, Cassie turned and walked hurriedly across the street to the bonnet shop.

She stopped at the sign overhead proudly proclaiming "Mrs. Bodie's" in bold black letters. As Cassie entered the shop, a little bell tinkled merrily over the door, announcing her entry.

The smiling, plump proprietress turned at the sound. "Cassie, how nice to see you again. What may I help you with today?"

"Good morning, Mrs. Bodie."

Cassie crossed to her and endured the usual exuberant hug from the older woman. Mrs. Bodie greeted all her known customers in the same predictable fashion. The especially strong scent of lilacs wafted up to Cassie's nose, almost making her sneeze. Blinking her eyes and trying to hold back the sneeze, Cassie stepped back.

"You've gotten in a new shipment of bonnets, I see," she remarked, crossing the few feet to examine the display of bonnets in less heavily scented air.

"Yes," Mrs. Bodie answered with pride. "Aren't they lovely? I'm especially fond of that dove gray one for myself."

Cassie admired the gray velvet bonnet the woman pointed out. A delicate band of black lace accented the top, culminating in a broad array of lace at the back, and black and gray ribbons hung down just waiting to be tied under a customer's chin. However, Cassie knew for certain that before the day was out, that particular bonnet would likely grace the head of Mrs. Bodie. The proprietress always picked out one bonnet from each shipment to keep for herself.

"It is pretty," Cassie answered, making sure to properly admire the favored bonnet.

She dutifully examined the rest of the new display. Fine lace and multi-colored feathers adorned the four additional bonnets of assorted shades of blue, pink, rose, and black. Along one wall hung rows of ribbons in a brightly colored rainbow, and laces and trims decorated a second shorter wall. As usual, the little shop was ablaze with color.

Cassie enjoyed the beautiful colors around her, and her gaze landed on a silver coronet in the display case. The perfect item.

"I, ah, I was looking for a coronet," she said, slowly. "Perhaps a silver one?"

"I have one right over here." Mrs. Bodie bustled over to the display counter and handed Cassie the bright silver coronet.

Cassie took it and smiled her thanks. "This is exactly what I was looking for."

"Oh, while you're here, you absolutely must see the new order of dolls that came in," Mrs. Bodie insisted, gesturing to a side corner. "I only received them this week. Already I've sold eight. They are going to be quite the thing for Christmas.''

She led Cassie to the other side of the store where a display of china dolls sat on a shelf. Picking one up, she handed it to Cassie.

"Careful," Mrs. Bodie cautioned. "They're hollow, but the workmanship is unsurpassed."

As she carried on, extolling the virtues of the newly arrived dolls, an idea began to form in the back of Cassie's mind. She pondered it for a few moments. Mrs. Bodie had said that the china dolls were hollow inside. Her idea just might work.

The head and body of the doll could carry quite a bit of morphine if one tried. Dolls were given as gifts all the time. Why just last month, she'd been part of a group that had sent a package of dolls to an orphanage in Virginia. She ticked off the reasoning in her mind. And who would suspect dolls for the orphans of carrying life-saving morphine for the Confederacy?

"I'll take six of them," she told the proprietress, mentally figuring how much powder each doll would hold. "No, make it seven." She added one for luck.

"I'll box them for you." Mrs. Bodie gathered up the requested dolls and headed for the counter.

Checking the time, Cassie noted it was exactly eleven o'clock. Time for her meeting with Will. She paid for her purchases and left the store with the box of dolls in her arms. They would solve her problem of Mama's morphine shipment. Now all she had left to do was give the papers to Will.

Almost the instant she exited the shop and walked away from the door, Will Radford approached her coming from the opposite direction. Cassie tightened her hand over her velvet reticule nervously. Stuffed with the packet of papers she'd retrieved from Jared's bedroom, the velvet bag was a little heavier than usual. However, the documents she'd hidden inside crinkled reassuringly beneath her fingers.

"Cassie, what a pleasant surprise." Will stopped in front of her.

She smiled up at him. Surprise, my foot, she thought. Although he did manage to carry off the deception well, she admitted. However, the fine art of persuasion was only one of the tools a good lobbyist used. And Will Radford was good at his job as a lobbyist.

"Why, Will Radford, where have you been keeping yourself?" she said for the benefit of anyone who might be within hearing.

"I've been away on business, and I only returned late last night. I'm sorry I missed seeing you." He lowered his voice. "And may I say, you're looking beautiful today."

The words and intonation caught Cassie off-guard. Aunt Vangie's insistence that Will had been "smitten" with her sprang to mind instantly. Could her aunt be right about Will? Or was she now seeing things that weren't there because of her aunt's comments?

For the first time, Cassie questioned if his words held a deeper meaning. Did they go below the social niceties they implied? Or was she imagining things just because of her Aunt Vangie's meddling?

Cassie stared at Will, studying him closer than she ever had before. Dark hair curled over his forehead and covered the tops of his ears. He'd grown side whiskers, like so many of the Northern men wore. She recalled hearing that at one time, a full growth-beard instead of side whiskers had been a way to tell the newly arrived Southern spies who had travelled North. Now the whiskers helped to hide one of those spies.

Not a handsome face, Cassie thought. Quiet, unassuming would describe it much better.

Another thought prompted her mind. Aunt Vangie had remarked that she wouldn't refuse him a dance herself. Was her aunt possibly interested in Will and trying to hide that interest?

Her long space of thoughtfulness prompted Will to lean closer.

"Cassie? Are you feeling well?" he asked in a low voice. A puzzled frown marred his face. "Nothing's wrong, is it?"

"No, I'm fine," she assured him, chiding herself for listening to her aunt and her chatter.

"And the papers?"

"I have them." She motioned to her reticule.

"I may be being watched," Will warned her in an uneasy voice.

"Then—"

He cut her off with a sharp exclamation. "For now it would seem to be best for you to keep the papers until I can devise a new route for their delivery."

Cassie opened her mouth to deny this, but quickly shut it. She couldn't very well confess that she'd already had the papers stolen from her once by a handsome and daring Yankee thief, could she?

"I'll get a message to you when I think it's safe for you to deliver the documents. Don't worry, I'll be in touch, Cassie." He lightly touched her hand.

With this, Will strode away down the street. She watched him walk away. Surely her aunt was wrong about his interest in her, wasn't she? Or was it a ploy to cover Aunt Vangie's own attraction to the lobbyist?

As the papers crinkled under her grip, more important concerns pushed the thoughts planted by her aunt out of her mind. Will Radford had left her with the stolen packet of papers. Oh, great, she thought to herself, and meanwhile I'm supposed to hide the most dangerous papers in the city of Washington. At this rate, she was going to run out of hiding places in the house.

Keeping a tight hold on her reticule and hugging the packet of china dolls close to ensure that they couldn't be jostled out of her arms, she crossed the street. Suddenly, she wanted the security of being with her mother and aunt. Not to mention that she was eager to be as far away from her meeting with Will as possible, before she chanced running into anyone she knew and having to face any curious questions.

If Will were being watched as he suspected, then perhaps she might be as well. She shifted her hold on the box of china dolls. She'd have to explain their purchase to her mama and inquisitive aunt. Hopefully, her mother would catch on to their real purpose and help divert Aunt Vangie's interest.

No matter what, she had to get Mama's morphine shipment delivered soon. It had to be out of the house before Aunt Vangie began searching for something else to "borrow" and found the bottles of morphine by mistake. Heaven only knew what might happen then.

Now, thanks to Will's suspicions, Cassie also had the dangerous packet of papers to contend with. How was she to keep the papers from anyone's sight if Aunt Vangie accidentally stumbled on the key to the safe?

Cassie nibbled on her lower lip in consternation. First, Jared had searched her room, then Aunt Vangie. What next?

Trying to shake off the feeling of impending doom, Cassie rounded the corner and ran right into Jared Montgomery's arms.

Eight

Cassie landed against a rock-hard male chest, clothed in a Yankee blue uniform. The force of their collision almost knocked her down, and she instinctively caught at his shoulder with one hand to steady herself, attempting to catch back her breath.

The palm of her hand against his broad shoulder tingled unexpectedly, and she glanced up into the face of Jared Montgomery. Quickly, she looked down while the shock of their meeting penetrated her mind.

Clutching the parcel of dolls tightly in one arm to keep from dropping them, she snapped her mouth closed. This couldn't be happening. It just couldn't. Please no, she prayed.

Then, to make matters worse, the drawstrings of her reticule slipped through her fingers. She made a hasty grab for it, but missed, her fingertips only brushing the edge of the strings. The little bag fell to the ground, landing with a thud at Jared's feet.

Oh, no.

Cassie closed her eyes in horror. Forcing herself to open her eyes again, she avoided what she knew would be an intense green-gray gaze. Unwilling to meet accusation or questions in those steady depths, she looked down to where the bag lay on the dusty plank.

The papers! She suddenly remembered they were tucked in the bag at her feet. Cassie's heart dove straight for her toes, this time she was certain of it. Could she even dare to hope that Jared wouldn't find out that the velvet reticule contained the packet of papers she'd stolen from him only last night?

She didn't have a hope if he felt the bag. Not daring to meet his eyes, she forced herself to raise her chin and focus on the second golden button on his uniform jacket. She couldn't look any higher.

Jared glanced from the small bag that had landed in the dust back to the woman who'd collided with him. What he saw stole the breath right out of his chest.

Cassie Van Dorn.

He felt like he'd been kicked in the stomach by a mule. In his arms, he held the very woman who'd broken into his house last night and stolen from him. And where were those papers now? Had she already passed them on? Was he too late?

Damn, he swore silently. The little minx

had beaten him again. He had to find a way to learn if she still had those documents, or what she had done with them.

Nodding a greeting to her, he bent down to pick up her drawstring bag. As his fingers closed around the velvet, he heard the sound of papers crackling beneath his firm grip. Leaning down more to conceal his actions from her eyes, he pulled open the drawstrings with a jerk of his thumb. Paper wrapped in a red ribbon rested just inside the bag, and scribbled drawings showed clearly on one corner of the documents.

She hadn't passed the packet of papers on yet.

Hiding his smile of triumph, Jared pulled the drawstrings tightly closed before he straightened back up. The reticule was heavier than he'd expected. Obviously, the little velvet bag hadn't been made to hold documents as well as a lady's personal items. He handed the bag to her and looked fully into her face for the first time.

"Good morning, Cassie," he said the words in a low voice.

"Good morning," she parroted his greeting.

She had a hard time forcing the words out past her lips. Was she still smiling? She was so numb with fear that she couldn't tell. Had he felt the papers? Surely, he'd say something if he did, wouldn't he?

"I see that you must be feeling better."

Jared couldn't resist toying with her just a bit.

"Better?" Cassie asked, unsure of his question. What exactly did he mean?

"From your headache last night," he offered in explanation, waiting for her answer.

"Ah, my headache. Yes. It's much better. Thank you for asking."

In truth, her head was beginning to throb in time with her pounding heart. That's what she got for lying last night.

"Good, I'm glad to hear that," Jared answered. "I hope nothing broke when you dropped your bag."

Cassie tightly locked the fingers of her free hand around the drawstrings of her reticule. "Oh no, it's fine. I'm sure."

Jared smiled at her tell-tale actions. He couldn't resist asking, "Are you certain you don't want to open it and check?"

"No." The denial rushed out before Cassie could stop herself.

At Jared's raised eyebrow, she added, "It's sturdier than it looks. And I don't remember having anything breakable in it."

"If you're certain." Jared held back the laughter that threatened.

He noticed how Cassie's cheeks flushed a becoming pink. From guilt, he'd bet. He noted that her eyes still held a hint of stunned surprise. Obviously, she'd never expected to meet him this morning. Not when she still held the papers she'd stolen last night.

Admittedly, she was the last person he'd expected to see upon his walk back from Willard's Hotel. Luck had most assuredly been with him. Now he knew for certain the exact location of the papers. All he had to do was to keep Cassie in his sight, or one of his men's sight, from now until she passed on those documents, and he'd have the man he sought.

She glanced around, as if looking for an escape. In fact, she looked to Jared like she was ready to take flight given half an opportunity. However, he had no intention of allowing that to happen.

Noticing the parcel held tightly in her hands, he took advantage of the opportunity it presented.

"Here, let me take that," he offered, the soul of politeness, as he deftly removed the wrapped parcel from her grasp.

She wasn't going anywhere as long as he held possession of something of hers, he knew that for a fact.

"But—" Cassie attempted to protest.

Jared shifted the parcel to under one arm and placed his other arm around her back, stilling the protest on her lips.

"Don't drop it," Cassie cautioned.

"What on earth is in the package?" Jared shook it slightly, now curious. Her nervousness was a dead giveaway that she was up to something.

Cassie caught his arm. "Oh, no. Please, don't shake it."

Her hand on his arm was so unexpected that Jared almost dropped the box. He'd been unprepared for the feel of her small hand gripping his forearm. The muscles tightened under her fingers, and his breathing became ragged. At this moment he couldn't care less what the package contained. He stared down at her, unable to tear his gaze away.

She wore a dusty rose morning dress that instantly brought to mind the tempting pink nightgown that was fast threatening to become an obsession with him.

She's a thief, he reminded himself. She's involved in the secession plot.

The reminder did no good, no matter how hard he tried to concentrate on the fact. The unexpected feel of her touch persisted in pushing all thoughts of her illegal activities from his mind.

All he could see with his eyes was the way her gown caused her blue eyes to darken to the color of a rich sapphire gem. The rose gown brought out the velvet darkness of her hair, and he longed to run his hands through the soft curls that framed her face.

The bodice of the dress hugged her figure lovingly, and he suddenly wished it was his hands cupping her breasts instead of the fabric doing so. He knew that he could span her slim waist with both his hands, and he longed to prove it. Admittedly, he longed for anything that would allow him to touch her in return.

"They're breakable," Cassie rushed to explain the contents of the parcel, feeling embarrassed by her sudden outburst. "They're china dolls that I bought for an orphanage."

Just as quickly she removed her hand from his arm, unconsciously rubbing her fingertips. They felt as if she'd gotten too close to where lightning had struck.

Yes, she thought to herself, Jared Montgomery was every bit as dangerous as lightning.

Why did he have to be a thief up for sale to the highest bidder? She continued to rub her fingers. Wasn't that what Michael Jones had told her last night? She'd have respected Jared more if he'd at least been stealing the packet of papers for the Union.

Guilt suddenly washed over her in waves. *She* had been the one stealing last night. And from Jared.

Did he know yet? Had he discovered that the reticule held the papers? She searched his face for any sign of condemnation, but found none. Instead, she met blatant appreciation, a sudden darkening in his green-gray gaze, and desire.

The realization of that desire jolted her. It wasn't the look she'd been expecting to receive from him. It left her unsure of herself and strangely tingly from head to foot.

Anxious to return their unexpected meeting, and her traitorous body, back to a more proper encounter, she swallowed and stepped back a decisive step. Instead of taking her lead, Jared tightened his hand's hold on her waist, startling her into realizing his hand still rested there. Unbelievably, she'd practically forgotten it was there.

His hand at her waist had felt so right that she'd grown accustomed to its presence until he moved his fingertips against her waist. The skin beneath his fingers responded to his touch even through the layers of clothing. Her waist, then her entire back, heated to a warm pleasant glow. His hand seemed to radiate heat to her. And her body responded to it like a homing pigeon flying straight back to its roost.

Unable to resist the orders her traitorous body was issuing, she took another step—this time towards him. Then another step.

"I, ah, I do volunteer work there. At an orphanage." She gave a futile last attempt to break the power he seemed to have over her. It failed miserably.

"Cassie," her name was a mere whisper on his lips, yet the sound was deep and melodious.

She watched him form her name on his lips, enthralled. She was lost, she thought to herself. Totally and completely lost. Then his head lowered towards hers, and everything else fled from her mind.

"Cassie?" This time the voice belonged to her mother.

Cassie jerked her head back away from Jared's approaching kiss. She spun around in a fluster of swaying hoop and rose-colored skirts.

"Mama?" Disbelief echoed in her faint voice.

Cassie struggled to regain her composure and control of her galloping senses at the same time. Horror and embarrassment at the situation she'd been caught in flooded over her.

Gathering her poise about her, Cassie raised her chin to meet her mother and Aunt Vangie's distressful stares. As her aunt opened her mouth, Cassie cut in and quickly performed the introductions between Jared and her mama and her Aunt Vangie, hoping to forestall her aunt's caustic comments.

"If you'll excuse us, Captain," her mother spoke, "I think we should be getting home."

Cassie looked at her mother and wondered just how long it was going to be before she began voicing her questions. Avoiding her gaze, she turned to Jared.

"Thank you for helping me with my parcels." She held out her hands for her package, praying that he would release it to her quickly. Right now she wasn't up to any verbal sparring.

He complied without argument, handing her the parcel. He didn't wish to raise her suspicions. Little did she know that he intended to know her every move from this moment on. She would be watched—either by him or someone who he knew he could trust.

"Until next time, Cassie," Jared said softly.

Her mind flew back to the last time he'd said those words. It had been the first night they met. The night he'd broken into her bedroom and stolen the papers from her. Was there another meaning behind his reminder?

Without realizing that she did it, Cassie nibbled on her lower lip in nervousness. As she walked away with her mama and Aunt Vangie, she could feel Jared's gaze on her back.

Cassie knew without the slightest doubt that there would be an "again" with them.

The carriage ride home was tense and strained. Aunt Vangie was the first one who spoke out.

"Cassie, I can't believe you would allow yourself to be caught up in such an improper situation. Tsk, Tsk." Aunt Vangie clicked her tongue in dismay and shook her head at her niece.

Without giving Cassie the chance to respond, she continued on. "And a mere captain."

Vangie gave the word "captain" a decidedly disdainful sniff.

"What was this captain's name? I didn't catch it before." Her aunt frowned.

"Jared Montgomery," Cassie answered.

"Oh." Vangie seemed taken back for a moment. "He doesn't look much like his brother."

"His brother?" Cassie turned to face her aunt. She hadn't been aware that Jared had a brother. In fact, she knew very little about him. Except that he was a very tempting thief.

"Oh, yes," Vangie answered. "Bryan was quite smitten with me." She patted a curl into place, before her eyes narrowed a moment, then she added, "For awhile."

Surprise prevented Cassie from responding. Aunt Vangie and Jared's brother?

"I met him when I was here visiting a couple of years back." Vangie tossed her head in a dismissive gesture. "But, I hear he's dead now."

Cassie recalled that visit quite vividly. It had been her father's first Christmas away from them, and her mama and Aunt Vangie had gotten into an awful argument the day after the new year began.

"But a captain, Cassie? You could do so much better, my dear. Please, do try and set your standards a little higher—"

"Vangie," Alicia snapped at her sister's interference.

"Well, it's true, Alicia. She could do better, if only she'd try. At the reception, my first night here mind you, she danced with a clerk. A government clerk."

Vangie turned on the seat of the carriage in a flounce of her ruffled skirt.

"Do either of you know how much a government clerk earns? Well, let me tell you it is most definitely not enough for you to be bothered with. Alicia, I must insist that you take Cassie in hand. Or, I will be forced to do so myself."

"Vangie." Alicia's voice raised noticeably this time when she said the name.

Cassie clenched her teeth tightly together in order to force herself to remain quiet. As long as Aunt Vangie was in such a dither over Jared's rank, she would notice little else, and not ask questions.

"I've already told you that the only ones who will have any real money left after this dreadful war is over, will be the Yankees. Mind you, Cassie, your mother and I don't object to you consorting with the Yankees—"

A gasp came from her mama.

"Just, please, do try and watch their station in life. My dear, do try harder."

Cassie was saved from any further Vangie-style advice by the welcome halt of the carriage at their house. Thankfully, she exited the carriage.

"Yes, Aunt Vangie. I'll try," Cassie answered obediently, in an attempt to pacify her vocal aunt and to waylay a further argument between her mama and Aunt Vangie.

Cassie threw her mama a sideways glance. A troubled frown creased her mother's dainty features and drew Cassie's full attention. That was always a sure sign that her mama was deep in thought over something that was greatly bothering her. How much longer was her mother going to remain silent? And how was Cassie going to answer the questions that were sure to come?

They entered the house in strained silence. It seemed to Cassie that the house itself even held its breath waiting for whatever was to come next.

"Well, I'm going to put up my new gowns," Aunt Vangie announced, with a long look at Cassie.

Cassie knew that the look from her aunt was an invitation to accompany her for a "talk." She tactfully ignored it.

"I'll put up my packages, too." She made an escape to her bedroom.

However, she had scarcely crossed the

threshold of her room before what she'd been dreading happened.

"Cassie?" her mama called out from her bedroom doorway. "Can you come in here? I'm having trouble with the knots on this one package."

Cassie crossed to her bed and sat the parcel of dolls down on the feather mattress and straightened up. She tightened her fingers around her reticule. She wasn't about to leave it unattended. Not with Aunt Vangie about.

"Cassie?"

As surely as she breathed, Cassie knew that her mama's words were an order not the mere request that they sounded like. It was one she couldn't very well ignore like she had her aunt.

She took a deep breath, brushed her hands down her skirt, and crossed the highly polished hallway to her mother's bedchamber.

"Dear, come in and please close the door." Her mama motioned to her.

Cassie did as she asked, dreading the questions that were sure to follow.

"Dear, about last night . . ." she paused.

Last night.

Cassie's heart plummeted. Her mother's first words were what she'd least expected and precisely what she'd dreaded answering the most.

Caught off guard, she froze, unable to move and scarcely able to breathe at her mother's words. Her heart beat a rapid cadence in her chest. She feared that the pounding was loud enough to be heard in the bedroom.

"Last night?" Cassie stammered, not daring to meet her mother's gaze.

How had her mother learned of last night? And even worse, how was she to explain why she didn't come directly home last night? There was no way on this earth that she could tell her mama where she'd gone. That was out of the question.

"Cassie, are you listening to me?"

"Yes, Mama," she answered.

"I think Vangie is sneaking out to see a new beau," her mama announced in an overloud whisper.

"What?"

A frown creased Cassie's brow. What on this earth was her mother talking about?

"Vangie—"

"Cassie, dear, aren't you listening?" she asked again. "We're talking about last night. I said that I think Vangie is sneaking out to see a man."

"Vangie? We're talking about Aunt Vangie?" Cassie held back her sigh of relief.

"Yes, dear." Her mother sent her a puzzled glance. "As I said, last night after we'd returned home, I got to thinking here in my room. I really was too hard on Vangie last night. And all because I didn't want to attend that party. She had her heart so set on it."

"You had a good reason," Cassie reassured her mother.

"Well, I shouldn't let my worry over your father's safety ruin Vangie's time here. So, I decided that I really should go and apologize to her. She's so much more high-strung this visit. I'm worried about her."

As she paused to nibble on a fingertip, Cassie prompted, "And?"

"Oh, yes. Well, I knocked on her door, and there was no answer. When I entered, she wasn't there!"

Cassie blinked, startled at the announcement.

"Where did she go?"

Her mother shrugged. "I don't know. Much later, I heard someone come in, but I didn't get up to check. I didn't want her to think I'd been spying on her."

Cassie bit down on her sigh of relief over her mama's decision not to intrude on Aunt Vangie. More than likely she would have caught her sneaking up the stairs, not Aunt Vangie.

"Now we have even more to worry over." Alicia caught Cassie's arm. "Please keep an eye on her. We don't know what she might be up to," she said in a dramatic tone. "I fear it's another one of her clandestine affairs."

"Now, Mama—"

"Cassie, while she's sneaking in and out, she could stumble onto one of my shipments. And heaven only knows what she would do."

"One of your shipments?" Cassie forced herself to lower her voice to a whisper. "How many more shipments are there?"

"Oh, don't worry."

The words sent a chill all the way down Cassie's spine. It settled in her toes.

"Mama—"

"There's just the one that we hid. But it does need to be delivered. I—"

"No!" Cassie stared at her mother. She was going to refuse to budge in the slightest on this. She wasn't about to let her dainty, impulsive mother attempt to deliver the morphine across the enemy lines.

"I am taking care of everything. Just like I promised," Cassie assured her.

"But, I had planned to—"

"Today, I purchased several china dolls for the orphans—"

"That's nice dear, but right now we should be concerned with my shipment."

"Mama," Cassie bit back her frustration. "The dolls are hollow—"

"Really, dear. I'm certain that your little dolls are quite nice, but—"

"Mother." Cassie caught her mother's hands in hers to get her attention. "The dolls are to be used to hide the morphine in. The soldiers won't suspect a few dolls for an orphanage of containing morphine." She spelled out the details.

"Oh, Cassie. That's very bright."

"I've been thinking, and with Petersburg and Richmond under siege, it will likely take me about two days to deliver the shipment and return back home."

"Oh, dear."

"And, Mama, I will need Aunt Vangie away from the house so that I won't be missed."

"Oh, dear," her mother said again.

"Mama." Cassie squeezed her hands reassuringly. "I have it all figured out. You and Aunt Vangie will go on a shopping—"

Her mother groaned.

"A shopping trip to New York. If you suggest it, I know that Aunt Vangie won't be able to resist going. I'll stay behind on the pretext of wanting to help out at the local orphanage. When you add together the train ride to New York, shopping time, staying overnight at a hotel, and returning on the train the next afternoon, it should be about right."

Cassie waited for her mother's response to her plan.

"I don't look forward to this, you know. Vangie will be simply impossible in New York. And the train ride with her will be—"

"Mama," Cassie interrupted. "Be sure that you don't catch an earlier train than the afternoon. And if I'm not here when you arrive, make the excuse that I'm at the orphanage."

"Oh, Cassie, that would be lying."

"Mama—"

"Very well. I'll make the suggestion to Vangie. When do you want to go?"

"Tomorrow."

"Tomorrow?" her mama gasped. "So soon?"

"I've already caught Aunt Vangie snooping in my bedroom once. We've got to get your morphine out of the house before she finds it."

"Very well. Go on. Don't worry, I'll see to Vangie," her mother promised.

Somehow that promise was overshadowed in Cassie's mind by her mother's words of "don't worry." Every time without fail, when her mama said "don't worry," there was sure to be trouble brewing.

"Oh, Cassie?"

The words stopped her, the uneasy tone in her mother's voice freezing her in place. Here it comes, Cassie thought, wondering how she could explain her body's traitorous reaction to the Union Captain Jared Montgomery.

"Yes, Mama?" Cassie swallowed down the sudden lump that had formed in the back of her throat.

"About today," she paused, a blush staining her cheeks. "Dear, try not to give Vangie anything else to be upset about. She gets upset so easily."

"Yes, Mama."

Cassie sighed in relief under her breath. It seemed that Aunt Vangie's tirade, combined with her nocturnal disappearances had given her mother more important matters to think on than her daughter right now.

Hugging her mama, she slipped out of the room and walked down the hall to her own bedchamber. Deep in thought, Cassie passed her aunt's room, scarcely noting that the door was tightly closed.

Worried over her mother's activities, and concerned about Aunt Vangie's disappearance at the time she was likely retrieving back the papers, Cassie turned the knob to her closed bedroom door. Who had her aunt been sneaking out to see? Was there any possibility that her aunt had seen her last night? She closed her fingers over the doorknob, tightening her hold.

Odd, she didn't remember closing the door behind her when she'd gone into her mama's room. She pushed the door open.

The first thing Cassie saw when the door swung inward was the back of a brightly-colored fuchsia gown of the woman at the side of her bed. She knew who it was immediately. Aunt Vangie. She was bent over the bed, rummaging through the package of china dolls.

"Why, Aunt Vangie," Cassie swallowed down her shock and forced out a polite inquiry for her aunt. "Can I help you find something?"

She would have rather bitten her tongue. Her aunt's insistent snooping was going to land them all in trouble soon.

Nine

Vangie Maitland spun around, almost knocking the parcel of dolls off the bed in her haste. She quickly righted the china dolls, busying herself by arranging them in the center of the feather bed.

"Cassie, I simply couldn't resist a look at these pretty little dolls," Aunt Vangie announced without the slightest degree of embarrassment or hesitation upon having been caught snooping. "I was certain that you wouldn't mind."

Her aplomb amazed Cassie. Aunt Vangie held one doll up to examine it closer in the light. She fingered the muslin dress and the ribbon edging the skirt.

"They are absolutely exquisite. Where did you find them?"

Vangie turned the doll into her arms, holding it like one would a real baby.

"At Mrs. Bodie's shop," Cassie answered. "I bought them for the orphans." She mentally crossed her fingers over the lie.

"The orphans?"

Cassie leaped at the opportunity her aunt's question presented. Here was her chance to lay the foundation for her trip tomorrow. If she could successfully do that, then her aunt was less likely to question Mama without mercy as to why Cassie wasn't going along with them on their shopping expedition.

"Yes, I do volunteer work at one of the orphanages. And when I saw the dolls I couldn't resist purchasing some of them."

At least both of those statements were true, Cassie reassured herself. She did volunteer and help out at the orphanage in Washington. And she hadn't been able to refrain from buying the hollow china dolls—not once she realized that they could be used to smuggle her mama's morphine south.

"How nice, dear." Aunt Vangie carelessly tossed the doll back down onto the bed.

Cassie released a barely audible sigh of relief at her aunt's surrender of the doll, thankful that it hadn't broken. She'd also been half afraid that Aunt Vangie was going to want to keep one for herself.

"Well, dear, as much as I'd love to stay and talk with you, well, I had best be getting back to my room and put away my purchases," Aunt Vangie said, without a hint of regret or guilt to her voice at her snooping of her bedchamber.

Cassie presumed that since her aunt hadn't found anything of interest, and had been caught at her snooping as well, that she was likely more than ready to leave Cassie's bedroom.

"I'll see you at supper." Aunt Vangie gave a cheery wave and sauntered out the door.

Cassie shut the door after her aunt, then leaned against the wood. Thank goodness she'd taken her reticule with her to her mama's room. She shuddered to think of the possibility of her aunt coming across the packet of papers in her snooping.

Heaven only knew what trouble they would all be in then. She only hoped that everything would now proceed according to plan for the shopping trip tomorrow.

Much to Cassie's amazement, the impromptu shopping expedition started off without any problems. Vangie had warmed to Mama's suggestion immediately, eager to see what the New York shops had to offer. Their carriage set off for the train station right before mid-morning.

By the time they'd been gone an hour, Cassie had filled the china dolls' hollow bodies with the morphine powder and placed them in an open basket, cushioned with a brightly colored fabric. It wouldn't do to try and hide them. The success of her plan depended on the dolls being in plain sight. Everyone knew that the sentries suspected any type of contraband to be cleverly hidden away, not displayed in the open for them to ably see.

She'd estimated her purchase of the number of dolls correctly. It took exactly six of the little china dolls dressed in their pretty muslin dresses in order to hold all of the powdered contents of the bottles from her mama's shipment.

Good, she had plans for the seventh doll. Leaving it empty, she positioned it in the center of the others, except that this one stood up higher in the basket. It would be an easy matter to pull out the doll when the time came, and she needed it for a diversion.

Slipping the drawstrings of her reticule over her wrist, she retrieved the key to the safe from its hiding place in the armoire and crossed to the safe. Reaching inside, she first withdrew the pass that her father'd had made up and sent to her and her mama. She bent down and folding it, tucked it into her slipper. The pass would insure her safety within the Confederacy.

Next, she withdrew a second pass from the safe—this one for the Union. Will Radford had obtained it for her several weeks ago. This pass was signed by President Lincoln himself.

She'd never asked Will how he came to be in possession of the pass, and now she was too thankful to have it to care how he'd acquired it. However, she suspected that Michael Jones had assisted in its delivery, not that it mattered. The pass would make her trip past the Union patrols much easier. It meant that she could travel openly without fear of being turned back by the Union sentries.

She placed the second pass in her reticule, then withdrew the packet of papers from her velvet bag. Laying them in the safe, she closed and locked it. That should keep them secure until her return.

Crossing to the armoire, she replaced the key on the tiny ledge. Then she rearranged the clothing inside to completely hide the wooden ledge and key.

Cassie paused to glance about the room and brush her moist palms down the skirt of her muslin day dress. A ruche of white lace trimmed the neckline, and after smoothing down the lace, she nervously trailed a finger over the gown's paisley pattern of blue and white. She'd forgone her hoop in favor of an extra petticoat.

It would be more manageable on the long trip. If everything followed according to plan, she'd be back home by tomorrow evening. Crossing her fingers, she gathered up the basket of dolls, turned, and headed for the door.

Mama had arranged for their phaeton to be readied for her, and the four-wheeled carriage stood waiting, the two horses pawing the ground. With the scheduled pretext of going to the orphanage and spending the night at a friend's house to cover her absence, Cassie climbed up into the seat and took the reins.

The pass from Will Radford worked every bit as well as she'd hoped it would. In practically no time at all she was on the outskirts of the city.

A light breeze tugged on a curl at her cheek, and she was glad that she'd chosen to wear her hair caught back in a chignon and topped with the dainty blue velvet bonnet, even though she'd had to secure the bonnet with her silver bonnet pin to hold it on. The open carriage would most assuredly have allowed the breeze free rein with her hair if she'd worn it loose.

She drove the carriage with complete assurance, having driven it many times in the past. Now she needed every bit of that assurance to face whatever might come up during her illegal trip.

She left the city of Washington behind and had been travelling for about half an hour before she was challenged by a Union sentry.

"Halt."

She obediently drew the horses to a stop, the opposite of what she wanted to do. She wanted to run as fast and as far as she could. However, she knew without a doubt that there was nothing for her to do but stop.

Putting her best, most defenseless smile

into place, she forced herself to smile down at the uniformed soldier who approached her with his rifle in hand.

"Ma'am, do you have a pass?" he queried.

"Yes, I do. Let me get it for you."

Cassie made a show of opening her reticule and searching through the little bag for a minute. It gave her the time she needed to attempt to still her racing heart and force her ragged breathing to return to some semblance of normal.

"Oh, here it is."

She pulled the pass out of her reticule and handed it over to the sentry. Meanwhile, she held her breath while he scrutinized the pass.

He looked it over thoroughly, before returning it to her.

"May I inquire where you are going, ma'am?"

"I'm delivering some dolls to the orphanage. The children have so little."

She hoped he wouldn't be the chivalrous type and offer to see that she was given an escort to the orphanage. That was the last thing she needed.

She forced herself to smile sweetly at him and wait.

"Ma'am, would you mind handing that basket down here to me?"

"Why, whatever for?" she asked, a hint of injured dignity to her voice. "They're only dolls."

"I need to check it."

"Check it?" she asked with a show of wide-eyed innocence.

"For contraband," he explained.

"Oh, why of course. How silly of me not to understand."

She hated the insipid tone of her voice, hated pretending to be helpless and dumb. However, it was quite necessary, she assured herself, if she was to keep the soldier from getting suspicious.

Pretending an embarrassment she was far from feeling, she gathered up the basket from where it sat on the seat beside her.

"Here, you are."

She lifted the basket across her lap, mindful to ease the one special doll out from the rest of the dolls, making certain that it rested precariously on the top. As she handed over the basket to the sentry, she tilted the entire lot to one side.

Just as she'd anticipated, he'd been unprepared for the sudden angle of the basket. He grabbed the handle and attempted to right the basket, but the top doll tumbled out of the cushioned basket and fell to the hard-packed ground. The empty doll shattered into several pieces at the soldier's feet.

"Oh, no," Cassie quickly began to scramble down from her seat in the phaeton. "Oh, no."

"I'm sorry, ma'am." The soldier held the

basket carefully and helped Cassie descend from the carriage. "I didn't mean to break it. I was just checking—"

Cassie snatched the basket from his grasp, cradling it close to her. "Oh, dear. I understand it was only an accident, but please be careful. Those dolls are for the orphanage."

She scarcely felt the twinge of guilt her lie caused. It appeared that lying came easier the more a person did it. She hated that possibility, and hated the act of lying even more— no matter how necessary it seemed to be.

Ignoring the Union soldier, she bent down and carefully picked up the broken pieces of china, placing them on top of the remaining dolls and hidden morphine still left in the basket. She intended to keep the broken china as evidence of their innocence for the next too-curious soldier she might meet up with on her journey.

As she straightened back up, she faced him. "As you can see, they are nothing but china dolls. Or do you want to break another one to check them?"

"Ma'am—"

"Oh, I'm sorry," she quickly apologized, wringing her hands.

The apology wasn't difficult to give or fake. She truly hated pretending to blame the sentry for something that she had planned herself.

"It's just that I hated to lose even one of the dolls," she continued. "And—"

"Ma'am—"

"The dolls are so pretty and so fragile."

Cassie made a show of blinking away the beginning of a flood of tears, hating herself for her subterfuge.

"Ma'am, everything will be fine, I'm sure. Let me help you back up onto the seat."

"But, don't you want to check the rest of the dolls?" She extended the basket to him unsteadily, all the while praying that he wouldn't accept her offer.

"No. No, ma'am, you can go."

He stepped forward and helped her up to the seat of the phaeton. Nodding, he waved her on.

Cassie held her breath as she passed the other sentries, scarcely daring to believe that her ploy had actually succeeded. As she drove the carriage on and out of their sight, she resisted the whoop of victory she wanted to give.

Hours later, Cassie came to the fork in the road and drew the phaeton to a stop. To one side lay another road leading her back to Washington. To the other was the more dangerous route further south.

The temptation to turn back to the safety of the city pulled at her, but she staunchly resisted its lure. She had a job to do, and she'd see it through to the end. No matter what the danger.

She knew as surely as she breathed that if she turned around now, her mama would simply set out and deliver the shipment of morphine herself. Cassie refused to allow that possibility to even arise.

Flicking the reins sharply, she set the carriage in motion down the road south.

The trip through the lines to reach her father's encampment proved longer and more involved than Cassie had at first anticipated. After a night's stay at a simple farmhouse with peeling paint, which was in reality a smuggling station that she'd only heard whispers about, she'd set out that morning for her father's field hospital.

The pass he'd had made out for her and her mama proved itself useful, now that she dared to pull it out of her slipper. In fact, she was called upon to show it more than once.

Hours later, she reached the Confederate encampment. Showing the pass her father had obtained for her use, she requested directions to where Major Thomas Van Dorn was working.

The sentry obliged her, and with a smile of appreciation, he waved her forward into the camp. Drawing the carriage to a halt, she jumped down from the seat. She could scarcely contain her eagerness to see her father once again.

Catching up her skirts, she covered the short distance to where his tent stood. A tall, older dark-haired man stood at the tent's entrance, a pipe in hand. Cassie's breath caught in her throat at the sight of her father. Although he'd aged since their last visit, he had never looked more welcome to her eyes.

"Cassie?" her father's voice held a note of disbelief that it could be her.

She bit her lower lip and nodded her head, unable to speak. Tears burned at the back of her eyes and threatened to brim over. Her father was safe. And alive.

As much as she'd refused to acknowledge the fear, she had been afraid that she might find that he had perished in the fighting. The casualty lists that were sent out were not very up-to-date, and sometimes they were less than accurate.

"Cassie!"

Thomas Van Dorn held out his arms, and Cassie ran into his embrace. As he hugged her close, the tears which had merely threatened earlier now trickled down her cheek. She sniffed them away, not wanting him to see her crying.

At the sound of her sniffles, he drew back and looked down into her face.

"Cassie, what's wrong?" His voice caught. "Is it your Mama?"

Cassie shook her head. "No, she's fine. Nothing's wrong. Well, not too wrong."

"What is it? Why on earth are you here?"

"I . . ." she paused, suddenly unsure how to proceed now that she was actually standing face to face with her father.

How was she supposed to tell him that she was smuggling morphine across the lines for her mother?

"Cassie, what are you doing in Virginia?" he asked bluntly.

She'd known the question was coming, but had tried to push it out of her mind on the long trip here, since she hadn't been able to come up with a good answer. Now it had at last been spoken, and her father stood waiting for her response.

Cassie took a deep breath, then blurted out in a low voice, "I was delivering Mama's shipment of morphine."

Her father's eyes widened and suddenly his mouth gaped open.

"No," he whispered.

Biting her lower lip, Cassie nodded her head in confirmation.

"Please, tell me your mother isn't involved in this."

Cassie grimaced. "I'm afraid she's involved up to her pretty neck. I only just found out about it a few days ago. I wouldn't let her try to deliver anymore shipments herself."

Her small shudder said more than any words could as to her fear over her mother's unexpected new scheme she'd become involved in.

"So, to stop her, I delivered it myself," she finished.

"Cassie!"

"Everything went fine, Papa."

"Do you have any idea how dangerous—"

"Yes, I do."

She patted his arm reassuringly. Anger began to tint his cheeks, and she decided it might be best to give him a moment alone to digest the information she'd just relayed to him.

"You just wait right here. I'll be right back. I have to get something from the carriage."

Cassie spun around and dashed for the relative safety of the carriage and horses. She wanted to give her father time to deal with what her mama had gotten them all into this time.

Once at the side of the carriage, she took her time gathering up the basket of china dolls. She could scarcely believe that they had made the trip with the life-saving morphine still safely intact. The only casualty had been the one doll she'd set up in advance as a decoy to throw off the suspicions of any Union sentries.

Cassie straightened the dolls in the basket and arranged the brightly colored material that trailed over the edges of the basket. Knowing that she had delayed as long as she reasonably could, she retraced her steps back to her father.

Thomas Van Dorn appeared to be in a state of shock. His face was unusually pale except for two bright spots of color on his cheeks.

"Papa?" Cassie said softly as she approached him.

"Yes, Cassie?" He smiled wanly at her, then his gaze caught the basket of dolls.

"Mama's morphine," she explained. "The dolls' heads and bodies are hollow. Well, they were hollow when I bought them." She held the basket out to her father. "Before I filled them with the morphine."

He took it from her, then called over a soldier and handing the basket of dolls over to him, quickly explained the contents. He issued orders for the care of the precious cargo.

Thomas Van Dorn sighed and turned back to his daughter. "Come on inside the tent. We'll be more comfortable there." He also wanted his daughter away from the curious and too appreciative eyes of the soldiers in the camp.

Cassie obeyed and ducked inside the tent opening. Once inside, her father pulled a straight-backed chair away from a table and gestured for her to sit. He sat down on the edge of a cot facing her.

Cassie looked around the tent with unabashed curiosity. She'd thought of her father so many times and tried to picture his surroundings. The real thing was a far cry from her imaginings.

A fine layer of dust seemed to hang in the air of the encampment, covering everything no matter how hard anyone tried to prevent it. She could see her father had tried to keep the tent's interior clean in spite of the persistent dust. The bed was covered and neatly made with a dark blanket on top. A framed picture of Mama sat on the desk, along with a stack of her letters. Cassie smiled at the loving sentiment displayed there.

"Cassie?" Her father leaned forward and caught her hands in his.

At the concern in his voice, Cassie rushed on to assure him. The last thing she wanted was to cause her father more worry right now.

"Papa, I was only doing it this one time," she promised. "Somebody had to do it. Aunt Vangie was snooping around—"

"Evangeline is visiting?"

Cassie nodded.

"What more could go wrong?" he asked. "There is always trouble when she visits."

"I'm taking care of Mama. Don't worry."

She inwardly cringed at her use of her mama's troublesome phrase.

Right now, that phrase meant precisely the same thing it did when her mother used it. It practically boasted of more trouble brewing.

Cassie clamped down on the almost overwhelming urge that rose up to tell her father of her own involvement in the secession plot, and the papers, and the trouble she had gotten herself into. But she knew she couldn't do it. There was nothing that he could do to help from his position at the field hospital, and all telling him would accomplish would be to make him worry. And he most assuredly didn't need that.

"But how did you get through the patrols?" he asked, hugging her close once again.

Cassie told him of the little china dolls and her trip to his camp, making sure that she left out any mention of Jared Montgomery.

They talked for another hour, with Cassie giving her father every piece of news of her mother that she could think about, then he stood, signalling an end to their time together.

"As much as I hate to see you leave, it's time for you to be getting home."

Cassie noticed the film of tears before her father blinked them away. She had to fight back her own tears that burned at the back of her eyes.

Not yet, Cassie wanted to cry out.

"I want you to promise me that you won't make any more trips delivering morphine?" he insisted, his tone and stance demanding her acquiescence.

Cassie was happy to agree to his request. She had no desire to even attempt another delivery.

"I promise."

"It's time you were headed back, Cassie. God go with you, daughter. It seems that Grant is doing his best for Lincoln's election."

He caught her close, and she could hear the tears in his voice.

"Take care of yourself and your mama for me. Promise?" he asked her.

Cassie could no more have refused his request than she could have decided to stop drawing breath. She knew her father was counting on her to keep her mother safe from her own impulsiveness.

Guilt and a renewed sense of determination filled Cassie. She'd do anything she had to in order to help end the war sooner. Anything.

A mental picture of Jared sprang unbidden to her mind, and she resolutely pushed it away. She knew she could not allow herself to be swept away by the man her heart demanded she love. It could bring everything tumbling down around them. And she couldn't risk that.

She'd given her father her word, and she intended to keep it. No matter what.

After pressing another kiss on her father's cheek and one last hug, she walked back to where the phaeton was waiting. Climbing into the carriage seat, she turned the horses and set off for Washington.

It was nearing dusk as Cassie approached the Union encampment on the far outskirts of Washington. She wondered how her mother and Aunt Vangie's shopping expedition had progressed. She hoped that there hadn't arisen any problems.

At least, for now, one problem was no longer of any importance. Her mama's morphine shipment was out of the house and safely delivered. Aunt Vangie could snoop to her heart's contentment and not find the shipment of white powder.

However, the papers were still tucked away in her bedroom, a little nagging voice reminded Cassie. What was she to do with them?

Thoughts of the packet of papers brought Jared Montgomery to her mind with a force that took her breath away. As her heart beat faster, she forced herself to remember that he was a thief. And a Union officer.

She had to attempt to keep her heart safe from him, no matter how thoughts of him affected her. As a Union officer, he would surely interfere with her Rebel activities. She shuddered to think of what he might do if he knew of her involvement in the secession plot.

Deep in thought, she allowed the horses to slow their pace. Then she heard it. Hoofbeats sounded on the road behind her. She turned back to look, but could see nothing in the gathering dark.

A sense of unease crept over her. She pulled the reins back, drawing the phaeton to a halt, and listened. The only sounds came from the encampment up ahead. Still, the vague apprehension remained with her.

She flicked the reins and started the horses and carriage forward again. Within minutes, she thought she heard the sound of someone behind her again.

Throwing a glance over her shoulder, she could have sworn that she saw the outline of a figure several yards away. Fear swept over her, and she tamped it down. It would do her no good to let panic overtake her now. She needed to think clearly.

She glanced back again and saw that the figure was staying with her. This time fear loomed, closing off the breath in her throat.

Someone was following her.

And she had no idea who that person might be. Or why.

Seeing a scattering of tents and lights off to her right, away from the Union encampment, she slapped the reins and made for the tents.

She only prayed that she'd make it.

Ten

Jared took another sip of his half-cooled coffee and sighed. He leaned back, and the legs of the wooden camp stool tottered unsteadily beneath his weight.

Looking up from the sheaf of papers in his hands, he studied the Union encampment around him. While he'd been reading, it had began to darken with the approaching dusk. Now, it was nearly getting too dark to read without the use of a lantern, but he wasn't ready to return to the tent yet.

The faint sound of a harmonica playing a lonesome tune could be heard across the camp. It made Jared think of Cassie, and he tried to put her image out of his mind. He had work to do. Voices, movements, and low laughter came from a nearby tent.

Jared rubbed the knot of tension that had settled at the back of his neck. The past two days had been rough. He'd spent long hours in meetings with commanders and more long hours gathering information, and then going over the facts into the wee hours of the morning. He was tired, dusty, and frustrated.

While he'd succeeded in his mission of gathering information to put together a report for the President as the man had requested, Jared wasn't one step closer in his search for the head of the secession plot—the man who'd killed his brother. It seemed that he'd been met with a dead-end at every turn he'd taken in his search.

The rumble of a carriage moving at a rapid pace alerted him, and he surged to his feet, the wooden stool teetered then resettled itself. Jared instinctively reached for his pistol. Across the open field, he noted a single occupant in the carriage. A woman.

The combination of light wind and the horses' speed had knocked the little bonnet on her head askew, and dark curls cascaded out from underneath her bonnet. The dark hair and a certain tilt to the way she held her head reminded him of Cassie.

He rubbed the knot of tension that had increased at the back of his neck. This mission must have taken more out of him than he'd thought. He shook his head as if to clear his vision. He seemed to be picturing Cassie more and more.

He studied the carriage and its occupant more closely as it drew nearer. If he didn't know better, he'd swear that the woman driving the carriage was Cassie Van Dorn. But that was impossible.

Cassie was safely tucked away back in Washington. He was certain of it, wasn't he? Besides, what earthly reason would she have to be driving a team pell mell out here when she belonged back in Washington tucked safely in her feather bed?

The errant thought of her in bed brought back the reoccurring picture of Cassie clothed in the pink nightgown, her dark hair flowing loose about her shoulders in a mass of curls taunted him. That image of her the night he'd broken into her bedroom continued to haunt his waking thoughts.

For the life of him, he couldn't seem to keep his mind free of her and dedicated only to his mission like he should be doing. Thoughts of Cassie insisted on coming to him at the worst moments. Such as now.

He chalked it up to his missing her these past two days and his latent guilt over not telling President Lincoln of Cassie's theft of the papers. But he still didn't regret his decision to keep her involvement quiet for just a little longer.

Surely that was the reason for him thinking he'd seen Cassie out here, Jared assured himself. The woman driving the carriage with her fancy bonnet all askew couldn't have been Cassie Van Dorn.

He glanced over to the outlying tents with

their bright lights of invitation and noted that the carriage was headed away from the Federal encampment and destined for one particular tent.

No, it definitely couldn't have been Cassie. She would never be headed for *that* particular tent.

Assured that the carriage and its mysterious occupant presented no threat to the encampment, Jared sat back down on the rickety wooden stool and turned his attention back to mentally recounting the papers he'd been studying before the interruption. He needed to have everything set clearly in his mind before his return to Washington in the morning. He attempted to push the woman in the carriage out of his thoughts.

Cassie headed the carriage for the nearest lighted tent, the phaeton's wheel's kicking up a wall of dust behind her. Pure instinct ordered her to steer clear of the Union encampment.

Instinct or guilt?

She pushed the nagging question aside. She'd only done what was needed to keep her mama safe. Right now she had more serious concerns than mere guilt. Someone was following her, and she intended to reach the safety of more people before whoever was following her caught up with her.

As she drew up to the side of the tent, she could hear the reassurance of voices and boisterous laughter coming from the large tent. Light poured out the opening where the tent flaps had been fastened back, beckoning her inside to the safety it so willingly offered.

She snatched at the invitation, pulling the carriage to a stop and jumping down in a quick movement of raised skirts and ruffled petticoats.

The sign over the entrance to the tent proclaimed, "The Crystal Chandelier."

Oh, no! As luck would have it, she'd chosen a saloon tent to seek safety in. Any port in a storm, she thought to herself, mentally reciting the old saying that she'd heard her father use many a time.

Not taking precious minutes to smooth her chignon or resettle her bonnet about her wind-blown curls, she dashed through the tent opening. At the scene that greeted her within, she stumbled to a stop.

"Oh, no," she muttered under her breath.

Talk about going from bad to worse, she chided herself. While the tent was filled mostly with men, the few women that strolled about or sat on the men's laps were scantily clad. Cassie had no doubt as their profession. She was experiencing her first close-up view of what Mama referred to as "soiled doves."

The women in the tent plied their trade

without the slightest hint of embarrassment or hesitation. Instead, it was Cassie who felt her cheeks heat with mortification. She forced her gaze away from the women.

She forced her attention on the tent's interior. A half a dozen or so small wooden tables were scattered about the inside of the tent. Men were seated at the tables, either playing cards or drinking amber-colored liquid from tall-necked bottles—or doing both.

From the top tent pole, a crystal chandelier hung, its candles burning brightly in the gathering dusk. The candlelight softened the harsh interior of the tent as if trying to hide what truly went on within the canvas structure.

However, when her gaze took note of a pallet of blankets laid out in the far corner of the tent, Cassie couldn't stop the small gasp that escaped her lips. There wasn't enough candlelight in the entire Union to disguise what use that pallet was intended for.

She felt her cheeks heat even more. The impulse to simply turn around and run out of the tent swept over her. Taking a step backward, she caught herself. She couldn't leave. No telling what or who was waiting outside for her. In spite of what this tent was used for, it presented the only safety she could count on at this moment. She had to stay. For a while.

Taking her courage in hand, Cassie walked

across the tent to the only unoccupied table. The instant she sat down in the wooden chair, an older woman, fully clothed, strolled across to her.

"What'll you have?"

"I was just admiring your pretty chandelier," Cassie answered, trying to stall for time.

The woman glanced up to the tent pole and then back at Cassie.

"I brought it all the way from New Orleans," she informed her. "I used to have a place there. A real nice place."

Cassie glanced around the tent, trying to decide her course of action. Much as she hated to stay here, she didn't have much of a choice.

"So, what'll it be?" the woman asked bluntly.

"What?"

"Searching for business, a drink, or just looking?" She gave Cassie a thorough once over. "I don't need another girl, and lookers aren't much welcomed—if they're not buying."

"I'll have something to drink. A . . . a sherry." That should be safe enough, Cassie thought. And it would give her an excuse to stay a while longer.

The woman laughed and slapped her on the shoulder. "No fancy drawing room sherry here, missy."

"I don't suppose you have cocoa or—"

Harsh laughter cut off her request.

"Missy," the woman paused to look her up and down. "All I serve is whiskey. Good, strong, and not watered."

At Cassie's disbelieving look, the woman added, "Well, not much it isn't."

"I—"

"If you aren't drinking, you aren't staying," the woman cut in. "Understand me?"

Cassie nodded her agreement.

"So, what'll it be?"

"I'll have a whiskey," Cassie answered quickly.

Right now, a sip of whiskey didn't sound half bad to her rattled nerves. Her mama occasionally took a sherry to settle herself when she was upset. After all, how much different could the amber-colored liquid be than Mama's sherry?

She didn't have long to wonder about that. Within a couple of minutes the woman appeared back at the table with a glass of that amber liquid.

Cassie paid for the drink, then picked it up in her hand. A thought of how horrified her mama would be if she were to see her now flashed through her mind.

Taking a deep breath, Cassie raised the glass to her lips and took a swallow. A bitter taste was her only warning before fire blazed

its way down her throat all the way to her
stomach, robbing her of all breath.

Cassie gasped for air, and tears came to
her eyes. It felt as if she'd just swallowed a
hot fireplace poker. She'd swear that even
her toes burned from the whiskey.

She coughed, and more tears flooded her
eyes. The tears trailed a path down her
cheeks. Suddenly, a spasm of coughing
wracked her, and she caught the edge of the
wooden table.

The woman clapped her on the back. "Try
just sipping it," she advised with a wide
smile. "It'll go down better."

"Thanks," Cassie whispered in a strangely
hoarse sounding voice.

The woman smiled at her for the first
time. "Girl, you got guts. I like that. Name's
Massie if you need anything else."

Cassie nodded weakly and tried to give the
woman a smile in return. Her effort came out
wan and slightly watery. She wiped the tears
from her cheeks with the back of her one
hand. In her other hand, she still held the
half-filled glass. She didn't honestly think she
was capable at this moment of uncurling her
fingers from it. That would take more
strength than she could muster at this instant.

Whiskey was definitely a far sight different
than a sip of Mama's sherry. Cassie blinked
again and sucked a breath of air through her

mouth. Her throat still burned as if it had been scalded.

A few minutes later, she was trying to get up the nerve to try another sip when a disheveled soldier pulled out the other chair at her table and dropped into it. Cassie sent him a questioning glance, hoping to discourage him. It bounced right off the sergeant stripes sewn on his shoulders.

"Haven't seen you here before," he said, leaning over the edge of the table.

He reeked of alcohol, and Cassie pressed back in her chair, trying to put as much distance between her and him as she possibly could. She feared it was going to take a lot of doing to discourage this man.

"This is my first time here," she answered in a cold, disinterested voice. "And I'm most assuredly not looking for company."

He burst into laughter at her remark. "Hey, I like the way you talk. All uppity sounding." The last two words came out slurred together.

Oh, good gracious, the last thing she'd wanted to do was encourage him into liking anything about her. Cassie sent him a quelling frown.

"If you would excuse me—"

"Name's Charlie Parker. Sergeant." He gestured to his rank. "Hey, let me buy you a drink," he offered, dropping one hand beside hers on the table.

Cassie pulled her own hand back, placing it in her lap safely out of his reach. "No, thank you."

"Aw, come on, now," he persisted.

"I haven't finished the one I have." She lifted the glass in her hand to show him the amber-colored whiskey still remaining.

He reached out his hand and snatched up her hand, glass and all. "Forget that, girlie. Why don't we have us some fun? I could show you a real good time."

Cassie cringed inwardly at his coarse words. She jerked her hand out of his grasp, not caring that the whiskey sloshed over the rim of the glass and spilled onto the table.

"Hey, you sure aren't being very friendly, are you?"

Cassie narrowed her gaze on his. "I'm not feeling very friendly right now. I'm tired and not feeling very well," she offered the additional excuse, hoping to discourage his persistent advances. Maybe if he thought her ill, he'd lose interest.

It didn't work. Instead, he leaned closer and reached for her hand again.

Cassie pulled her hand back just in time to avoid his groping fingers. A tiny fissure of fear began to settle in at the base of her spine. The sergeant was proving to be more tenacious than she'd anticipated.

The soldier laughed and leaned farther over the table. His drunken breath fanned her face. The fear grew and raced up her back.

The situation was fast getting out of hand. She fired a glance around the tent, but knew instinctively that she wouldn't be getting any help from any of the patrons in the tent. The woman named Massie turned away when she looked to her.

Most assuredly, there was no one here who would be coming to her assistance, Cassie thought. It was up to her to make her own way out of this.

Damnation. Which was the worse of her two choices? Staying here with the drunken soldier's advances, or leaving the tent and facing what awaited her outside?

For an instant, a picture of Jared so tall and strong and striking came to her mind. She wished he were here, he'd handle this problem.

The sergeant reached for her again, and she made up her mind. Jared wasn't here. She was on her own, and it was time to leave.

As she started to scoot her chair back, the soldier grabbed her arm. Cassie raised her other hand and threw the remainder of the drink in his face.

Jared stepped through the tent opening just in time to see the disheveled soldier jerk his head back from a dark-haired woman sitting at a back table. Amber-colored liquid dripped down from his chin a moment before the man knocked the glass from her hand. It smashed against the canvas side of the tent.

From where Jared stood all he could see clearly was the back of the woman's head, covered with a blue bonnet. A cluster of dark curls hung loose from under the bonnet. She reminded him of Cassie, but it was most definitely the woman he'd seen driving the carriage in such a hurry to reach this tent.

Whoever she was, the woman was asking for trouble, he thought. He still wasn't sure why he'd felt the sudden impulse to tuck the sheaf of papers into his jacket pocket and stride across the field to check out the saloon tent. He told himself that he'd done it solely because he was thirsty. It most assuredly couldn't be because he still thought how much the woman carriage driver had reminded him of Cassie.

"Hey, girlie, you sure messed things up." The soldier caught her small hand with his beefy one. "We could sure have had us some fun together. Now you're gonna make me play rough."

Jared watched the interplay between the soldier and the woman. She pulled her hand back and appeared to be pretending to hold out. Probably trying to get him to offer more money. Once again, he thought how she was asking for trouble. It wasn't smart to make the drunken soldier mad at her.

Sure enough, the disheveled sergeant made an angry grab for her, catching her shoulder with his hand.

"Get your hands off me!"

Jared's head snapped up at the woman's voice. While he knew it was impossible, he'd swear that for a moment she'd sounded just like Cassie.

A slap resounded from across the room.

"Hey, girlie—" The soldier staggered to his feet.

He grabbed the woman's arm, roughly hauling her up to his side.

"Let me go!" she demanded. "Or I'll—"

Her bonnet tilted backwards, and Jared got his first clear look at the dark-haired woman's face. His mouth dropped open.

Cassie Van Dorn.

The silly fool, Jared thought, the instant his mind cleared enough for him to think coherently. What in the hell was she doing in a place like the Crystal Chandelier?

Didn't she have any idea what this tent was intended for? The Crystal Chandelier had an unsavory reputation for miles around. Didn't she have any sense of self-preservation at all?

Jared strode across the floor of the tent toward the obviously drunken soldier and Cassie.

"Let her go," he ordered.

Cassie's gaze locked with his, and he heard her shocked gasp of disbelief.

"Jared?"

She stared at him, hardly daring to believe that he was real and not just her wish coming true.

"Jared," she breathed his name in a sigh of relief.

"Hey, buddy, leave it be," the sergeant shouted. "This is between the girlie and me. I got first claim." The soldier yanked Cassie toward him. "She's mine."

"I said let her go." Jared's voice chilled by several degrees.

The other man ignored the icy warning, squeezing Cassie's arm. She winced at the sharp pain and tried to pull away, but he tightened his grip on her.

"Can't do that. I already paid Massie my money for the night with one of her girls."

Keeping his attention firmly fixed on the other soldier, Jared reached into his pocket and withdrew twenty dollars. He laid the money on the table.

"Consider it a repayment. With a nice profit."

The soldier laughed off the offer. "Not interested."

"I'm not one of her girls," Cassie denied.

The soldier ignored her, and Jared sent her a look that plainly told her to be quiet.

"I'm not one of the girls," Cassie repeated

louder this time, trying to stop the fight she could see brewing.

Jared slowly extended his hand to her, catching her wrist gently. He urged her toward him. Cassie obliged willingly, taking a step away from the soldier.

Instead of releasing her, the sergeant tightened his hold, pulling her back toward him. Held between the two men, Cassie felt like the wishbone on a chicken, being pulled in two directions at once, just waiting to break.

She'd had enough.

She'd been frightened, insulted, and now made the bone of contention between two men. She wasn't going to stand there helplessly while they tugged at her.

Raising her foot, she kicked out at the drunken soldier's shin as hard as she could. The impact of the ball of her slipper-clad foot caused him to yelp in pain, and tears of pain to come to her eyes.

Swearing profusely, the soldier released her. Cassie jumped back away from him, determined to get out of his reach. Jared quickly caught her wrist again and pulled her towards the tent opening.

The next instant all hell broke loose in the tent. The soldier bellowed in rage, and Jared shoved Cassie out of the way. As he turned around to face the soldier, the man charged at him. He caught Jared full in the stomach, sending him stumbling backwards.

"Jared!" Cassie screamed.

He straightened and shot a glance her way. The next instant the soldier's fist connected with Jared's chin. The force of the blow sent him back two steps.

"Jared!" Cassie yelled again.

"Cassie, get out of here," he ordered her, not daring to turn his attention away again from the sergeant facing him.

This time when the man lunged for him, Jared was ready. He swung, his fist connecting solidly with the man's stomach. The soldier doubled over, then reared up, fists thrashing the air.

Jared sidestepped the blows, landing a sharp right to the sergeant's chin. His head snapped back, then he shook his head and charged again, swinging a beefy fist at Jared. This time the punch went wide, missing him.

The tent erupted into a brawl of swinging fists and shouted curses. Cassie spotted Massie and her soiled doves quickly ducking out the front of the tent. Above them, the chandelier swayed precariously for several seconds before it finally slowed to a stop.

All around the tent, fights broke out. Cassie watched almost spellbound until she saw a heavy-set man lift a chair over his head and turn toward Jared. In a flash, she snatched her bonnet pin free and stabbed it firmly in the man's rear end. The man yelped and jumped, dropping the chair harmlessly to the floor.

She pulled the pin back and moved away toward a tall, stringy man who was wielding a whiskey bottle and approaching Jared from his blind side. Before the man could reach him, she closed her fist tightly around the pin and thrust out her hand.

Once again, the bonnet pin found its mark. The man howled, dropped the bottle, and spinning around swung in her direction. Cassie dodged to the side, and luckily the blow only grazed her shoulder. However, it carried enough force to send her tumbling to the floor.

Before she could rise, someone made a grab for her. She recognized the beefy hand that grabbed for her. Damnation, that sergeant was persistent. She stabbed his hand with her bonnet pin.

As he pulled back, she vowed that she'd never leave the house again without at least one bonnet pin in her possession. They sure came in handy.

She glanced up in time to see Jared plant a solid punch at the overly persistent sergeant. The man stumbled, then fell backwards. She scarcely had time to roll to the side out of his path before he landed on the tent floor.

Scrambling to her feet and pushing down her rumpled petticoats, Cassie realized that she'd lost her bonnet and dropped the pin in her haste to roll away. She searched the tent floor and saw a gleam of silver from the bonnet pin. There it was.

As she bent down and closed her fingers over the pin, Jared caught her by the waist. Pulling her toward the tent opening, he shouted at her, "Get out of here."

"I—"

The words froze in her throat as she saw a man charging at them with a broken bottle in his hand. She screamed a warning.

Jared released her and swung at the man. His fist connected solidly with the man's chin, and he crumpled to the ground.

This time, Jared gave her a shove towards the tent opening.

"Wait for me at the carriage." He turned away from her to keep his attention on the brawl still going on inside the tent.

"But—"

She wasn't about to leave him.

"Cassie—"

"You need someone to watch your back."

"Don't argue. Now go!"

"Aren't you coming?" she asked, still uncertain of whether to leave him or not.

"Yes. Now go!"

Cassie obeyed his shouted order and ducked out the tent opening. Strangely enough it was peacefully quiet outside, but she knew it wouldn't remain that way for much longer. She caught up her skirts and ran for the carriage.

At the side of the phaeton, she stopped to look back for Jared, but he hadn't appeared outside yet. Climbing up onto the seat, she loosened the reins and turned the carriage around, then urged the horses back toward the front of the tent.

She'd scarcely reached the tent when Jared hurled himself through the tent opening.

"Here," she yelled to catch his attention.

Jared climbed into the carriage. Taking the reins from her, he slapped them, sending the horses off at a gallop. Shouts and curses sounded behind them. A bottle whizzed past their heads.

Jared flicked the reins again and turned the carriage towards Washington. They travelled in silence for the better part of five minutes before either of them spoke.

"Do you want to tell me what the hell you were doing in the Crystal Chandelier?" Jared asked in a tight voice.

Cassie's heart raced for her toes. What in the name of heaven was she supposed to say? That she was on her way back home from delivering an illegal shipment of morphine to the South? She didn't think so.

"Thank you for rescuing me," she answered instead, trying to sidetrack his questions until she could come up with a suitable answer.

Beside her, Jared stiffened. She could almost feel his anger as he withdrew from her.

"You were great in there," she added.

"And you owe me twenty dollars," he answered in a cold voice.

"What?" Her own voice raised in disbelief.

"I said you owe me twenty dollars." He enunciated each word clearly.

"Whatever for?"

"That's what I paid for you back there."

Cassie gasped and snapped her mouth shut. She vowed to remain silent the rest of the way to Washington. Of all the damned nerve. This had to be the worst insult she'd ever received in her life.

Eleven

The longer the wheels of the carriage continued to turn, the angrier Cassie became. What right did Jared have to be mad at her?

After all, she hadn't intentionally gone into the saloon tent. She hadn't tried to catch the sergeant's attention. And even more, she hadn't asked Jared to interfere.

Finally, she could stand it no longer. Seething with anger, she turned to Jared.

"I didn't get you into a fight on purpose. And I didn't ask for your help!"

"Oh, and I suppose you were doing fine on your own, too?" he asked with a hint of sarcasm.

"As a matter of fact, I was."

His harsh burst of laughter startled her.

"Like hell you were." He slapped the reins hard on the horses rumps.

"I was," she argued back.

"If that's true, would you rather I turned the carriage around and gave you back to them so you could prove that fact?"

Cassie bit back her sharp retort. He just

might carry out that threat. She crossed her arms over her chest and glared over at him. She even contemplated not speaking to him for the remainder of the ride back to Washington, but knew her anger would never let her hold her tongue that long.

"I saved your back a couple of times if I happen to remember correctly," she said haughtily with a toss of her head. Her dark curls tumbled free about her shoulders, albeit without her bonnet.

"And I saved your—" he bit off the rest of what he'd been about to say.

"How dare—"

"Don't start something you're not ready to finish, Cassie," he warned.

"I'm not the one who started this." She sat back in the seat, her arms still crossed.

"Look out or I may finish it."

Cassie snapped her mouth shut on the retort she'd been about to give, recalling the old saying her father often quoted about not pulling on a tiger's tail when he was angry. Somehow she felt that advice most definitely applied to Jared Montgomery at this moment.

"Are you going to tell me what you were doing in the Crystal Chandelier tent? And don't give me any story about being out for a ride." Jared sent her a demanding look.

She decided that her best course was to tell the truth—partially.

"I was visiting someone."

"Who?" Jared fired the single word at her like the crack of a rifle shot. He could wait and learn the answer from the man he'd assigned to follow her, but he wanted to know now.

Was that jealousy she heard in his voice, she asked herself in surprise? One sideways glance at his set face assured her she'd been wrong at the thought. The only emotion she could read on his face was anger. Pure and simple.

Cassie drew in a breath and answered him. "My father."

"Your father? Do you really expect me to believe that?"

"Why not? It just happens to be true."

Cassie raised her chin a notch, insulted at the inference behind his question.

Jared tightened his hands on the reins, and the horses jerked their heads. He quickly released his harsh grip, loosening the reins.

"If you were meeting your father, what in the hell were you doing in a place like that saloon tent?"

Still angry with him, she pretended to ignore his question. He could just wonder until snow fell for all she cared right now.

"Don't you have a brain in your pretty head?" Jared asked in frustration.

Her breath rushed out in a burst of anger. "Don't you dare talk to me that way!"

"Cassie, answer me. What were you doing in the Crystal Chandelier?"

"It looked safe—"

"Looked safe?" he sputtered in disbelief.

"Yes!" she shouted back at him.

Cassie could see him shaking his head, even in the dark.

"Well, it did. At first."

"Cassie, do you know what the Crystal Chandelier is?"

"Of course I do. Do you think I'm a fool?"

Jared's cheek muscles tightened as he clenched his jaw. He answered her through his teeth, "You wouldn't like the answer I'd give to that right now."

She decided to change the subject away from her meeting with her father. "If I recall correctly, I was doing just fine with my bonnet pin."

His answer of harsh laughter grated on her nerves.

"Well, I was."

Jared pulled the carriage to a halt and turned to face her.

"You little fool."

"I—"

"Dammit, Cassie," he growled, catching her shoulders in his hands.

She fell silent, her eyes meeting with his dark ones. Anger, confusion, then desire flared in his gaze. She couldn't have looked away from him if her very life depended upon it.

Jared drew her to him, and his lips crushed hers beneath his in a punishing kiss. However, heat immediately seared between them, like a campfire taking hold after kindling, and the kiss changed almost instantly to one of hunger and desire.

Cassie clenched her hands in her lap, forcing herself not to give in to the sensations running pell mell through her body. If she did, she'd throw her arms around Jared's neck and hang on for dear life.

If he didn't let her go soon, she might still do that.

She felt the sharp prick of her bonnet pin in her clenched hands. That would surely prove her point that she could take care of herself. There was her answer. Her salvation.

One stab of the sharp pin, and Jared would be sure to release her. She gripped the silver pin in her hands, then released it, letting it slip through her fingers and drop to the floor of the carriage.

She couldn't do it. She couldn't stick him with the end of the sharp pin merely to prove her point. If she did, he might surely stop kissing her, and if he did that she thought she might die.

Cassie gave in to the overwhelming longing to throw her arms about his neck. She felt the strength of his shoulders beneath her fin-

gers and revelled in it. Then she curled her
hands about the back of his neck, her fingers
sinking into the thick pelt of the hair at the
back of his neck. A sigh broke free from her
throat.

Jared released her suddenly, pushing her
to her side of the carriage. He ran a hand
distractedly through his hair, and she noticed
that his hand was none too steady. Turning
away, he sent the horses onward again.

Cassie felt as if she'd just been doused
with cold spring water. Whatever had
prompted his sudden change? Hot kisses one
minute and cold distance the next.

"Do you have any idea what kind of danger you put yourself in?" he asked in a low,
tight voice, answering her question.

Cassie bit down on the shiver of fear his
words brought to her as she recalled the sergeant's hands on her and his threats.

"I—"

"Dammit, Cassie."

"Yes," she answered with the only thing
she could—the truth.

"When I think of what could have happened to you back there." Jared ran a hand
through his hair again. "I don't know rather
to shake you or love you. Oh, Cassie, what
in the hell am I supposed to do with you?"

"Love me?" She was certain she'd only
thought the unexpected words, but one

glance at his face, and she knew she'd said them aloud.

Her cheeks flamed at what she'd done. Where had that thought even come from? Much less the words?

She couldn't want him to love her. She couldn't. He was a Yankee. And a thief. And . . .

The rest of what she'd been thinking trailed off, leaving her with only the single word "love" left echoing in her mind. She was fast falling in love with the devastating Yankee sitting so proud and straight beside her. When had it happened? Likely as not, it had happened the instant she laid eyes on him at the Admiral's ball when he'd taken her hand in his, she thought. Or perhaps, when he'd first caught her stealing the papers and pulled her into his arms upstairs in the Admiral's bedroom?

Cassie moistened her lips. "Jared?" she whispered, longing in her voice.

He jerked the carriage to a sudden halt and pulled her into his embrace. "Oh, Cassie, my sweet."

He kissed her hard and long. Dragging his hands through her hair, he buried his fingers deep in her lush curls. Then, he rained small kisses along her cheek, her chin, her throat. Continuing downward, his lips brushed back and forth along the lace-edged ruche above her bodice. He dipped his tongue between the valley of her breasts, and Cassie moaned against him, straining to get closer if possible.

Cupping her breasts in his hands, he kissed them through the muslin of her gown. Unable to help herself, Cassie tipped her head back. Jared took the invitation she gave and ran his tongue up to the white column of her throat.

Cassie gripped his shoulders, hardly able to stay upright under his loving foray and the flurry of unknown emotions now coursing through her with every beat of her heart.

As if her action had drawn him to his senses, Jared eased away from her. Cassie moaned in mute protest.

"Come home with me, Cassie?" he asked in a husky voice.

She could no more have refused him than she could have refused her heart to beat. At that moment in time, nothing else mattered more than the look in his eyes and the beloved catch in his voice.

"Yes." Her answer was no more than a whisper of sound on her lips.

Taking a moment to settle her carefully in the seat, near enough to him so that his leg brushed hers, Jared then flicked the reins and sent the carriage into motion. Under his guidance, the horses galloped into the night.

As the phaeton wheels rolled into the streets of Washington, Jared slowed the coach. Mere minutes later, he drew the carriage to a halt at his house.

Climbing down, he raised his arms and lifted Cassie down from the seat. From over his shoulder she saw the outline of his brownstone in the night. It seemed to loom out of the darkness, chastising her.

What was she about to do, she asked herself? He was a Yankee officer, and a thief, and she loved him. Heaven help her.

Cassie stiffened in his arms, and Jared could feel her sudden indecision. He lowered his head to hers, brushing a gentle questioning kiss across her lips, leaving the decision up to her.

If he had demanded, she could have refused. Would have refused, but the simple, questioning kiss was her undoing. Cassie answered him by returning the pressure of his lips, her arms slipping around his neck. She could not refuse him now.

Jared turned and carried her into the house without breaking stride. His long legs quickly ate up the distance to the bedroom.

Once there, he gently lowered Cassie to the bed. Pausing only long enough to shed his greatcoat, Jared joined her on the feather mattress. She felt the mattress give beneath his weight with a faint creak of the wooden headboard.

Suddenly, Cassie remembered the large wooden headboard behind her head and the

papers that had been hidden behind the
wood. She felt a moment of guilt over her
theft before Jared's lips claimed hers once
again, and all thought evaporated away like
dew drops under the brilliant sunshine of a
spring morning.

The silken hairs of his mustache caressed
her upper lip, and beneath it his lips were
smooth and warm against hers. So very
warm.

She could feel the heat course from her
lips throughout every nerve ending in her
body. She felt as if she were floating in a
cocoon filled with love. It radiated between
them, taking her very breath away.

It was as if nothing else in the whole world
existed at that moment in time. No war. No
packet of papers. No South or North. Only
the two of them wrapped in that cocoon of
warm loving.

She wanted the feeling to go on forever
and ever. When Jared eased away and sat up,
she moaned her disappointment. He leaned
forward and took the sound in a kiss that
just as surely stole her breath along with it.

Cassie felt his hands move between them
and realized that he was unfastening his buttons. One by one.

She reached down and hesitantly met his
hands, helping him unfasten first one gold
button, then another. She could swear with
each button freed that the temperature in the

room climbed. She felt for the next button, now more than eager to assist, but when Jared's hands dropped to his trousers, she blushed and turned her head.

Jared chuckled softly, and the sound was anything but an insult. It was deep down sensual, like the low rumble of a mountain lion's roar.

He stood in a quick decisive move and shucked his trousers and boots, then rejoined her on the feather bed.

Cassie felt herself blush all the way from her forehead to the tips of her stocking-clad toes.

Jared traced the pink of her cheeks with a fingertip. As her blush deepened, he lowered his lips to hers, erasing all embarrassment in a burst of loving desire.

"Now you, my love," he murmured, reaching for the first fastening of her gown.

Unable to resist the soft entreaty in his low voice, Cassie rolled to her side, facing him. Her movement gave Jared the access he needed, and the fastenings of her gown soon fell way to reveal her lacy chemise.

He lavished kisses across her shoulders and the top of the mounds of her breasts revealed by the lace edging. Slipping the gown upward, he swept it over her head and tossed it to the floor. Her petticoats followed to land in a pool of white on the wooden flooring.

He soon replaced the warmth of the garments with the touch of his body against hers. Easing the lacy fabric of the chemise upward, inch by inch, he placed kisses against the silken skin revealed by the undergarment's departure. Finally, he removed the chemise entirely and dropped it aside. He trailed his fingertips back down along the column of her neck, to her shoulders, along their gentle curve to her breasts.

Cassie floated on a wave of loving pleasure under the touch of his hands and his lips on her skin as he tenderly and slowly removed each of her garments. Oh, so very slowly.

Finally, she lay naked to his gaze. For an instant, feminine insecurity nibbled at the pleasure she felt. What would Jared think of her? Would he find her body pleasing? Was she slender enough? Voluptuous enough? No man had ever seen her naked before in her life.

"Beautiful," Jared murmured the word, making it sound like an endearment.

He tenderly smoothed a tendril of hair from her cheek, then ran his hands through her curls, spreading them over the pillow like a cloud.

All insecurity and uncertainty fled from her, faster than it had come on. In its place, desire swept through her as surely as his hands slid down her rib cage and over her hips.

As Cassie looked into his eyes, she could

see that very same desire reflected there. It darkened his green-gray eyes to deepest emerald, calling to mind a dark secluded forest. His gaze called to her, begging her to go to a secret place with him.

Once again, Cassie knew it was impossible to resist his silent request. This time, she was the one who initiated the kiss, pressing her lips against his, then deepening the kiss.

Jared took command like a soldier in battle. Slanting his mouth over hers, he brushed back and forth gently at first, then he increased the pressure until her lips parted under his. He slid his tongue into her velvet warmth until he had complete possession of her. With his hands, he drew her hips against his.

As his tongue sought and touched the roof of her mouth, she moaned her pleasure against his lips. It was all the encouragement he needed. Jared drew her more firmly against him, pressing his hardness against the welcoming softness of her. He nestled between her thighs, waiting, coaxing her with ever deepening loving kisses.

Cassie strained against him, her body demanding more. More of his touch, his feel, his love.

Jared obliged, laving hungry kisses along her jaw and down to her neck. Once at her collarbone, he shifted in the bed, positioning her beneath him as he trailed his tongue kisses lower to her breasts. Pausing to suckle

232 Joyce Adams

first one peak, then the other, he felt her thrash beneath him and smiled.

"Jared!" Cassie caught his head, pulling him snugly between her breasts. His teasing kisses of first one breast and then the other were threatening to send over the edge into what she wasn't sure.

"Yes, love?" he murmured before he took one nipple into his mouth.

Cassie cried out, clutching her hands into his thick golden hair. She writhed beneath his loving lips. In answer, he suckled harder, increasing the pressure of his firm lips.

She thought she would surely go insane from his touch. She had never felt anything like it in her entire life. She'd never felt so loved before.

His mustache brushed ever so softly against her breast, increasing the pleasure that she'd thought impossible to increase any more.

"Oh, Jared, I don't think I can take any more," she whispered in a hoarse voice.

His low chuckle sent shivers up her back—warm, sensual shivers. They ran the length of her spine, then pooled in a heated warmth between her thighs.

"Oh, love," he answered, his words muffled against her silken skin. "We've only just begun."

With this, he lowered his head to dip his moist hot tongue into her navel, and Cassie thought surely that she had died and gone to heaven. A moment later, he smoothed his hands back and forth along her thighs. The slightly rough calloused touch excited her more than she had dreamed a man's touch could ever do to her.

Easing her thighs apart, Jared ran his fingertips up and across her stomach, then began his course back downward. Lower, and lower he advanced, until he stroked her where she'd never been touched before. Again and again. And again, until Cassie thought surely she'd die from the new, unknown sensations he was causing to ripple through her body.

Finally, Cassie arched beneath him, and Jared took her mouth in a kiss burning with desire and a hunger that could not be denied. At the same moment, he eased himself between her legs. Probing gently, he pressed against her opening, then with a final thrust, he made her his.

He took her small cry of pain away the same magical way he did her very breath. Cassie clasped his shoulders tighter, digging her fingertips into the firm muscled flesh beneath her hands.

"Ah, yes, my love," he whispered in the shell of her ear.

Smoothing his hands over her body, he fondled her buttocks, and ran his palms upward over her hips and waist, coming finally to rest on her cheeks. He held her face, gently,

tenderly within his grasp before he took her
lips in another breath-stealing kiss.

Cassie was certain that there wasn't an inch
of her that hadn't felt his touch or his possession. She was totally, completely his.

She arched beneath him, instinctively meeting him thrust for thrust. Warm pleasure
rolled through her like a silken fabric unfurl-
ing from a bolt. It continued to roll and spiral.

Suddenly, small starbursts exploded for
Cassie, and she held tightly to Jared, shaken
to the very foundation of her being by his
loving. His cry of joyous release joined hers.

Cassie awoke the next morning to the sound
of faint movements within the room. She sat
up in bed, clutching the bedcovers to her.

Across the room, Jared turned to face her.
The loving look in his eyes stole her very
thought away.

"Morning, my love."

He crossed to her and sank onto the edge
of the bed beside her. His thigh brushed
hers, sending a thrill through her. He leaned
forward and brushed a tender kiss against
her love-swollen lips.

"Morning," Cassie murmured, noting that
he was fully clothed, his hair neatly combed
as well.

He smelled of the outdoors, and she suddenly wondered where he had gone so early

in the morning. Becoming aware of her state of undress, she clutched the bedcovers tighter, and felt her face heat with the red of a blush of embarrassment.

"I had hoped to be back before you'd awakened, my love."

"Back?" Cassie licked her lips in a gesture of nervousness and uncertainty.

This didn't go unnoticed by Jared.

"I'm sorry, but I had to deliver a report first thing this morning. I didn't want to disturb you. I had another way of waking you in mind." He said the last on a low breath of sound.

Reaching one hand to his chest, he began to unbutton his uniform jacket. Cassie watched spellbound as first one gold button, then another, and another gave beneath his fingers. The open vee of his jacket widened, giving her a close up view of his broad chest. She stared at it fascinated.

Jared pulled the wool jacket away from his waist, and Cassie's breath left in a soft rush of sound. She ran her hand across the muscles of his chest, and as she did so, the muscles rippled beneath her fingertips as if begging for more of her touch.

"Jared?" she whispered.

"Yes, love," he answered, pulling the jacket the remainder of the way off and tossing it heedlessly onto the floor.

Cassie stared at him, suddenly, unexpectedly at a loss for words.

Smiling at her silence, Jared kicked off his boots, unfastened his trousers and slid them to the floor. His gaze darkened as he watched her eyes widen.

"Yes, love," he whispered again, joining her in the bed.

This time they made love slowly, even more leisurely than last night. They touched, tasted, explored each other as neither had imagined possible. At that moment, Cassie knew that she loved nothing more than Jared's touch in the morning, and she gave herself over to his loving.

All too soon their idyllic time came to an end. The decision lay unspoken between them, but still there nonetheless. They both knew it was time for Cassie to return home.

She hated leaving the security of Jared's arms about her in the feather bed just about more than she'd hated anything in her entire life.

"I have to get home," she spoke the words out loud, more to convince herself than him.

The words fell in the quiet room like pebbles on a pond, the ripples destroying the stillness.

Jared leaned up on an elbow and gazed down into her face. "I know, my love."

Other words hung between them, waiting for either to speak them while Cassie and Jared dressed. When he cleared his throat one time, she held herself perfectly still, waiting for his words of love to come. But he remained quiet. Suddenly hesitant to voice her feelings, she remained equally silent.

They walked to the door together, and Jared waited until they'd reached the carriage before he took Cassie in his arms one last time. His kiss was all the reassurance she needed, and then some. However, still she withheld her proclamation of love.

Jared lifted her into the carriage and placed the reins in her hands. Regretfully, she drove the carriage away. His image stayed with her on the drive home, and she completed the trip in a daze of precious memories.

She was in love. Truly. Completely. Totally. And forever.

Once home, and still smiling to herself, she turned the phaeton and the horses over to a servant's care, then slipped quietly into the house. Luck was with her, and she reached her room without being seen by any servants or her inquisitive aunt. As soon as she had a few minutes to freshen up, she would let her mother know she'd arrived back safely.

While straightening her tousled hair, her eyes strayed to the safe. She really should check on the safety of the packet of papers, a nagging thought told her, although it was likely as not completely unnecessary. However, in spite of that assurance, the persistent worry refused to go away, so she finally gave into it.

After retrieving the key from where she'd left it, she crossed to the safe and opened the door. Shafts of sunlight from the French doors filled the partially darkened interior thoroughly revealing the contents, and her breath left her in a cry of distress.

Cassie stared at the compartment in disbelief. It was empty of any papers. Empty—save for the dried, single red rose from Jared.

Jared.

No, she wanted to cry out. Please, no.

She dropped her head into her hands and closed her eyes briefly. She had to think this through. She had to.

The papers had been locked away in the safe before she'd left to deliver Mama's morphine. She was positive of that. No one else knew of her hiding place for the key. Lowering her hands, she glanced around the room. That's when she spotted it.

A dark pool of fabric lay in front of the French doors leading to the balcony. Without taking her eyes from the cloth, she crossed the room, hardly daring to breathe. Reaching the closed doors, she bent down and picked up the black silk mask. She recognized it immediately.

Jared. The mask belonged to Jared.

She closed her fingers over the fabric, squeezing them tightly. Her fingernails dug into the palm of her hand, and tears suddenly burned at the back of her eyes.

However much she wanted to deny it, prayed it wasn't true, the proof of his deception lay in plain sight for her to see. Only a fool would deny it.

The sense of betrayal cut deeper than she'd imagined possible, and the pain hit her so hard that she felt she might shatter from it.

All the while he'd been making love to her, he'd been planning this. Planning to slip away from her before dawn this morning for the time he needed to retrieve the papers—the time he'd been gone to deliver his so-called report this morning.

Jared had only been using her. The thought cut deep and sharp. Cassie wrapped her arms about her waist, as if by holding on she could somehow withstand the pain of his betrayal better. It failed.

The sheer anguish she felt almost drove her to her knees.

What they had shared had meant nothing to him. And everything to her.

Twelve

"Cassie?"

Cassie recognized her mama's voice and heard the door swing inward, but couldn't turn around to face her mama. Not just yet.

Instead, she clenched her hands into fists, striving for some outward show of calm. Her fingernails scored half moons into her palms, but she ignored the pain. It was nothing compared to the pain that still tore at her at the remembrance of Jared's deception.

"Cassie? Is everything all right?" her mother asked, concern weighing down her voice.

Cassie wanted to scream out, no, nothing would ever be all right again. But she forced herself to remain silent the extra moments she needed to compose herself enough to face her mama.

Her mother crossed the room and laid a hand on her shoulder. It was almost Cassie's undoing. The desire to turn into her mama's embrace and cry her eyes out almost over-whelmed her. Instead she swallowed down the temptation and raised her chin in silent determination.

"I'm . . . fine," Cassie mouthed the lie that would reassure her mother, not even flinching at the deceit this time.

Maybe what people said about lying getting easier the more you did it was true, or maybe she hurt too badly right now to even care.

"Cassie . . . is . . ." her mama's voice broke, and she raised a hand to cover her mouth.

Silence blanketed the room for the space of several seconds.

A tiny sob came from her mother, and Cassie turned to her in sudden concern and guilt.

"Mama?"

"Thomas? Was he . . ." her mama cut off the rest, and another sob tore through her.

In that instant Cassie understood what her mother had been trying to ask. She shook her head, rushing to assure her.

"Papa's fine. He sends his love."

Her dainty mother almost crumpled with relief at Cassie's words. Cassie led her to the bed and helped her to sit down.

"You're sure? You're not just saying that, are you?" Alicia caught her daughter's hands in hers, demanding an answer to the fear that plagued her. "You're not saying so just to help me?"

"No, Mama." Cassie squeezed her mother's

cold hands. "Papa is fine. Honest, I swear it. I saw him, and I talked with him."

"Oh, dear." Alicia laid one hand over her heart. "You gave me such a scare." She stared up into Cassie's face. "You're certain?" she asked once again.

Cassie smiled back at her mama. "Quite certain. I even saw the framed picture of you that you sent him. It was sitting on his desk, in a place of honor." She lowered her voice to a conspiratorial whisper. "And there was a stack of your letters saved beside it."

Her mother blinked away a sudden rush of fresh tears. "Thank you, dear," she murmured. "I can't tell you how relieved I am. I still can scarcely believe that you really saw Thomas and talked to him."

"In fact," Cassie added, "I have even been ordered by Papa not to let you smuggle any more."

"Oh." Worry etched her mother's face a moment, then was almost instantly replaced by a radiant smile. "Yes, you really saw him."

"Yes, Mama." Cassie sat down beside her mother on the bed. "He is fine. A little older looking maybe. But very alive and well. In fact, I don't know when he ever looked better to me."

Her mother blinked and gave her a watery smile. "Oh, that's good. So good." She sniffed. "I do miss him so very much."

"I know, Mama."

Suddenly Alicia straightened and raised her chin in a gesture Cassie recognized. Trouble was coming.

"And where were you last night, Cassie?"

Cassie's stomach tied in a big knot at the question. How was she to answer her mama's question?

"I . . . I . . . spent the night with a friend," she said softly.

It was the truth, Cassie told herself, ordering her conscience to be quiet.

"Your friend, Jane, from the orphanage?"

Cassie remained silent, but that was enough of an answer to satisfy her mother.

"That's what I told Vangie, but I don't think she believed a word of it." Alicia's voice clearly showed her dismay and distress.

"Oh, no."

"I fear she's going to be even more curious now than she's been before. If possible," her mother added under her breath.

"I'll see what I can do to dispel her suspicions," Cassie assured her, nibbling on her lower lip.

"Vangie was quite upset that you didn't accompany us shopping, and she made quite a scene. You'll have to make certain that she knows you're home today. Oh, once you've cleaned yourself up."

"Of course, Mama. I'll take care of it."

Alicia nodded her head. "Good. I've had about all of her I can take for awhile. I swear she ran me nearly ragged. Let her show you her purchases. Please, Cassie? I don't think I can bear to look at another bright-colored gown this morning.''

Cassie smiled at her mother's remarks, biting back the new rush of tears that threatened. It appeared that everything had gone along normally while she'd been delivering the morphine. And it seemed that everything in the house had returned to normal.

Except for the heartsick pain from Jared's betrayal that was now to be her constant companion.

''I'll be sure to go and talk with her, Mama,'' Cassie promised.

''You don't mind too much?''

''No, not at all.''

Actually Cassie was looking forward to the upcoming frivolous conversation with her aunt. It would take her mind off of Jared and his duplicity for at least a short while.

She scarcely noticed when her mother stood to leave. In fact, she was so deep in thought that her mama called out to her.

''Cassie?''

''Umm, yes.''

''You're sure you are all right?''

''I'm fine. Just tired.''

In truth, Cassie felt as if the very life energy had been drained from her. She'd felt that the moment she'd realized how Jared had used her and the love she'd given him.

Her mama turned back to the door, then stopped. "Oh, dear, I almost forgot. This was left for you." She extended a note.

Cassie took the folded piece of paper her mama held out. Uncertain of what it might contain, she held her breath as she unfolded it and read the message.

Meet me at the usual place at three.

The brief missive was signed "W."

Cassie closed her eyes, seeking a moment's peace. She hadn't thought that things could possibly get worse, but it appeared she'd been wrong.

The message was from Will Radford. He wanted to meet her this afternoon at Mrs. Bodie's shop. And he was most assuredly to ask about the packet of papers. In fact, he might even be awaiting their delivery from her this very afternoon. How was she to tell him that she'd lost the papers?

However, she couldn't share this with her mama. She'd just have to face it alone.

Alone . . . alone . . . the word echoed in her mind, mocking her. She'd never felt so alone before in her entire life.

At five minutes before three, Cassie paced the block encompassing Mrs. Bodie's bonnet shop for the second time. She'd arrived early, so glad had she been to escape the house after her required time with Aunt Vangie.

Instead of the distraction she'd hoped for, the conversation had turned into an ordeal. Today, Vangie Maitland had been in high form—chatty and overly inquisitive.

Aunt Vangie had questioned her on practically every single thing in her life. Cassie had been unbelievably relieved when her aunt had finally pleaded a headache, and she'd had the chance to leave her company.

In truth, Cassie had virtually fled the house, so eager was she to leave behind the questions and the memories of Jared that hovered there. However, her attempt had failed, for Jared's memory persisted in following her like an unwanted haint.

She'd been so caught up in thoughts of the handsome, deceitful Union captain, that a couple of minutes ago she imagined that she'd even seen him once from across the street. However, when she'd turned back for a second look, the uniformed officer had been gone. Jared even had her very mind playing tricks on her now.

"Cassie?"

She spun around, startled by the sound of Will Radford's voice. She'd practically forgotten her reason for being here, she'd been so caught up thinking about Jared Montgomery. Damn him anyway.

"Cassie?" Will stared down at her, concern written on his face. "Are you all right?"

She bit back the sharp retort that sprang

to her lips. If one more person asked her that question this day, she would likely as not scream.

"I'm fine," she answered, her voice coming out sharper than she'd intended.

Everyone's sudden concern over her well-being combined with the uncertainty of the missing papers had her more agitated than she liked to admit.

"Cassie?" Will caught her hand in his.

She jumped at the contact.

"Listen, I don't have much time. About the papers—"

Here it comes, she thought, her stomach twisting into a knot.

She opened her mouth to make her confession, but not a sound came out.

"You're to deliver the packet," Will continued, oblivious to her distress, "tomorrow night."

Finally, her voice broke free. "But—"

"I can't stay any longer," Will cut her off, throwing a nervous glance over his shoulder.

"But—"

"We'll talk tomorrow," he assured her. "Don't worry. I'll get word to you of the time and place later."

"But, I—" Cassie let her confession trail off.

Here was her opportunity to tell Will of the loss of the packet of papers. Still she paused, nibbling on her lower lip.

On the other hand, she had just been given a reprieve if she'd but take it. Cassie decided.

Not one to ignore the gift she'd been given, she mentally grabbed it and held on with both hands. Smiling up at Will, she gave his hand a thankful squeeze.

Perhaps she could find a way to retrieve those papers. Again.

Jared watched as Cassie reached out and caught the other man's hand. His gut twisted at the contact he observed. He could scarce believe what he was seeing. Mere hours after the tender lovemaking the two of them had shared, she was meeting another man for a tryst. He should know—he'd been with her, her unseen shadow, from the moment she left her home this afternoon until this minute.

At the sight of Cassie secretly meeting with another man, jealousy almost overwhelmed him. Hadn't their lovemaking meant anything to her? It appeared that it hadn't meant a damned thing to her, while it had shaken his very world to its core.

In Cassie's arms, he had forgotten all thoughts of the war and the revenge that, until then, had eaten at him constantly the past two years. Their loving had begun to heal the pain that had been a constant companion. However, once again, his need for vengeance for his brother's killer rose up within him. Was Will Radford the murderer? Was he the man Bryan had been about to expose?

Jared watched the other man with Cassie. Jealousy, pain, and rancor swept over him, each emotion warring for eminence. Had their lovemaking only been a means to an end for Cassie?

After all, she'd stolen from him once before, he reminded himself. However, this time, she'd stolen his very heart and soul with her treachery.

It took all his training and discipline not to rush out and interrupt the tryst between Cassie and her lover. He clenched his hands into hard fists at his sides. He didn't know whose throat he wanted to feel his fingers around worse at this moment. Will Radford's neck or Cassie's slim throat.

Jared forced himself to remain in place and follow the orders he'd been given. He would uncover this damned plot and put an end to it. And Cassie's involvement along with it.

He held his ground like a soldier facing a coming battle. While it tore at him to do so, he watched every move, every touch, every nod of the head between Cassie and her other lover.

After a few minutes of observing them together, reason began to surface above the other more potent emotions. Jared narrowed his eyes in concentrated thought. Something nagged at him, like the persistent dripping of water after a rainstorm.

Something wasn't quite right.

The scene he was watching wasn't playing itself out the way it should between two lovers. Once again, the thought nagged at him that things were not exactly as they seemed on the surface. He looked deeper.

Abruptly, the answer struck him. Cassie and Will Radford were not behaving the way lovers would on a secret tryst. Yes, they had touched, but although Cassie had squeezed the man's hand, it had seemed a strangely impersonal gesture. In fact, there had been a distinct lack of the special, tender touching between Cassie and Will Radford that one expected with lovers.

Not once had Cassie reached up and tenderly brushed the other man's hair back from his temples the way she had with him this morning. Not once had she smoothed her hand along the other man's cheek like she had with him before she'd left today.

Suddenly, he knew with certainty that Radford wasn't his competition for Cassie. Will Radford wasn't her lover. Jared almost wanted to shout this out loud, so intense was his satisfaction.

The relationship between Cassie and Radford had a purely business edge to it, he was certain of that fact. However, exactly what was their business together?

Once again Jared vowed to uncover precisely how deep Cassie's involvement in the secession plot had gone. No matter what the cost to him might be.

She needed someone to protect her from herself and her actions.

Little did she know, he'd already volunteered for the assignment. For a lifetime.

Determined to find the answers to his questions and to Cassie's safety, he strode away from the rendezvous he'd been observing and walked the distance to Willard's Hotel. That would be a good place to start finding his answers.

By the next morning, Jared had his answers. At least part of them, he thought, staring out the window of the office he'd been assigned that morning.

Turning away from the window, he paced the length of the room. His questions and a bit of bribery last night had revealed the name of a traitor within the government.

It seemed that a certain government clerk, by the name of Michael Jones, had come into a fair share of money over the last six months—far more than he could have earned by merely doing his job. He also gambled heavily, and lost even more heavily. A further search had turned up evidence that the man harbored strong Southern sympathies.

Michael Jones had been placed under arrest and was, even now, undergoing questioning. Jared withdrew his pocket watch and checked the time as he'd been doing repeatedly over the past hour. What was taking them so long?

Jared reached a decision. He wasn't going to sit by idly any longer; he intended to find out what was happening for himself.

Turning toward the door, he'd taken two steps when a sharp knock sounded on the wood panel.

"Come in," he called out, impatiently.

To his surprise, Trevor Caldwell entered the room, closing the door behind him.

"Trevor, what are you doing here?"

His friend gave him a half-smile. "I heard about Jones and thought maybe you'd like someone to wait with you."

"Is there anything that goes on around here that you don't know about?" Jared asked in mock disgust.

Truthfully, he was glad for his friend's presence. The solitary waiting for news had him edgy and far too tense.

"Very little." Trevor crossed the room to join him. "How is it going?"

"I don't know yet. Care to pull up a chair and wait?"

Trevor nodded his agreement and dropped

into a nearby leather chair. Stretching out his long legs, he looked prepared to spend the day. Only Jared knew of the strained tension behind his casual appearance.

"Care to join me?" Trevor asked with a wry smile.

Crossing to his friend, Jared sank tiredly into a second leather chair. It had been a long night. He rubbed the knot of tension that had formed at the base of his neck.

When a knock sounded at the door, both Jared and Trevor surged to their feet and called out, "Come in."

A short, stocky officer bearing the rank of captain entered the room. Jared recognized him instantly as the man who'd headed up the questioning of the prisoner.

"Yes, Captain Evans?" he asked in a deceptively casual tone that belied none of the tension beneath.

"You were right." The shorter man clapped Jared on the back in congratulations. "He's our man. Mr. Jones was more than willing, after a little persuasion, to tell us the identity of the man he's working for."

Jared nodded, waiting for the answer that was to follow.

"Name's Will Radford."

The words dropped into the tense silence of the room, seeming to echo off the walls. Jared stiffened at the revelation, clenching his hands into fists.

At last he knew the identity of the man who had murdered his brother.

Revenge was so close that Jared could almost taste it.

"Captain Montgomery? Did you hear me?" Captain Evans asked.

The question jolted Jared out of his reverie. Oh, he'd heard all right. Most definitely. And he intended to do something about it.

"Yes, I heard," he answered with a deceptive quietness to his voice.

"Any instructions?" the other man asked, well aware that in spite of rank, Jared had been picked by the President for this job.

"Not yet. I'll let you know." Jared's voice held a firm command.

"Yes, sir." Captain Evans nodded and walked to the door.

As soon as the other man left, Trevor turned to his friend. "You're planning something."

"Am I?" Jared's voice sounded cold, even to his own ears.

"Don't play that game with me," Trevor shot back. "I know you too well."

A deep sigh shook Jared's chest. His friend was right. They knew each other far too well for any subterfuge.

"I'm going after Radford."

"Jared—"

"Don't try and talk me out of it. It won't

do you any good. Trevor, this is the man who killed Bryan. I can't let him go."

"I don't expect you to—"

"I'm setting a trap for Radford." Jared turned away and stared out the window.

"And what about Cassie Van Dorn?"

Jared spun back around at the mention of Cassie, but met his friend's question with silence. He didn't have an answer to that right now.

"You've found something with her," Trevor persisted. "Something worth fighting for. Trust me. I can see it in your eyes. Don't throw it away."

Jared faced his friend squarely. "Trevor, I have to do this."

"Well, remember that revenge doesn't always taste sweet," Trevor warned. "It can be quite bitter."

"Not this time."

"Jared?" He caught his friend's arm. "Don't let this revenge cloud your judgment. Or destroy the love you've found."

As Trevor's admonition echoed and re-echoed in his brain, Jared questioned if it was a warning or a premonition.

However, it mattered little. He had no choice. He had to do this.

Thirteen

Jared, himself, led the planned capture of Will Radford. With a hand-picked group of men under his special command, he entered the sixteen-story Willard's Hotel shortly before noon.

As he strode across the lobby, the blood coursed through his veins in a raging heat of anticipation. Within minutes, his two-year long search would be at an end, and he would, at long last, be standing face to face with the man who had murdered his brother, Bryan. His ever-present quest for revenge urged him onward, allowing no thoughts of a delay.

After one look at the hard, no-nonsense expression on Captain Montgomery's set face, the short, graying man behind the desk rushed to greet him. He was obviously eager to assist the officer and his Federal troops and possibly avert the scene, or duel, or whatever it was that was apparently about to erupt here in his lobby.

"How may I help you, sir?" the clerk

asked, a betraying nervous tremor in his voice.

"I'm here on special orders," Jared informed him curtly. "From President Lincoln."

The clerk gave an audible gasp of surprise, then nodded his acquiescence.

Armed with the knowledge of the location of Will Radford's lodgings, Jared didn't need to ask for the room number.

"I need the key to room number five forty-five." Jared sent him a look that almost dared the wiry man to refuse his request.

Smart enough not to chance interference, the desk clerk rushed back to the desk and extracted the correct key. He extended it to the officer, then waved him and his men on without any further challenge or questions. He had no desire to interfere or be a part of whatever it was that was about to happen upstairs.

Jared paused only long enough for a brief word of thanks to the obliging desk clerk. With long strides, he led the way to the fifth floor without the slightest show of nervousness or hesitation. In fact, no emotion whatsoever showed on his hard face.

He didn't pause until he reached the hall outside room number five forty-five—Will Radford's room. Forcing himself to ignore the surge of adrenalin that raced through his body and urged him on, he motioned his men safely back from the door. He didn't want to lose any of his hand-picked patrol should Will Radford begin shooting the instant he learned they were at his door.

Raising a fist, he pounded on the door. The demand was met with silence.

"Radford!" Jared called out.

All remained quiet behind the closed door.

Jared motioned his men to stay back and eased his pistol from his belt. Pistol in hand, he eased the key into the lock barring the door. A flick of the wrist, and the door's lock ceased to present a problem.

Securing his grip on the pistol, he turned the knob and thrust the door open. It swung inward with the force and banged against the wall with a loud thump.

Without a second's pause, Jared rushed the room. However, his effort was for nothing. The hotel room was empty.

Although Jared and his men searched the room thoroughly, they found nothing. Not a scrap of paper or a piece of clothing had been left behind.

Jared slammed his fist down on the bureau. The wood shuddered under his blow. Somehow, Will Radford had eluded their capture.

They had lost him.

The rattle of the glass in the balcony doors of her bedchamber startled Cassie. She swung away from the dressing table, wondering at the strong wind that had sprung up and was causing the window glass to rattle.

She looked over at the curtained windows, but saw nothing amiss. A sudden memory of Jared standing in the same balcony doors sprang unbidden to mind. She tried to dispel the image without success.

Damnation, even her brief glance at the French doors caused unwanted memories of Jared to rush back with a force that practically took her breath away. As long as she lived, she knew for certain that she would never forget how he had looked standing in the moonlight the night he had broken into her bedroom.

The black clothing had emphasized his size and strength rather than diminishing it. In fact, the dark color had made him look more devastatingly handsome than even his uniform. And more dangerously sensual.

She fought back the surge of turbulent emotions the thoughts summoned up. They were as unwanted as a conjured haint or apparition would have been to her.

The effort did no good. Tenderness, love, and then pain filled her being—each emotion stronger than the one before.

Cassie quickly grabbed up the hairbrush out of desperation and pulled it through her hair. Anything to try and rid herself of the unwelcome images that persisted in forming before her mind. She tugged the brush through the back of her hair.

The bristles caught in a tangle, and she winced, tears coming to her eyes. She blinked them away, telling herself they were only caused by the sharp tug of the brush caught in her hair, not by the memories of Jared.

Another sudden rattle of the windows caused her to jump and drop the hairbrush. It bounced and clattered across the wooden floor, the noise overly loud in the quiet bedchamber. She told herself that she was being foolish to be so skittish.

As she bent down to retrieve the brush, the same noise rattling repeated itself at her balcony doors again. She jerked upright. That had been no wind.

Jared!

Her breath caught on the thought. Had he returned to see her again?

The clatter of pebbles tossed against the window glass sounded again, capturing her wandering attention. Catching up the skirts of her full gown, Cassie dashed across the room to the window.

Once there, she scolded herself, ordering her racing heart to slow to a natural pace. However, it didn't listen to her any more than her mind had when she'd commanded it not to think of Jared these past days.

Hurriedly, she pushed the billowing curtains aside and opened the French doors. She paused a second to attempt to gather her composure, then clenching her hands tightly at her sides, she stepped out onto the balcony.

She urgently searched the yard, looking to find Jared's tell-tale golden hair. Inwardly, she held her breath, hoping against hope that he'd come to her. If he had, surely that meant that he cared. Meant that he . . .

Instead of Jared's dark blond hair, she spotted the dark head of Will Radford. Her breath passed her lips in a soft sigh of disappointment.

Will, not Jared.

Cassie swallowed and blinked back the sudden burning that signalled tears welling up. Damnation, she called herself every kind of a fool for believing Jared would return to her.

"Cassie?"

The harsh, loud whisper jerked her thoughts up short. Will sounded angry. This was the first time he'd ever sought her out at her home, much less attempted to contact her in this strange manner.

Something was definitely wrong.

The thought seared her mind. She bent over the balcony railing and waved down at him to let him know that she had heard his call.

He immediately motioned her to come downstairs and join him. Cassie tamped down the sudden rush of uneasiness his action prompted. She stepped back, closing the

French doors, and turned away from the balcony.

Without even pausing to gather up a cloak, she dashed out of her bedchamber and down the stairs to meet with Will. Whatever he needed to talk to her about, it had to be urgent.

She only hoped he wasn't here for the packet of papers. Tightening her hands into fists, she knew that it was time to tell him of the loss of the papers. Her sense of uneasiness increased.

Slipping out a side door of the house in hopes of escaping the notice of anyone inside, she hurried around to where Will was waiting for her.

Tonight there was none of his usual flattery or compliments. He greeted her curtly with a nod.

"What's wrong, Will?" she asked him as soon as he didn't speak.

"Did you bring the papers?" he asked in a short, abrupt voice.

Cassie knew what it felt like for a person's blood to turn cool in their veins, for that is exactly what she felt at that moment. There was no more postponing; the moment of truth had finally caught up with her.

She took a deep breath and blurted out, "No—"

"Well, hurry up and go on back upstairs

and get them," he ordered, cutting off what she'd been about to say.

"I—"

"Cassie, I don't have time to talk." He threw a nervous glance over his shoulder. "Go on and get me the packet of papers."

"I don't have them," she blurted the confession out, resisting the almost overwhelming impulse to shut her eyes against his coming anger.

"Didn't you steal them from the Admiral like I told you to do?"

She flinched inwardly at his use of the word "steal."

Will reached out and grabbed her arm. Pulling her after him, he rushed them over to the shadows afforded by the side of the two-story brownstone.

"Well?" he demanded.

Refusing to be intimidated by his actions, Cassie raised her chin a notch. "I retrieved them from the Admiral's jacket just like you told me—"

"Then what the hell are you trying to say? Where are the papers now? If you're trying to hold out for a payment—"

"Will! You know me better than that. I did it for the Cause, not for money."

"Then give me the papers." His eyes narrowed in a menacing gesture.

"I told you that I don't have them," she enunciated the words clearly for his benefit.

Jerking her arm out of his hold, she faced him straight on. "They were stolen," she stated flatly.

Disbelief, then anger marked his face. She could swear that his side whiskers even quivered with his suppressed fury.

He swore under his breath, raking an unsteady hand through his hair. Throwing back his head, he closed his eyes a moment.

"Will?" Cassie inquired.

He swore again, then met her concerned gaze.

"They're onto me, Cassie," he admitted to her in a hoarse voice. "Luckily, I was warned in time. I scarcely made it out of Willard's Hotel before a group of Federal troops broke into my lodgings. They were led by a Captain Montgomery."

Cassie sucked in a sharp breath of air. Jared had led the attempt. Now what?

Will picked up on her slight reaction to his mention of the officer's name. He narrowed his gaze on her.

"Cassie, just what do you know of this Captain Montgomery?" he demanded.

She bit back a response, refusing to give him the answer he wanted. Nothing could induce her to betray Jared, no matter whether he had betrayed her or not.

"I had heard a rumor of his interest in you from Jones, but I didn't believe it." He shook his head in disgust.

Cassie forced herself not to recoil from his abhorrence.

"And I thought I could trust you," he accused.

"You can," she answered back.

"Montgomery is the one who has the papers, isn't he?"

When she refused to confirm this, Will swore. "Don't bother denying it. Dammit, Captain Montgomery has gotten in my way once too often."

Before she could stop herself, Cassie blurted out, "What are you going to do?"

At Will's sudden tenseness, she wished she could call back her question.

"What I have to do," he responded in an unfamiliar cold tone. "Rid myself of the problem."

No! she wanted to scream out, but she knew it would do no good.

"Will—"

As he abruptly turned away, she knew she had to stop him, no matter what.

"Will!" she called out again, oblivious to whether or not her voice carried in the stillness. "If you proceed with this plan, I'll tell them everything I know."

Her threat caused him to pause.

"I swear it," she vowed.

Ignoring her, he strode away and vanished into the gathering darkness.

Aware that it would be useless to pursue

him, Cassie caught up her skirts and turning, ran back into the house. She had to get to Jared and warn him of Will Radford's threats.

Although Will had sounded serious and desperate, he wasn't a killer, was he? Surely Will wouldn't carry out those threats, would he? She knew that whatever the answer to those questions would be, she couldn't chance it. She had to warn Jared.

Running through the house, she took the wide stairs at a mad rush, one hand on the railing to steady her. She skidded to a stop on the stair landing outside her room, then rushed into her bedchamber, pausing only long enough to catch up her reticule and pull her dark blue cloak from the armoire. She didn't give a whit whether the cloak matched her pale turquoise gown or not. The cloak was warm and suitable. That's all that was important.

Rushing back out the bedroom door, she stopped with her foot on the first step as a sudden thought of her mama sprang to mind. She had to let her mother at least know that she was leaving. There wasn't time to explain everything to her, but she had to at least tell her something. Mama would be frantic if she simply disappeared.

Hating the delay, she crossed quickly to her mother's room, knowing it couldn't be avoided. She only hoped their discussion wouldn't be noticed by Aunt Vangie. The last thing she needed right now was her aunt's seemingly endless questions.

"Mama?" Cassie called out softly from the doorway.

"Dear, what's wrong?" Alicia crossed the room to her daughter, a hint of apprehension creasing her smooth complexion.

Cassie paused a moment. Heavens, was her mother up to something as well? She had scarcely seen her mother all day. It was almost as if her mama was avoiding her. She brushed off the ridiculous thought and got straight to the problem at hand.

"Mama, I have to go out," Cassie announced in a low, but firm voice full of determination.

"Whatever for, dear?" Alicia turned to face her.

"I can't explain now, but please, trust me. I *have* to go."

Cassie bit her lip, waiting for her mother's response. She most assuredly didn't have the time to go into a lengthy explanation of Will Radford, and his plan, and the danger to Jared. However, whatever her mother's answer would be, she was going to Jared. No matter what was said.

Jared's life could well be at stake.

She knew beyond a shadow of a doubt that there was no way on earth that she could simply stand by and chance that Will Radford might carry through with his threats against Jared. She could not—would not—allow anything to happen to Jared.

She had to get to him and warn him.

"Very well, dear," her mother sighed. "But when you return, we must talk."

Cassie nodded, then hugged her mama goodbye. Slipping away, she crossed to the stairs and took them as rapidly as she dared.

Once outside, Cassie dashed away from the house, all her concentration fixed on reaching Jared in time. She didn't notice that a curtain in an upstairs bedchamber moved back and forth slightly, checking on her progress.

Jared paced the confines of his office, restless to do something. Anything. But there was nothing further that could be done.

A further search of all possible known friends and acquaintances of Radford's had revealed nothing more. It now appeared that Will Radford had slipped through their fingers like the lost sands through a crack in a broken hourglass.

Perhaps what his friend, Trevor Caldwell, had warned him about revenge was true. Right now, his unsuccessful attempts at revenge tasted more bitter than sweet. He could only hope it didn't remain that way.

A knock on his door pulled him out of his reverie. He spun around and faced the door.

"Come in," he ordered.

A messenger entered the room. "Sir, the President would like to see you."

Jared's head jerked up. "Tell him I'll be right there."

He paused only long enough to run his hands through his tousled hair and straighten his uniform jacket. Then he strode out the door.

Scant minutes later, Jared stood across the desk from President Lincoln. The room had seemed to develop an even more somber note than at his last meeting with the President.

The room still held the same tall-backed chair he'd sat in many times, in front of the same broad desk, with the same leader waiting there. However, this time Jared could sense an almost imperceptible difference.

The tension was more tightly strung in the room, and the strain more evident on the craggy face of the man before him. However, the President's piercing gaze was as intent as it had ever been. Once again, he thought of how the critics of the nation's leader should see him like this. They would surely change their opinion on his suitability and compassion.

"So, Radford escaped us." President Lincoln sighed raggedly, motioning Jared into a chair.

"Unfortunately yes."

Jared's harsh voice told the nation's leader more than any words could how hard he had taken the loss of Radford.

"The secession plot still has to be stopped," President Lincoln assured him.

"Yes, sir." Jared's voice tightened as he recalled yet again how his brother had died attempting to stop the insidious plot. "I will find Will Radford," he vowed.

The President rubbed his long fingers over his chin in a habitual gesture that Jared had come to recognize.

"It's like cutting off the head of a snake, my boy."

"Sir?"

"Without his head, a snake is powerless to hurt anyone any longer," President Lincoln went on to explain. "If we get rid of Radford, the plot will whither and die without its leader."

He pinned Jared with his infamous direct gaze, and continued, "Or at least be delayed. In another few months it won't matter; it will be too late for the Confederacy to succeed with the plan by then."

Jared nodded his agreement. They both knew that this war could not go on much longer, and they longed for the time when it would be over.

"However, Radford must be captured before he can do any further harm." President

Lincoln leaned forward in his chair, crossing his long arms on his desk.

"Yes, sir," Jared agreed with him. "And I intend to see to it."

"I'll be awaiting news from you, Captain."

"Yes, sir."

Jared stood and took his leave with a firm determination to locate Radford and bring him to justice.

He returned to his own office in full agreement with the President. Will Radford had to be captured—too much was at risk to allow him to run free and continue to head up the secession plot.

Clenching his hand into a fist, Jared turned to the papers on his desk with the intention of reading over the information they'd received from Michael Jones again. He only hoped that he could find some small piece of information that they had overlooked that would lead them to Will Radford.

The minutes passed without any revelations. Jared read through each scrap of paper he had. However, it availed him nothing. There wasn't a single item that hadn't been checked at least once.

He rubbed at the knot of tension that had formed at the back of his neck. Nothing—they had absolutely nothing now to lead them to the location of Will Radford.

Gathering up a piece of paper, he crushed it and threw it across the room. It hit the far wall with a soft smack of sound, then fell to the wood floor. He left it laying there.

Damnation. He was no closer to catching his brother's murderer than he'd been before.

Jared leaned back in the chair and forced himself to try and relax the frustration that ate at him like a festering sore. It didn't do a bit of good.

Surging to his feet, he strode across the room and retrieved the wad of paper he'd tossed against the wall. He unrolled it and crossed back to his desk to add the paper to the stack on the scarred top of his wood desk.

As he turned away to glance out the window, he noticed the gathering darkness. Dusk had fallen, and the lamp had burned on unheeded by him.

Finally, noticing the lateness of the hour, he grabbed up his hat and strode out of the office. He wasn't going to be able to accomplish any good by remaining there and going over old, used-up information.

Safely away from the view of anyone in the house who might be looking, Cassie searched the area for a hired carriage. It took her costly minutes before she at last encountered one.

Luckily, the hour was still early enough for the hired coaches to be about. She gave the driver the address of Jared's house, then sat back and counted the minutes as each one passed by.

She had to be in time. She had to be. Cassie recited the thought over and over like a litany. She refused to even think of the possibility that she might be too late.

After what seemed to her to be an endless amount of time, the carriage pulled to a stop in front of Jared's house. Paying the coachman, she jumped down from the carriage without waiting for his assistance and rushed toward the front door of the waiting house.

"Cassie."

At the sound of her name, she spun around to see Jared striding up the street toward her. Her heart performed an unexpected flip-flop and dove for her toes. She stood rooted in place at the sight of him.

Suddenly, from the corner of her eye, she saw a movement beside the broad oak tree. She glanced over in time to recognize Will Radford. Before she could call out to him, he raised a pistol, aiming it at Jared.

"No!" Cassie screamed.

She threw out her hand in a useless gesture. Nothing she could do now could stop what was unfolding before her sight.

Spinning around to attempt to ward off Jared's approach, she knew she was too late. By now, he was already too close—well within the deadly range of a minie ball.

"Jared, look out!"

She screamed out her warning at the same instant the crack of the pistol sounded in the evening.

She watched, helpless to change what was happening, as she saw Jared's body jerk with the impact of the bullet.

Fourteen

Cassie grabbed up her skirts and ran toward Jared, heedless of any possible danger to herself from Will Radford and his pistol. She cared not a whit whether or not Will escaped right now. Her entire concentration was centered on Jared.

Before she could reach him, he crumpled to the ground.

"Jared!" she screamed.

She ran on, desperate to reach him. Her heart thudded and lodged in a large, unmovable lump in the center of her throat.

"J . . ." she tried to call out his name again, but the sound wouldn't make it past her lips.

He couldn't be dead. He couldn't be.

Reaching him at last, she crouched down beside his still figure. With hands that trembled, she clasped his shoulder to roll him over.

As a warm stickiness oozed between her fingers, she pulled her hand back. It came away darkened with his blood. Used to the sight of blood from assisting her father in the past, she was still unprepared for the jolt of horror that rocked her at Jared's blood covering her fingers.

Clamping down on the fear that threatened to overwhelm her and turn her into a helpless, simpering miss, she drew in a deep breath of the cool air around her, then reached out her hand again. This time she didn't pull away when her fingers encountered the blood that was easing down from his head. She carefully rolled him over, praying desperately that he still drew breath.

Her gaze flew to his face. His skin held a pasty pallor, but his eyes were open and alive. She caught back her cry of joy. Pain glazed his eyes, taking away the dark intensity she'd grown so used to. It frightened her more than she cared to admit.

"Jared," she whispered his name.

A trickle of red dripped down his temple to his cheek. She brushed it away tenderly with the edge of her white ruffled petticoat.

"Cassie?" He blinked up at her, wincing at even that first movement.

Nothing had ever sounded better to her than the sound of her name on his lips. He was truly alive. She swallowed the lump that had remained stuck in her throat until this very instant.

For a moment it was as if the wide chasm that had existed between them, brought upon by his betrayal, had closed. Cassie relished the instant of closeness it provided.

"You're hurt." Her heart leaped and her voice caught with unshed tears. She couldn't have uttered another word if she'd had to.

She gripped his arm, holding to him as though she expected him to be torn away from her at any moment, reminding herself that he had almost been taken from her once already this night. If Jared hadn't turned at the instant of time that Will Radford had fired the gun . . . a shiver coursed through her at the very thought of what might have been.

"Jared?" Her voice came out a hoarse whisper of sound, scarcely loud enough to be heard.

He raised his hand and felt the wound behind his temple, wincing at the pain the touch brought.

"It's nothing. Just a scrape," he assured her, sitting upright.

Cassie anxiously examined the wound. Although there seemed to be a lot of blood, it appeared that the bullet had only grazed him and passed on by, without doing very much damage. Still, her father had always warned that head wounds of any kind could be serious.

"Jared—"

"Don't worry—"

Those two words didn't give Cassie anymore relief when Jared spoke them than when her mother offered them to her.

"Cassie, it's only a graze. I've had a lot worse."

Instead of reassuring her, his words caused the lump to catch tightly in her throat again. The thought of Jared injured, bleeding, hurting shook her more than she wanted to think about.

In spite of everything that had happened between them, she knew for certain that she still loved him. No matter what he had done, or why.

Jared struggled to stand, shaking off the wave of dizziness that swept over him at the movement. Once on his feet, he searched the area around them with a quick gaze.

Whoever had shot him was gone now. Likely as not long gone from here. He clenched his jaw, certain that he could correctly guess the identity of his bushwacker—Will Radford.

As Cassie reached out to drape his arm across her shoulders, he turned to her with a question in his eyes. Just how much did she know? And how deeply involved in all this was she?

"Cassie?"

"Yes?"

Although she answered, she kept her head lowered, busying herself with arranging his arm over her shoulders and wrapping her own arms about his chest to steady him. Was she avoiding meeting his gaze directly, he wondered with sudden suspicion.

"Cassie, did you see who shot me?" He voiced the single abrupt question, then waited for her response.

Had she in fact seen his attacker? And if she had, would she tell the truth or cover it up with lies?

Jared waited, his gaze fixed firmly on her lowered head. Her dark curls hid her face from his sight, and he wanted to push the mass of curls aside and see her expression for his own eyes. Did she know the man's identity?

He hadn't realized that he had been holding his breath until he heard her softly spoken answer, and his breath rushed out in a sigh.

"It was Will Radford." She pressed her lips together after she had pushed the words out.

Shocked silence greeted her response.

"I . . . I tried to warn you," she rushed on, eager to make certain that Jared knew she hadn't been a party to Will's attack.

Tightening her arms around his wide chest, she forced the final admission out past frozen lips, "But I was too late."

Jared could scarcely hear or believe her words. Not only had she known the identity of his attacker—she had possessed prior knowledge of Radford's murder attempt.

That part hurt even more than the bullet that had struck him.

"Jared, we need to get you inside. You need to be cared for."

"By you?" The sudden coldness in his voice cut her deeply.

"By me."

She raised her chin in defiance. She wasn't leaving him until she'd seen that his head wound had been treated and bandaged. Her father's warning returned, bringing with it a cold draught of fear.

"Jared, we can talk all you want inside. First, we need to see how serious your wound is—"

"I've told you that it's a graze."

"If you don't mind, I'd like to see to that for myself," she announced in a tone that dared him to defy her. "My father is a doctor. I helped him many times in the past."

She hoped that added reassurance would turn him toward the house. It didn't. Instead, he stubbornly stood his ground, refusing to take a single step forward.

"Dammit, Jared," she shouted at him. "Get moving!"

His eyes widened at her demand.

"Or do you want to bleed to death here on the ground while we have a little conversation?"

Her sharp retort caused him to take notice of the trickle of blood that persisted in running over his temple and along the length of his cheek. He glanced down and saw that his uniform jacket had darkened with the copper stain of blood that was spreading and growing larger. He allowed her to lead him into the house.

After she had removed his jacket and cleaned his wound, checking it over thoroughly and bandaging it, Cassie knew that the time for answering his waiting questions had come at last. There was no way the unspoken challenge could be avoided any longer. Jared sat, propped up in the wide bed, waiting. She could tell that his patience was growing thin.

"Cassie."

The single word demanded all the answers she had to give. Clasping her hands together, she turned back from setting the bandages down on the bedside table and faced him.

"Give me one good reason why I shouldn't have you arrested?" he fired the demand at her.

Swallowing, she realized that she didn't have a single reason that he was likely to listen to. She said the only thing she could—the truth.

"Because I love you."

Haltingly at first, then with growing need, she proceeded to tell Jared of Will's earlier visit tonight and his threats.

"I swore that I'd tell everything if he went

through with his threat," she said earnestly. "But it didn't do any good. I couldn't stop him."

She turned a tear-filled gaze to Jared, willing him to understand and believe her.

"I believed in the secession plot. At first. It seemed like the surest way to end the war."

After that admission, the words tumbled out. Her concern for her father working in the Confederate field hospital, her promise to him to keep her mother safe, her mother's impetuous actions in the past three years, and her own fear of what might happen if her father didn't return home soon—the only thing she held back was her mother's involvement in smuggling morphine south.

She ended with, "You do believe me, don't you?"

"Yes," Jared sighed raggedly. That was the worst of it—he did believe her. But what was he supposed to do now? Have her arrested?

That was his duty, his obligation. However, as he stared at her earnest face, waiting for his answer, he knew that for the first time in his life, he couldn't perform his duty. He couldn't turn her in.

The only option that remained to him was to do everything in his power to keep her out of jail, and out of trouble, as well.

He met her worried gaze with a purposely

hardened one of his own. He had to make her agree with him.

"No more secret meetings with Radford. No more messages. No more stealing." He fired the orders off as if he were giving them to a new recruit. "You understand and agree?"

As she paused to nervously lick her lips, his gut tied into a knot. What was he to do if she refused?

"Yes."

Her answer was so softly spoken that he had to strain to catch it.

"Promise?" he demanded.

"I promise."

Relieved, he shifted his body, attempting to get more comfortable in the bed. The wait for her agreement had about tied his insides up in knots.

The movement drew Cassie's full attention and concern. "Jared? Are you all right?" she asked in a low voice, almost afraid that any more noise might cause him more pain. "Your head—"

"Is fine," he answered.

"My father always warned that head wounds could be more serious than they looked." She reached out to lightly touch his forehead, suddenly fearful of a fever coming on.

Jared caught her hand in his, holding it captive. His nearness called out to her in a

primitive way, and the atmosphere in the
room changed to the heightened tension of
an approaching lightning storm. The deeply
muscled legs that she knew lay under the
sheet pulled at her gaze, tempting her. She
hadn't helped him remove his trousers, instead she'd fled to the kitchen for bandages,
and didn't know if he'd taken them off while
she was out of the room or not. She wasn't
sure she wanted to know that answer either.

From his inviting eyes, to his bare chest,
to the sheet draped over his length—she took
them all in with a quick sweep of her lashes.
A whimper of all-consuming need escaped
her lips before Cassie could stop it.

He was too close. Sitting propped up in
the bed only an arm's length away. Too close.
The bedroom seemed to begin shrinking in
size, growing smaller and smaller with each
indrawn breath.

"Cassie." Jared's voice was low and throaty.
It stroked her nerve endings, setting them on
edge.

He shifted in the bed, and the sheet
dropped lower, revealing the full wide ex-
panse of his bare, muscled chest. She stared,
unable to force her gaze away.

Jared left the sheet lay where it had
dropped. As she raised her head, his darkened gaze trapped hers for the space of a
heartbeat. Clenching her hands into fists, she
forced herself to fix her eyes on the sheet

instead of the almost hypnotic demand in his eyes. With hands that trembled slightly, she reached out to draw the sheet back up. Her hand collided with Jared's, his stopping her movement.

Glancing over at him, she froze. The dark intensity of his eyes softened, caressing her. As her lips parted on a sigh, his parted in time with hers.

"Cassie." This time, her name was a ragged whisper on his lips as he leaned across to her.

She bent toward him in answer. Nothing could have stopped her from answering the pull of his voice.

His lips brushed hers softly at first, then increasing in intensity. Cassie let her eyelids drift closed, revelling in the wondrous feel of his touch. The kiss swept away all misunderstandings, almost blotting out every single thing around them. Almost, but not quite. The sickly sweet smell of blood caught at Cassie's senses, reminding her of his injury. She reluctantly opened her eyes.

Cassie was the one who drew away this time. She had to. As much as she loved him, she couldn't let him make love to her when there was the slightest chance that it might endanger him.

"I . . . I . . . should be going," she forced the hated words out. The last thing on this earth that she wanted to do right now was to leave him.

"Cassie." Jared held onto her hand, holding her in place.

"I'll come and check on you in the morning, if you'd like," she offered, suddenly hesitant.

"What I'd like—"

"Jared."

"I'd like that very much," he said softly.

Placing a kiss on his cheek, she reluctantly left him alone in the tempting bed.

Her trip home was completed in far too short a time for her. She wanted to savor the precious time they had shared together. Even though Jared had yet to make a declaration of his love, she brushed this aside, wanted to hold the memories of their time close to her without the worries that nagged at her.

Jared did love her, she reassured herself. Surely he did, didn't he?

Her questions and persistent worries were brought up short as the coach drew to a halt. Glancing up, she noticed that the Van Dorn two-story brownstone stood, awaiting her. Climbing out of the hired carriage, she walked up to the front of the house.

She had her hand on the door latch when she was unexpectedly pulled away from the door. A scream bubbled up, but was halted at the sight of her mother standing beside her.

"Cassie. Shh! Come quickly."

Alicia drew her daughter alongside and around a corner of the brownstone, out of view of anyone inside the house.

"Mama—"

"Oh, Cassie, something horrible has happened." She dug her fingers into Cassie's arm in distress.

Cassie's stomach lurched then righted itself. Her mother sounded more than a little distressed. In fact, she sounded frantic. She'd never seen her mama in quite this state before.

"Calm down, Mama, and take a deep breath," she tried to soothe her mother.

It didn't work.

If anything, her mother appeared to become more agitated. She tightened her grip on Cassie's arm.

Wincing at the cramping hold, she asked, "Mama, what is wrong?"

"Oh, dear, it's my new shipment."

"New shipment," Cassie parroted the words.

"Yes, dear—"

"What new shipment?" she interrupted her mother before she could continue blithely on.

"Cassie, dear, aren't you listening to me?"

"I'm trying to," Cassie murmured under her breath, then added in a slightly louder whisper, "yes, Mama, please go on."

"As I said, my new shipment—"

"Mother," Cassie stopped her in a rush of agitation. Where on this earth had her mother gotten hold of another illegal shipment of morphine?

It looked as if, once again, her mother's impetuous nature had landed her right in the middle of more trouble and danger.

She lowered her voice back to a whisper and asked, "Mother, just where did you get this new shipment?"

"Oh," Alicia drew the word out, stalling.

"Where?" Cassie demanded.

"I brought it back with me from New York. And hid it under your bed." The admission was made in a rapid staccato, as if by saying it fast, her daughter might let it pass by unnoticed. Or at least, she hoped, she'd take less notice of the acknowledgment.

"New York!" Cassie felt like a trained bird reciting the words after her mother.

"Dear—"

"You brought it back with you on the train from New York—"

"Yes, dear. When I was offered the opportunity to get another shipment so soon, well, I tell you, I was delighted. Do you know how unlikely it is to encounter morphine so easily?"

Cassie shook her head. She didn't want to know. Her mother took the action as agreement and proceeded to explain the nature of acquiring the life-saving white powder in more detail.

"M-m-mother," Cassie sputtered out the

word, bringing her mother's detailed explanation to a halt.

"Yes, dear?" she asked innocently.

Cassie closed her eyes against the frustration that she felt building with every new word her mother uttered. Right at this minute, she felt like screaming. However, the only thing that would accomplish would be to bring Aunt Vangie downstairs and into their little conversation. That was absolutely the last thing they needed.

Instead, she forced herself to take a deep breath and bite back the words she wanted to say. After all, she had promised her father that she'd do everything she could to protect her mama. Now it looked that this was the perfect time to fulfill that vow. Again.

"Mother," Cassie interrupted, with what she sincerely hoped wasn't a wail of frustration.

"Yes, dear?" Alicia turned to her with an overly innocent expression across her delicate features.

"Do you mean to tell me that you brought back a shipment of," she paused and then whispered the word "morphine" in a hoarse whisper, "all the way from New York with Aunt Vangie along?"

Cassie knew that her voice had risen on the last words, but for the life of her, she couldn't help it. Didn't her rash, impetuous mother have any idea of what the word danger meant?

"Don't worry, dear." Alicia reached over and patted her daughter's hand in a comforting gesture.

Cassie pulled her hand back as if it had been singed. There were those hated two words again. Every single time her mother told her "don't worry" in that guileless voice of hers, she knew it was long past time for mere worrying.

"I planned it all out myself during our train ride to New York," Alicia assured her.

Cassie closed her eyes against the complete sincerity and artless confidence she witnessed on her mother's pretty face. She could not believe what she was hearing. Her mother's idea of a plan could be counted on to be the farthest thing from an ordered strategy that a person could imagine. Her mother's "plan" always, in the past, had turned out to be a poorly thought out scheme designed to land them all in trouble.

"Mama," Cassie paused and bit her lower lip, "how could you have attempted to bring back morphine all that way with Aunt Vangie along?"

"That's what I'm trying to tell you, dear." Alicia added with an edge of irritation, "If you'll simply listen to me without interrupting."

Cassie clamped her teeth tightly together

to keep from saying anything more. If her mother got overly agitated, she'd simply turn around, walk back upstairs to her bedchamber, and refuse to say any more on the subject until tomorrow. She swallowed down the lump of fear this thought brought. If there was already trouble over the shipment, they might not have until tomorrow.

"Goodness, dear," Alicia patted her daughter's hand in a subtle reprimand, "Don't go getting all crosslegged on me."

Cassie tightened her jaws, grinding her teeth in vexation.

"Now, where was I?" Alicia tapped her fingertip on her chin and cocked her head in thought. "Oh, yes. The plan. Well," she paused to take a long breath, then rushed on, "while Vangie was napping, recovering from one of her headaches, I purchased the morphine and hid it away in my new hat box." Her eyes widened. "Do you know how much the cost has gone up?"

Cassie guessed that her mother meant the cost of the morphine and not the cost of a new bonnet and hat box. Wisely, she remained silent and waited for her to continue. If she tried to rush her mama now, she would likely as not shut her mouth and return to the house, leaving her wondering what this was all about. And unaware if there truly was any danger awaiting them.

When Alicia saw that her daughter was

staying obediently quiet, she continued, "The
price has gotten so extravagant that I might
have to try and find it unrefined next time.
And—"

"Mother," Cassie refused to remain silent
any longer.

She could not allow her mother to blithely
continue making more plans to buy additional morphine. She had given her father
her word, and she vowed to keep it.

"You're forgetting, Papa made me promise
that you would not smuggle anymore."

"Oh, that." Alicia brushed off the admonition as if it had no meaning to her whatsoever.

"Yes, that!" Cassie had to stifle the sudden
urge she had to stomp her foot.

"Oh, very well, dear. If Thomas insists—"

"He does. He most assuredly does."

"This will be my last shipment of morphine."

Cassie ignored her mother's dainty frown
of disappointment. She refused to give in to
her on this point.

"Mama, what about the hat box?" Cassie
urged her mother to complete her story before she could drift off onto another tangent.

"As I was saying before you interrupted
me," she chided her daughter, "I planned it
all out. I made certain to purchase a bonnet
for myself that Vangie hated on sight." A
girlish giggle slipped out. "That way, you see,
Vangie would never even consider snooping

in my hat box to snitch my new bonnet." She ended the last on a note of pride.

She waited for Cassie to compliment her on the wisdom of her plan, but Cassie remained silent, not wanting to chance encouraging her mother's schemes.

After a moment or two of waiting in vain, Alicia continued, "So, I was able to bring the shipment home without any chance of a mishap."

"Do you mean to tell me that at this moment there is a hat box, full of morphine, hidden under my bed?"

"Of course not, dear," her mother reassured her.

Cassie's sigh of relief was premature. Her mother's next words practically ripped the sigh from her throat.

"That would be far too easy to discover. I transferred the white powder to a spare horse collar we had stored away. And I put that under your bed."

Damnation. Cassie closed her eyes and drew in a deep, calming breath.

Things were progressing from bad to worse at an unbelievable speed. She felt as if she was trying to hold onto the reins of a runaway team of horses. And failing miserably.

She'd been able to keep hidden the first bottles of morphine of her mother's shipment, and she'd been able to explain away the little china dolls, but a horse collar?

There was no conceivable way on this earth that she would be able to explain away the horse collar concealed under her bed! Not to mention the fine white powder secreted inside the leather collar.

A sudden surge of laughter bubbled up in her throat, threatening to overflow. She swallowed with determination. Now was most assuredly not the time for hysterics. There would be plenty of time for that later . . . that was, if they all survived her mother's latest scatter-brained scheme.

Drawing in a breath for patience, Cassie faced her mother. She wanted to make certain that she knew exactly what they were dealing with this time, and the only way to be sure of that was to ask her mama specific questions that demanded a straight-forward answer.

"Mama, there's a horse collar of morphine hidden under my bed?"

Before her mother could form an answer, a horrible thought struck Cassie. Not only was the morphine-filled leather collar left unattended and unguarded in her room, Aunt Vangie was on the loose, alone upstairs.

"Mama," she rushed to ask, "is Aunt Vangie upstairs? Alone?"

Her mother gnawed on her lip and nodded her head vigorously. Cassie's heart stopped for the space of a full beat.

Suddenly, her mother caught her hands

tightly together, wringing them in a completely uncharacteristic gesture.

"I think Vangie may have discovered the horse collar earlier tonight," her mother whispered in a frantic voice.

Cassie made herself remain calm and not give in to the panic that almost overwhelmed her at the thought of her inquisitive aunt finding the morphine shipment. Heaven itself only knew what she'd do with it.

"Mama, what makes you think that Aunt Vangie may have found it?" she forced the words out.

"Because the horse collar is missing from under your bed."

Her mother's flat statement crushed any semblance of calm that Cassie had enfolded around herself.

Fifteen

The morphine shipment was missing.

Cassie attempted to still the tremor of fear that had started at the back of her neck, running downward, and threatened to sweep her away on a wave of panic. It lapped at her resolve, eroding what little calm she might have held onto, as surely as the Potomac did an outcropping of land that stood in its path.

She forced herself to breathe deeply of the night air and face her mama with as much outward calm as she could muster. Across from her, her mother continued to wring her hands together.

"Mama," Cassie caught her mother's hands in hers, stilling their nervous movements. "We have to find that horse collar."

Before Aunt Vangie could do anything that might draw the authorities' attention to it or the morphine hidden inside.

Cassie kept the thought unspoken, but it echoed and re-echoed in her mind. If her gossip-prone aunt let it slip during a chatty conversation with anyone, they would surely all be arrested or worse!

The haunting specter of Old Capitol Prison arose before her, and she repressed the shiver it brought with it. Her dainty mama would never survive a sentence behind the prison's cold walls.

Cassie knew it was up to her to keep her mama out of prison. She wondered if her father had the slightest inclination of how difficult her promise to him was going to be to keep.

A recollection of her other promise she'd made to him at the Confederate encampment sprang to mind. Damnation, she'd promised him then that her first and only delivery of that morphine to his camp would be her last.

Now what was she supposed to do?

In order to keep one promise, she'd have to break the other one. If she didn't find the morphine shipment and ensure that it was safely delivered herself, her mama was most assuredly to be arrested for her latest smuggling scheme that had gone awry.

"Oh, Cassie, what are we going to do?"

Her mama stood waiting for her to devise a way out of the problem—like she always did. Except that this time Cassie wasn't sure she had an inkling of how to get her mother out of the trouble she had so blithely catapulted them both into.

"Dear?"

Alicia stopped wringing her hands together, and instead clasped them around her daughter's right hand. She stood there, patiently waiting for Cassie to give her the answer to the difficulty they faced.

Knowing she couldn't let her mama down, Cassie tried to think clearly and come up with something—anything—that would reassure her mother.

"Mama, are you absolutely certain that the collar is not to be found in the house?"

"Yes."

A second later, Alicia nibbled on the tip of one fingernail in uncertainty. Cassie picked up on the nervous gesture immediately and pounced on it, desperate for any tiny morsel of hope.

"Mama?" she queried in a soft voice.

"At least I think so." Hesitation edged her mother's voice.

"Why don't we check it again? Together?"

Cassie felt a glimmer of hope. Perhaps if they checked the house over again . . .

A thought struck her. Where was Aunt Vangie and what was she doing right now?

"Where's Aunt Vangie?"

Her mother waved her hand in an arc. "She retired upstairs to her bed with the complaint of a headache hours ago."

"Retired? But she is always the last one up."

"I might as tell you. We had a frightful row this evening," Alicia confessed.

"What about?" Cassie mentally added the words, "this time" to her question.

"She wants us to attend another Union victory party. Can you believe that? Well, I—"

"Mama, we'll talk about that later. Right now, we have to search the house over thoroughly."

"Of course, dear. You're right."

Turning about, her mother led the way back to the front of the house. She paused at the door, with her hand on the latch.

"Cassie?" she whispered. "Where do we start?"

"At the beginning," Cassie whispered back.

After thirty minutes that progressed from thorough to frantic searching, Cassie and her mother had turned up two mismatched gloves, a lace handkerchief, and a broken cup. But not a single horse collar.

They had checked every nook and cranny in the entire house, with the exception of Vangie Maitland's bedchamber. The door had remained tightly closed, and Vangie had stayed in her room without once peeking out.

Cassie glanced back over her shoulders at the stairs and wondered if the complaint of a headache had been a fact or a ruse. Aunt Vangie was not above locking herself in her room if she was vexed enough. During a visit last year, her aunt had gotten into a quarrel with Mama, and Vangie had stayed secreted in her bedchamber for all of two days in a fit of anger.

Her aunt's bedchamber remained the only place left in the house that hadn't been searched. If she chose to stay locked within it, how on this earth were they to search her room, especially without Aunt Vangie knowing it was being accomplished?

Cassie turned away and followed her mother into the parlor. There they could safely discuss how to deal with her aunt's seclusion.

"Mama—"

"Vangie," her mother responded with a rush, looking past her daughter's shoulder. "I do hope you are feeling better."

As if Cassie's thoughts of her had conjured her up, Evangeline Maitland sauntered into the parlor. She favored Alicia with a cool nod before sitting into a chair and arranging the wide satin bow of her cerise dressing gown with undue care.

"Cassie, my dear, I am so pleased to have the chance to speak with you," Vangie turned to her niece, completely ignoring Alicia in a delicate snub, "about tomorrow evening's party."

Cassie practically groaned under her breath. The none too subtle gesture did not go unnoticed. It was quite obvious that her mother and her aunt were still at odds with each other over their latest quarrel.

"My gracious, dear," her aunt shifted in her chair, then smoothed the skirt of her dressing gown, "I do so hope that you can talk some semblance of sense into her—"

"Vangie!" Alicia's voice raised several degrees at the implied insult.

Vangie casually overlooked her sister almost as if she wasn't even aware that Alicia was in the room with them.

A nagging suspicion began to nibble at Cassie. Could Aunt Vangie have found the horse collar in one of her characteristic searches of Mama's and her rooms, and then hidden it out of anger to frighten and get back at her sister for their earlier argument? An argument it clearly seemed that Aunt Vangie had lost. And not forgotten about yet. Cassie recalled that her aunt was not above doing something spiteful if she felt she'd been slighted.

"As I have pointed out before, and quite correctly, too," Vangie raised her voice on the last words. "Cassie, your future is at stake."

"My future?"

"My gracious, dear, don't tell me you've already forgotten how many young men were more than willing to be your dance partner at that Union soiree I took you to? Now, don't thank me." She waved one hand in a lofty gesture. "It isn't necessary."

Cassie opened then closed her mouth at her aunt's blatant assumption. She was beginning to understand why her mother and her aunt argued so.

Aunt Vangie could be the most exasperating, frustrating, patience trying person on the face of the earth—

"So, you see, this will be even better," Vangie concluded.

Cassie snapped her head up at her aunt's ending words. Whatever had she missed by not paying her full attention to her aunt's chatter?

"I'm sorry, Aunt Vangie. What was that?"

"Cassie, dear, do pay attention. After all, it is your future which is at stake here."

"Yes, Aunt Vangie," she answered automatically, not wanting to chance losing out on her aunt's explanation of what she'd missed.

"As I was pointing out, this party is avidly rumored to be anticipated to be an even larger event than the soiree we attended." She winked. "With more eligible men. And, you know how well you did at that other one."

Cassie felt her cheeks heating and knew without looking in a mirror that her skin had surely turned red at the remark.

Vangie stood to her feet and patted Cassie on the shoulder, startling her.

"Why, I do declare, the young men were practically standing in line to be introduced to you at that delightful soiree." Patting a mahogany curl into place, she giggled girlishly. "And, if I do recall correctly, a few of them were quite wealthy. Why, my dear girl, if you just try a little harder—"

"Vangie," Alicia's voice carried a distinct hint of a warning to it.

Vangie snapped her mouth closed, then rolled her eyes in disgust. "Oh, Alicia, don't be so proper."

Cassie could feel the tension in the room rising.

"My gracious, my dear girl," Vangie turned back to Cassie. "I do hate to speak ill of your mother, you know, but I can't simply stand by and chance letting her ruin your chances."

"Ruin her?"

"Yes, Alicia." Vangie spun around, turning her attention to her sister. "I said 'ruin her'. And that's precisely what you are going to end up doing, if you keep on the way you have been. As I pointed out before, you haven't yet found Cassie even one suitable prospect for a betrothal."

"Vangie—"

"You know what happens if you wait too long—that's precisely what happened with Bryan and I. And, you are behaving far too protectively towards her, as well. Why, I swear, a young man hardly has a chance to even speak to her."

Cassie's lips twitched with the threat of a smile. Quite obviously her aunt had forgotten all about finding her in Jared Montgomery's arms the day of their little shopping expedition.

"My gracious, dear, you will never make a suitable match if you don't get out and about and meet eligible men. And this Union party will be the—"

"Vangie, we are not attending another Union party or soirée or whatever you call it this time. I absolutely forbid it."

"Alicia, you know I hate to interfere, but you simply must not be allowed to ruin Cassie's chances of making a good suitable match. Not without someone pointing it out to your attention. Need I remind you of what happens if a lady misses the opportunity?"

Vangie sniffed and dabbed at her eyes delicately with a lace-edged handkerchief. "Why, just look at me, and what I have had to endure. Always losing the man I love to someone else." She threw a glance at her sister, before adding, "Someone younger."

As usual, the reminder of Vangie's unmarried state silenced Alicia. Exactly as Vangie had intended it to do.

"Oh, my gracious, we really should be getting our rest if we are to have Cassie at her best for tomorrow evening's party."

"You may do whatever you wish, Vangie, but Cassie and I will not be attending."

"Oh, yes, we will," Vangie replied airily with a gay wave of assurance.

As Vangie spun on her heel and headed for the parlor door, Alicia stopped her with a hand on her elbow.

"We are not finished with this discussion," she informed her sister.

Vangie whirled about. "How dare you lay a hand on me!"

Cassie glanced from her mother to her Aunt Vangie, as they faced each other in a heated blaze of anger. They were fully engaged in what would most assuredly turn into a shouting match. Definitely since Aunt Vangie appeared to be angrier than usual.

Her earlier suspicion returned to nag at her. Could the horse collar be hidden away upstairs in Aunt Vangie's bedchamber?

While the two sisters were fully occupied in their growing altercation, Cassie backed slowly out of the parlor. The women didn't even appear to notice her departure. Good.

Now to check out her suspicions, she thought to herself.

Slipping around the corner, she took the stairs as quickly as possible. Once upstairs, she turned to the bedchamber located between her own and her mother's—the one that was always occupied by Aunt Vangie on her extended visits.

Careful to ease the door open slowly, Cassie ducked inside the bedchamber, then just as cautiously eased the door closed so as not to make a sound. Grateful that her aunt had left the lamp burning, she surveyed the room.

It looked as if the bedchamber had been ransacked. However, Cassie knew that the room merely held the stamp of ownership from Vangie. Brightly colored gowns lay tossed every which way over each and every possible surface. A wrinkled peacock blue ball gown even laid in a discarded heap in a far corner. Obviously, her aunt did not intend to ever wear the blue gown again.

Cassie shook her head in disbelief. The room was typical Vangie.

Now, where to start searching?

Gnawing on her lower lip in consternation, she surveyed the room again, this time looking for possible hiding places. It didn't take long to realize that the horse collar could be concealed almost anywhere in the messy room. The tossed aside items could hide just about anything in the clutter.

As she continued to mentally search out possible hiding places, a long ago recollection came to mind. Mama had remarked, after one of her sister's visits, that Evangeline Maitland lacked two things—a husband and an imagination.

Was it too much to hope for that Aunt Vangie had simply hidden the purloined collar in the exact same spot in this room that she'd stumbled upon it in the other bed-chamber?

Resisting the impulse to tightly cross her fingers, Cassie crossed the room on tiptoes, careful to avoid making any of the floorboards creak. She stopped at the side of the bed and murmured a prayer.

Hoping against hope, she knelt down and pulled up the ruffle of the coverlet. She had to bend low to see under the bed and peered underneath, all the while hardly daring to breathe for fear that she'd find the space empty.

The space beneath the feather mattress was far from empty. She pulled out two pair of satin slippers, another bright blue gown with black embroidered trim, a rumpled petticoat and . . .

Cassie gasped. And a horse collar.

She shut her mouth on the yelp of triumph she wanted to let free. Luckily, Aunt Vangie had lacked every bit of imagination that Mama said she did.

Cassie pulled on the collar without success. Finally, lying flat on the floor, she pulled and tugged until the leather collar was out from under the confines of the feather bed.

Careful to try and replace the clothing back under the bed exactly as she'd found it, Cassie doubted if her aunt would even be aware that the horse collar was missing.

Aunt Vangie wasn't prone to housecleaning, and unless she purposely pulled every item out from under the bed, she'd never be able to tell that the collar wasn't still hidden there.

Cassie dusted herself off, then hefted the leather collar up in her arms. Hauling it back to her room, she shoved the bulky collar in her armoire between two gowns. Quickly she pulled her blue velvet pelisse over the protruding leather bulk.

Standing back, she surveyed her efforts. Not a corner or a strap of the leather showed for anyone to see!

She knew that she couldn't leave it hidden there for long; she had to get the morphine moved out of the house, not to mention, safely delivered before anything else happened.

For now, she had also better get herself back downstairs before she was missed, and Aunt Vangie got suspicious of her disappearance. As she opened her bedroom door, she could hear the reassuring sound of women's voices still raised in anger.

Cassie crept down the stairs and eased into the parlor, all the while attempting to do so as quietly as she possibly could. She stood perfectly still, not wishing to chance doing anything that would draw her aunt's attention.

Thankfully, the argument had continued on undisturbed during her absence upstairs, with neither of the women appearing to have noticed that she'd even slipped away.

Cassie watched it in amazement. Her mama and Aunt Vangie stood toe to toe, glaring at each other.

"Very well, dammit—"

Cassie jerked her head up at the amazing sound of her mother swearing.

"We'll go to your Union soiree. But, that is absolutely the last thing I give into you on, Vangie. Tears or no tears. Do you understand?"

"Yes, Alicia." Vangie's voice reeked of victory.

However, she did hug her sister tightly before she sailed out of the room with a yawn. Pausing at the doorway to glance back, she added, "Remember, we need our rest to look our best tomorrow night."

Tomorrow night. The words echoed in Cassie's mind as she gathered her scattered senses. It appeared that they would be attending a Union party tomorrow night.

A smile tipped her lips. Surely Jared would be attending as well, wouldn't he?

"Cassie."

Her mother's loud whisper jerked her out of the pleasant path her wayward thoughts had taken.

"Did . . . did you find it?"

Cassie smiled and nodded for her mother's benefit.

"Oh, thank goodness." Alicia placed a hand over her heart in a dramatic gesture of relief. "Where?"

Cassie's lips twitched with suppressed laughter before she answered, "Under her bed."

"Under her—" Alicia broke into soft laughter. "That's our Vangie. Not a whit of inspiration."

"Mama," Cassie chided with a smile.

"Well, I'm right."

"Mama," she sobered, all laughter gone from her voice now, "we have to get the morphine out of the house. Tonight. Before Aunt Vangie realizes that it's missing."

"Of course, dear. I'll have the carriage readied," she paused, tapping a fingernail against her pursed lips. "It would be best to have the collar on the horse for the trip. That way, I can—"

"Mama, I'll deliver it."

"But, dear, you haven't the faintest of an idea where it needs to go. When it's hidden in a horse collar—"

"Mother," Cassie's horrified gasp stopped her. "Are you telling me that you have done this before?"

Alicia shrugged in a delicate movement of her shoulders. "Just once."

Cassie shut her eyes tightly closed. She wanted to pray that this was all a dream and

that she'd wake up soon, but knew it wasn't.
No matter how hard she might wish it so.

She faced her mother with determination.
"You've delivered morphine in a horse collar
before?"

"Dear, aren't you listening? I only did it
that one time. It was really quite simple."

"How . . . how did you do it?"

"Why, I just drove the carriage south to
that little place where the river narrows so
much. I forget what it's called. Oh, dear."

"Never mind, Mother. I know the place
you're talking about. Go on."

"Oh, yes, well as I was saying, at that point
there is a farmhouse. The lady there—her
name's Martha, a dear sweet woman—she
takes the collar and gives me an empty one.
Then she has it rowed across the river to another farmhouse. From there, it—"

"That's enough for now, Mama. All I need
is exact directions to this Martha's farmhouse."

"Oh, no, dear. This time—"

"This time, this *last* time," Cassie emphasized, "I will take it."

"But, dear, I—"

"No." Cassie defied her mother for the
first time in her life.

"Cassie!" A look of shock colored her
mother's cheek a bright pink. "What would
your father say at you taking that tone with
me?"

"Mama, remember, Papa absolutely forbade you to smuggle anymore."

A petulant frown marred her mother's pretty face. "But—"

"No, I promised Papa that I would take care of you for him, until he returns. To do that, I have to deliver the morphine. Not you."

"Oh, very well," her mother gave in reluctantly.

The next few minutes were taken up in detailed explanation for the delivery of her mama's precious shipment. Cassie listened intently, committing every word to memory.

Following her mother's directions, Cassie found the farmhouse without undue difficulty. She'd had a few tense moments as her arrival had awakened several dogs, and they had promptly barked their warning, alerting anyone within hearing that an intruder was present. The sound had been overly loud in the darkness, and she feared it would draw every eye to her arrival. However, Martha had shushed the dogs, quickly swapped the morphine-filled horse collar for an empty one with assurances that it would be passed on, and sent Cassie back on her way home. All in all, the delivery had been surprisingly simple. Just as her mama had said it would be.

Luck had seemed to be with her. The entire trip, while exhausting, was uneventful. Cassie returned home, relieved and more than ready to collapse in her soft bed.

She overslept well into the next morning, missing her meeting with Jared to check on his progress. By the time she arose, the house was a flurry of activity in readiness for their attendance at the Union party that evening.

When, at last, the three women stood in the decorated foyer of the party, Cassie noted with a smile of pleasure that for once they had dressed in varying shades that complemented the soft rainbow of colors they made standing together, instead of clashing in disharmony. She hoped that this was a good sign of a calm, pleasant evening ahead of them.

Alicia was gowned in a deep gold that reminded Cassie of Jared's dark blond hair. She smiled at the memory.

On the far scale of the shade, as if to emphasize their differences, Vangie had dressed in the gown of deep russet that she had been so set on buying during their shopping trip together. Black fringe and fancy embroidery trim ensured that the gown was far from demure.

While Cassie's own gown left most of her shoulders bare, and a goodly deal of bodice displayed, she felt fully covered in contrast to her aunt's daring decolletage. Glancing away

from her aunt's conspicuous display of her
charms, she ran a hand down her own gown.

A brief wandering thought of what Jared
would think of her gown passed through Cassie's mind. She had chosen a shimmering
ball gown of soft apricot, trimmed in creamy
lace. Tiny diamond chevrons were scattered
across the wide full skirt, and they caught
and reflected back the lamplight from the
gaily lit foyer.

"Well, let's not stand here doing nothing,"
Vangie proclaimed in a loud voice. "We are
here to find a man for Cassie."

Not a man, Cassie silently corrected her
aunt, there was only one man she was interested in finding tonight. She scanned the
ballroom, searching through the numerous
guests for that one particular man. Jared.

She'd almost reached the disappointing
conclusion that he wasn't present, when the
glimmer from the overhead chandelier
picked out his dark blond hair, seeming to
add an extra sheen to his hair. Her heart
thudded in her chest, and she cared not a
whit whether or not her eyes lit with pleasure. Or rather or not anyone else noticed.

The room seemed to empty, although she
rationed that the party guests hadn't really
parted, it only appeared that way. Only appeared that Jared, standing in his dark uniform, was the only other person in the entire
long ballroom.

Cassie simply stared at Jared This time it was she who surveyed him, his every move, his every breath. He stood as tall and proud as ever, and just as strikingly handsome as the first time she'd seen him from across a similar ballroom.

She noted that the bandage was missing from his wound and experienced a moment of concern, until he drew nearer and she could scarcely locate the barely discernible break in the skin. She sighed in relief.

He was alive and well. And coming straight towards her with a no-nonsense stride that ate up the distance between them.

Sixteen

Before Jared reached them, Aunt Vangie clasped Cassie's arm.

"Oh, my gracious, there is a senator that you simply must meet, Cassie. He just so happens to be a widower." She smoothed a curl into place, then stepped away. "Hurry, dear. We must be quick before another younger girl snatches his attention."

Without giving her a chance to respond, Aunt Vangie pulled Cassie along in her wake, almost causing her to stumble with the force of her aunt's insistent tug. Short of causing a very noticeable scene, there was nothing to be done but to follow along and meet the senator.

However, it was about to be the shortest introduction on record, Cassie vowed.

She looked back over her shoulder for Jared, but the crowd had shifted, and she could no longer see him. Damnation.

Cassie endured her aunt's very obvious matchmaking attempts with thinly veiled indifference. One waltz, a polka, she didn't even bother to count the dances or the partners foisted on her. She wanted to dance with Jared, not any of her aunt's "suitable prospects." However, although she continued to search for Jared, it was several minutes before she spotted him again.

Cassie gasped and stepped on her partners toes. Aunt Vangie had Jared backed into a corner near the veranda. She was chatting away, and Cassie shuddered to think of what her aunt might be saying at this very moment. With Vangie, one never knew.

The moment the music ended, Cassie sought out Jared. With a wide smile, he nodded gallantly to her aunt and walked away.

This time, he strode toward Cassie without a single break in his stride, in spite of the people he had to move out of his way. A smile tipped her lips. She always had admired the man's determination.

He reached her without delay this time, and smiled down at her. "May I have the pleasure," his smile widened, "of this dance?"

"Yes," Cassie answered, relief obvious in her voice.

The next moment, she was in his arms and moving to the soft strains of a waltz. His arms enclosed her in a private haven. As Jared drew her closer in his arms, the waltz music seemed to fade, then drifted away all together.

It shouldn't feel so good, Cassie told herself, but, damnation, it did.

It felt so very right for her to be in Jared's arms, as if it was the one place in the world were she completely belonged.

"For a devout secessionist, you sure have a way of showing up at your share of Union victory parties," he whispered in her ear.

Cassie drew her head back and met his questioning gaze with a firm one of her own.

"It's not my doing." She glanced across the room to her brightly gowned aunt. "Talk to my party-loving Aunt Vangie about it."

"If you don't mind, I'll pass on that particular pleasure right now."

Cassie raised her delicate eyebrows at his unusual remark.

"Are you forgetting that your overly protective aunt already cornered me once this night? It was quite an," he paused over the next word, "enlightening . . . conversation. We, or rather she, discussed my rank, my future plans, and my intentions toward you."

Cassie gasped. So *that* was what Aunt Vangie had been so avidly discussing with Jared near the veranda doors! She wished she could slip into a crack in the wood of the dance floor.

For some unknown reason, Aunt Vangie was being overly persistent in her intention to find a "suitable prospect for a betrothal" for her. It appeared that her aunt couldn't seem to get her married off fast enough. She wondered at the reason behind the sudden rush.

"Oh, no, she didn't?" she muttered, horrified at her aunt's audacity and sheer nerve.

"Oh, yes," Jared stated firmly.

"I'll . . . I'll have a word with her," she promised him. "Not that I truthfully believe it will do a whit of good."

"Never mind." Jared drew her back against his body. "I'd much rather hold you in my arms any day."

So would she.

"I missed you this morning," he murmured against her ear.

"This . . . this morning?"

"You said you would come and check on me." His voice held a hint of reproach.

The exhaustion from her long and nerve-wracking ride to deliver her mama's morphine shipment had taken its toll, and she had overslept this morning. But she couldn't very well explain that to Jared, could she?

Besides, Aunt Vangie had occupied almost every moment of her time today until the party with suggestions and offers of loaning her colorful ostrich plumes and fussing over her.

Cassie nibbled on her lower lip. "I'm sorry. I really wanted to come. Aunt Vangie—"

Jared held up a hand to stop her. "Never mind." He shot a glance over to where her aunt stood, watching their dance. "I'd just as soon talk about something else, if you don't mind."

Cassie smiled in complete agreement. "She can be . . ."

"Yes, she can be."

Jared whirled her around in a movement that left them standing near one of the far left veranda doors. "Come on," he suggested with a devilish smile. "Let's elude her for a few minutes."

He caught up Cassie's hand in his and drew her past the few dancing couples separating them from the veranda and the waiting dark outside. Like naughty children, they slipped through the wide, open doors and out into the yard.

Without pausing, Jared led the way past carefully tended shrubs to where a towering oak tree stood. Its broad trunk was more than wide enough to conceal the two of them from any prying eyes within the house.

"Jared," Cassie laughed at his eagerness.

As he stepped closer, she retreated a step. Her back came up against the broad tree. She felt trapped between the tree trunk at her back and Jared's wide shoulders. It was a most thrilling and pleasant trap.

With an intensity that she knew would brook no denial, even if she'd wanted to refuse, he lowered his head to hers. However, refusing was the farthest thing from her mind. Behind him, the moonlight was blotted out as surely as every other single thing in the world around them. She awaited the coming touch of his lips against hers with held breath.

His kiss blotted out everything. The war, the problems, even her aunt's meddling. There was only Jared's lips on hers. His kiss was more intoxicating than the drink she could taste on the roughness of his tongue. Far more intoxicating.

Cassie leaned into Jared, and he caught her even closer. She hadn't thought it possible for two bodies to be so close together without becoming one person.

His mouth devoured her. Cassie felt lost in the sensation. Jared's strength reached out to her, pulling her, drawing her into him.

She uncurled her hands from the front of his uniform jacket. She didn't have a clue as to how her fingers had come to have such a tight hold on the wool jacket covering his chest. She smoothed the material, enjoying the feel of the muscles under her fingertips.

She recalled how his strength had impressed her from the first. If possible he seemed even stronger, utterly competent now. She drew her arms up and wrapped them around his neck, burying the fingers of one hand into the thick hair covering his nape.

In return, he ran the palms of his hands over her back and around to cup the sides of her breasts in his hands. His sure touch left no doubt as to his manly expertise. Instead of being put off by the fact, it intrigued Cassie.

Jared groaned softly against her mouth. She continued to stroke the hair at the nape of his neck, petting him like the large sleek mountain lion he reminded her of. Only he was much more dangerous than any wild cat could ever be. She knew this as surely as she breathed against his mouth.

At another groan from him, Cassie gave herself up completely to the pleasure of his oh-so-loving kiss. He increased the pressure of his mouth on hers, slanting his mouth, urging her lips to part to him. To accept him. And she did.

Instead of thrusting his tongue into her mouth as she'd expected, Jared teased the tip of her tongue with his. Lightly brushing, tempting. He ran his tongue along the curve of her teeth, then dipped quickly inside, pulling out just as rapidly.

Cassie's breath came in short bursts. She whimpered against him and didn't care if he heard. She wanted more, craved more from him.

Jared swept Cassie up into his arms in a liquid smooth movement that didn't even break their kiss. Well aware of the layout of the house and grounds where the party was being held, he strode off with Cassie held firmly in his arms.

His destination was a small barn situated
to his right. Still carrying her in his arms,
he kicked the barn door open, and strode
with her to a far, empty stall.

Once there, he gently lowered her to the
soft pile of fresh hay. Cassie felt her body
sink into the softness beneath her. It cradled
her, warming and soothing at the same time.

Jared knelt beside her on the fresh, fragrant hay and drew her into his arms. The
next instant his lips were on hers. His kiss
was gentle, questioning. It clearly asked, and
yet dared her to refuse him.

His lips brushed hers as softly as the evening breeze through the nearby woods. Cassie
had the sensation of being treasured. She
luxuriated in the feeling. She could think of
nothing in the world more wonderful than
being treasured by Jared Montgomery.

Her hands had instinctively laid against his
chest when he first drew her into his arms.
Now she raised her own arms, wrapping
them around his neck, burying her hands in
the thickness of his dark blond hair. She
smoothed and caressed the curls at the nape
of his neck. Ah, wonderful, she thought.

Jared pulled back and his gaze caressed
her. When he reached out to run his thumb
down her cheek, she saw that his hand was
unsteady, and she trembled inside. The pad
of his thumb was slightly rough against her
skin.

As he rubbed his thumb along her jaw, he tilted her chin up so her eyes met his. Cassie could have lost herself in the intensity of his green gaze.

"Oh, Cassie," he murmured, his breath brushing her lips. "It's up to you to tell me to stop, my dear love."

"I can't," she answered, her voice a mere whisper of sound.

She knew beyond a shadow of a doubt that she could not utter the words that would make him stop. Not even if her very life depended on it, and right now, she thought that just perhaps her life depended on him making love to her and never stopping.

Jared stiffened, raising his chin, and for a moment she thought he was going to turn away. Then he looked down into her face and groaned.

"So help me, I can't either."

He lowered his head until his lips stopped less than an inch from hers. Cassie ached for him to complete the journey. Her insides felt as tightly drawn as a violin string. Tight, and taunt. And aching.

"Last chance, my love," Jared offered.

In answer Cassie drew his head down to hers. As her lips touched his, Jared groaned his agreement. All thought left her, leaving only feeling too deep for words or thoughts.

He returned her kiss and the hunger beneath his lips startled her. Startled and excited her. He slanted his mouth over hers, deepening the kiss. But she could sense his restraint, and she wouldn't allow it. She didn't know if it was the love she felt for him, or the rush of excitement that came from hiding from the world and laying with him in the soft hay, but she craved all he had to give.

Cassie caught at his hair, pulling his head down, meeting his kisses. He crushed her lips under his, plundering her mouth.

Sensations rolled over her in waves, like the Potomac swelling and absorbing the banks. Jared eased his weight over hers, and she trembled beneath him.

As he drew back slightly, shifting his weight, she felt his warm, moist breath on her cheek and moaned in response. He trailed his lips across her cheek, along her jaw and down to her neck. Gently, tenderly, he placed feather-light kisses along her throat.

Once again Cassie had the awareness of being treasured. She'd never felt so cherished in her life. She marveled at how he could be so tough and yet so tender.

Sighing, she closed her eyes. She loved him so much. Her heart skipped a beat at her admission. And what of his feelings for her?

His lips moved down, lower, and the feelings inside her changed, stopping anything she might have said or asked. Desire rippled through her in waves of exquisite pleasure as he brushed the lace edging her gown's bodice aside with his tongue. He drew the gown down her shoulders to reveal the thin, fine chemise beneath.

She ran her fingertips down the cords of his neck, and explored the muscles along his shoulders and back. They rippled and flexed under her fingers. She caught her breath.

As his tongue touched her sensitive peak through the fine material of her chemise, she arched against him. She could feel Jared's lips lift into a smile against her skin. The knowledge brought an answering smile of pleasure to her own lips.

Jared raised his head and stared down at her, taking in her beauty. She'd never looked so beautiful as in this moment. It radiated from her. Head leaned back against the golden-colored hay, her hair cascaded over her shoulders in ripples of shimmering waves of deepest black velvet.

As if sensing his gaze on hers she opened her eyes, and her eyes met his. Need, desire and love flowed between them, wrapped around them.

Jared leaned back and quickly shed his jacket, then his trousers. Within minutes, he had removed her clothing that separated their heated bodies, leaving only her chemise, then returned to lay with her.

Cassie ran her hand down his stomach and

his muscles tightened at her touch, making her feel powerful. And vulnerable. She could lose herself in him. So very easily. The thought frightened her for a moment. In spite of the heat that coiled in her and enveloped her, she couldn't stop the slight stiffening of her body.

"Please don't ask me to stop," he murmured against her cheek, pulling away slightly to gaze down at her with loving tenderness and desire.

His request washed aside all hesitation as a wave gently lapping over the grassy banks of the river. She could no more have asked him that than she could have stopped the blood from flowing through her veins or stopped her heart from beating.

Cassie drew his head back down to hers, giving, taking, asking for more. She met him kiss for kiss and touch for touch.

Jared drew her upward to fully cradle her in his embrace, raining kisses along her neck, pausing a second to drag in a shuddering breath as the sweet familiar scent of her enveloped him, almost taking him beyond the point of no return. He laved kisses along her collarbone and downward to the lace barrier that he now regretted leaving in place.

With infinite tenderness he lowered her back to the bed of hay, following her down and covering her with his own body. He supported his weight on his elbows, almost afraid of crushing her, so strong was his desire. It raged and burned in him, threatening to incinerate them both. He'd never felt anything so powerful in his life. He felt as if it could ignite the hay beneath their bodies and the very barn itself.

In an attempt to slow down and regain some sense of self-control, he shifted his weight to the side and ran his fingers through her hair. The strands shimmered to life, the curls springing around his hand, almost caressing him in return for his loving touch.

With a groan he surrendered. Running his hands down her ribs, he smoothed and caressed the silken skin beneath the pads of his fingers. She moved and snuggled beneath him making him think of warm liquid honey. His very blood heated in response to the image.

He could stand no more. Sliding his hands up to her shoulder, he slipped the wide straps of her chemise downward. Beneath him, Cassie arched to help him remove what wisp of clothing she wore that separated her from his full touch.

She longed to feel his skin pressed against hers. Leaning up, she rubbed her naked breasts against his chest, enjoying the feel of his rock-hard chest against her softness.

It was all the encouragement he needed. He lowered his body fully on to hers, pressing her backwards into the soft hay blanket beneath them. Cassie welcomed the weight and firmness of him, pulling him closer. She clenched her hands over his shoulders and revelled in the ripple of the corded muscles beneath her touch.

Jared tasted her mouth, his plundering hers, devouring her, stealing her very breath away. He stroked her bare breasts, cupping first one in his palms and then the other. Ending the kiss that had her melting into him, he slowly lowered his mouth to her breasts' ripeness and drew the tip of one between his lips.

Cassie arched against him, whimpering her need for more of him. She gave freely of herself, her touch becoming bold in return as she brought her hands around to his stomach and then followed his tight muscles downward. She delighted in the feel of him beneath her fingertips.

Her touch seemed as if to ignite the very air around them. The air became so charged that it could have stopped time on a fine gold pocket watch.

Jared parted her legs, and with a surge, he entered her, filling her. As she gasped in wonder, his murmured endearments filled her ears and mingled with her own sighs of pleasure. He loved her body thoroughly, wildly passionately and completely. When she thought she'd surely die from the sheer pleasure of the release sweeping them, she arched upward, tightened her arms around his neck and cried out his name.

Jared captured the sound, drawing it to him just as he'd drawn that same name to him the first night in her bedroom when she'd recognized him. Their loving washed away the pain and despair of the last years of war, replacing it with memories of this night and of love. For she was his. He knew that as surely as he knew that he was hers now.

Seventeen

The next day dawned bright and clear as if in celebration. Cassie stood at the parlor window, staring out at the bright sunshine outside. It seemed to make the very air outside shimmer and sparkle with a special added warmth.

Was the day so bright and beautiful because she felt so loved and beautiful herself today? Cassie wondered. Or was the day a special gift to commemorate the love shared between Jared and her?

A secret smile tipped the corners of her mouth at the memory of being loved so thoroughly by Jared last night. If she closed her eyes, she could still smell the fresh, fragrant hay and see the light of love and desire in Jared's green-gray gaze.

He had yet to profess that love, but she refused to let that bother her. Not on such a beautiful and promising day such as this.

Cassie opened her eyes to see the unexpected reflection of a bright splash of color in the window glass. It caused her to whirl around to face the person standing behind her. She caught her breath at the sight.

"Aunt Vangie?"

Today, Vangie Maitland had chosen to wear a sea-green day dress. The color was most becoming on her, however, the puffed sleeves with pleated frills edged in ruffles and the long ribboned sash and bows made Cassie blink her eyes in stunned surprise.

She stared at her aunt's uncharacteristic mode of dress in barely concealed amazement. The day dress most assuredly had been designed with a younger woman in mind. A much younger woman.

A sudden thought crossed Cassie's mind. It was as if Aunt Vangie was attempting to appear younger than her years. Something she had never seen her aunt try before. Instead, in the past, her dazzling aunt had seemed to ignore convention, age, and anything that went along with either one of them.

Whatever had prompted the unexpected change in Aunt Vangie? She had been behaving more oddly than usual lately.

"Good morning, my dear. My gracious, isn't it a beautiful day outside?"

Vangie smoothed the contrasting green, wide ribboned sash into place, causing her hooped skirt to sway to and fro erratically. She crossed to stand beside Cassie and gaze out the window.

"Um huh," Cassie answered, unable to say much more at the moment as she watched the brightly colored skirt's wide sway.

She continued to study the changes in her aunt. For the first time ever, Vangie Maitland appeared to be nervous, maybe even worried about something.

"Did you enjoy the party last night?" Vangie inquired, reaching down and steadying her skirts.

Cassie knew that her cheeks had reddened by the heat that she could feel suffusing her face. She longed to lean her hot cheeks against a cool glass away from the view of her aunt.

Swallowing down her reaction, she turned her head, hoping that the redness would vanish before her too-observant aunt noticed anything amiss.

"It was very nice."

Cassie brushed at her own sash to her blue gown, wanting to direct her gaze to anywhere but at her aunt for right now.

Had Aunt Vangie seen her and Jared slip out the veranda doors last night? Did she have any inclination that they had . . .

Cassie felt the heat of a blush steal up her cheeks again. She tried to will it away without noticeable success.

"My gracious, dear, you were quite the belle of the ball. I do believe that my assistance with your toiletry helped, if I do say so." Vangie preened, awaiting confirmation.

"Why, yes, thank you, Aunt Vangie." Cassie hoped that the flattery was what her aunt had expected. And that it would distract her attention.

"Oh, you're very welcome, my dear. That is what I am here for, you know. To help you."

Vangie patted a curl into place, then continued, "Although next time, I truly believe that you should wear a coronet. Yes, it would be stunning in your dark hair, with two or three ostrich feathers. That would be so much more eye catching, dear girl."

Cassie would most assuredly agree with the fact that several dyed ostrich feathers would be eye catching. However, she had no intention of wearing those bright-colored plumes. Anywhere.

"The senator was quite taken with you. Although, you didn't need to rush off so fast." Vangie turned a reproachful gaze on Cassie. "I know he isn't much to look at, but remember, dear, he is a widower. And, after all, that fact does count for something."

Vangie flicked open the green fan that had been dangling from a cord on her wrist. She fanned it back and forth a few times, deep in thought.

"But, truly I can't blame you, my dear. I know I wouldn't be so eager to take on his four children. And all under the age of ten, too."

Vangie snapped the fan closed as if for emphasis. However, a moment later, she opened it again and waved it back and forth.

Cassie noted the uncharacteristic nervous actions with curiosity. Whatever on this earth was her aunt up to this time?

"Aunt Vangie—"

"Oh, no, dear," she interrupted. "I agree with you on the senator. He is most definitely not the man for you. Why the way that he was dancing with every woman he could lay his hands on . . . tsk . . . tsk." She shook her head. "It could take a man like that months to even decide to ask for a girl to marry him, much less to carry through with it. No, he is not the man for you."

Cassie snapped her mouth closed at this.

Not that her silence mattered a whit. Her aunt continued on as if there was no one else present in the room.

"Let me see, the senator is out. And that government clerk you danced with before wasn't even there. Not that you would want to settle on a mere clerk if you didn't have to.

"It really is too bad that the good looking Major Caldwell is married. He would have done quite nicely. Oh, my."

Cassie could scarce believe her ears. Her aunt was going down a list of her so-called prospects and ticking them off one by one.

"Now, mind you, not that it has to be at least a Major. I have been thinking, and I must say that I have reconsidered that point. Take that nice handsome Captain Montgomery—"

Cassie's heart raced for her toes at the mention of Jared's name from her aunt.

"Why, my gracious, I'm sure that he must be ambitious, and that would count for something. He wouldn't intend to remain a mere captain all his life. And, all it would take would be one promotion to bring him up to an acceptable level. And he does remind me some of his brother, my darling Bryan."

Cassie bit the tip of her tongue to force herself to remain silent.

Beside her, Aunt Vangie tapped her fingertips on her chin, most assuredly deep in consideration of something or other. Then, she started, as if jerked out of her reverie.

"Yes, your Captain Montgomery does seem a most suitable prospect. Don't you agree, my dear?"

"Um huh," Cassie forced the required agreement out.

Whatever was her aunt going to come up with next? She wasn't sure she wanted to know. In fact, she was certain that she *didn't* want to know.

"Oh, well, dear. Don't worry." Aunt Vangie patted Cassie on the shoulder. "If he doesn't

propose soon, we will come up with someone. Soon."

With this, Aunt Vangie spun around and
sailed out of the room.

Cassie stared after her, stunned and sure
that her own mouth was ajar. It was most
assuredly clear that Aunt Vangie was determined to marry her off before she returned
to her own home.

Cassie was left to puzzle over the strange
conversation. Something was definitely going
on with her Aunt Vangie.

But what?

"Cassie, dear. Here you are. I've been
looking all over for you." Her mother said
the words in a flustered rush.

Cassie's heart plummeted, and she was certain that it didn't stop its descent until it
reached her toes. At least that's how it felt.
All thought of her aunt and the differences
in her vanished to be replaced by real concern for her impulsive mother.

What trouble had her mama gotten them
both into this time?

Cassie chided herself for the unpleasant
thought, but it refused to leave. Oh, dear,
what had gone wrong this time?

Not another shipment? Please, no, she prayed
in silent supplication.

"What—" she choked the word out.

"Did you see the note?"

"What note?"

Alicia leaned forward and brushed an errant curl away from Cassie's shoulder, seeming not to have heard her question.

"What note?" Cassie repeated, a sudden uneasiness beginning to creep down her back.

"Why, the one I put on your dressing table over an hour ago, dear."

The words "dressing table" echoed in Cassie's mind. Her dressing table was upstairs and so was overly inquisitive Aunt Vangie. Alone.

The last time Aunt Vangie had been left alone upstairs for any amount of time, the horse collar filled with morphine had vanished to reappear in Vangie's bedchamber. The recollection of that plagued her. It was followed by a horrible thought.

Was the note still upstairs on the dressing table? Or . . .

Cassie cut the thought off. Whirling about, she ran from the parlor. Practically holding her breath with hope, she dashed up the stairs and into her room.

Quickly, she surveyed the dressing table, but there was no folded note laying on it. Not a single piece of parchment was in sight. One look at the floor around the dressing table confirmed her worst fears.

The note was gone.

She tried to slow her suddenly racing heart. Maybe her mother had put the note somewhere else in the room. She glanced over at the bedside table, but it was empty of any pieces of paper, as well.

At the sound of a footstep behind her, Cassie whirled around. Her mother breezed into the bedroom.

"Whatever is your hurry, dear?"

Cassie swallowed down her trepidation and crossed to where her mother stood beside the dressing table. Her mama picked up a perfume bottle, removing the stopper and taking an appreciative sniff.

"You know, dear, I really do like this scent. I must remember to purchase some for myself next time we go shopping. I like this far better than the rose one I've been using. And this is much nicer than what Vangie has been wearing. Why, I—"

"Mama," Cassie cut in, breaking off her mother's discussion of perfumes. "Are you certain you put the note on my dressing table?"

"Why, yes, dear."

"Maybe you—"

Alicia pointed to the dressing table. "I put it right here on your . . ." The words trailed off. "Oh, dear, it's gone."

Cassie and her mother looked at each other and whispered one word, "Vangie."

That was the only possible answer. Had her

aunt been snooping and found the note? Cassie's stomach performed a flip flop at the thought.

The uneasiness she'd felt earlier grew to a genuine concern, then an outright fear as she thought of the possibilities. The missing note could have been from Jared. Or from one of Will's men. Her heart doubled its beat. Or the note could have been from Will Radford himself.

Covering her mouth with one hand, in a half-hearted attempt to keep her worries from spilling out, Cassie turned away and stared at the French windows where sunlight poured into the room.

Suddenly, the bright sunny day outside the window glass didn't look as bright as it had only minutes before. Now it held a vaguely sinister quality.

Heaven only knew what was in the note that Aunt Vangie had intercepted.

And there was no way on earth that Cassie could ask her.

Jared swung down from the saddle with ease. Looping the reins of his horse around a protruding branch of a nearby tree, he turned towards Cassie's home.

He could imagine her upcoming surprise at his calling, but he had stayed away from her as long as he possibly could. He longed to see her again, to hold her in his arms, and kiss her sweet lips.

Smiling to himself at the memory of their passionate lovemaking last night, he started for the front door with long strides.

As he saw a figure in a dark blue cloak slip out the side door of the two-story brownstone, Jared halted in mid-step. In the dim half-light of dusk, it was difficult to make out the woman's features.

Cassie?

He took a step towards her immediately, but she turned away from him, instead moving quickly in the opposite direction as if she hadn't seen him. Or was eager to avoid being seen by anyone.

"Cas . . ." he bit the word back.

Instead, he instinctively stepped back into the early evening shadows to watch her actions. Cassie was wearing the same dark blue cloak he'd seen her wear the night of the celebration party—the same night she'd stolen the papers from his bedroom. This time, she had the hood pulled up over her head.

What was going on tonight? Why was Cassie stealing away from the house so suspiciously?

A half hour ago, he'd given in to the urge to call on Cassie that had hounded him all day long. Now he was greeted by the sight of her slipping away into the night on some sort of rendezvous.

Just where was she sneaking off to? And
why?

He fully intended to find out. After more
tightly securing the reins of his horse, he set
off on foot after her. The blue cloak was easy
to follow in the not-quite dark of approaching evening.

He remained a safe, indiscernible distance
behind her, while still keeping her within his
line of vision. Cassie was behaving most suspiciously. A sense of unease haunted him,
drying his mouth and throat.

Where was she going?

Jared followed her for the better part of
ten minutes. He was just about to call out to
her and stop her when the clackety-clack of
carriage wheels alerted him to an approaching coach.

She stopped and appeared to be waiting
for the coach. However, she didn't have long
to tarry.

The coach came around a corner and drew
to a halt. A man leaned out the side, and
the moonlight showed dark hair and tell-tale
dark side whiskers.

Jared knew the man's identity instantly.
Will Radford.

"Darling?" Radford's loud whisper
reached even Jared's ears several feet away.

He flinched at the overheard endearment.
Had he been wrong about Cassie and Will
Radford having only a business relationship?

In the next instant, he had his answer. The blue cloak swung in an arc as she took off at a run for the man in the coach. Will Radford swept her up into his arms, and Jared's heart froze for a beat, then hardened into a cold lump of granite within his chest as he watched the exuberant greeting.

His Cassie had just ran into another man's arms. Damn her.

This was no business arrangement he was watching. The two lovers embraced and kissed as he stared on.

They drew away, and the crack of a whip broke the spell that had held Jared in its grasp, but it was too late. The horses took off at a hard gallop. Mere seconds later, the coach disappeared around a corner.

Jared knew it would be useless to attempt to follow the fast-paced coach on foot. Clenching his hands into powerless fists, he stared off into the darkness.

He called himself every kind of a fool. For that had surely been what Cassie had thought him to be when she'd used him. Used him to see that her lover went free.

He vowed to see that they were both brought to justice. Any way he had to.

No matter how much hurt it caused him.

"Jared?"

Captain Nathan Evans paused at the door

of the office, hesitant to disturb the concentration of the man behind the desk. Jared's head snapped up at the question.

"Come in," he invited, laying the paper he'd been studying down on the desk top.

He motioned the other man towards a single straight-backed chair opposite the wooden desk.

"We have a new lead on some missing documents," Nathan announced before entering the room. "It seems that Michael Jones is more than willing to tell all he knows now."

Jared smiled at the news. "Good."

He wondered for a moment if that new information would mean that he'd need to retrieve those documents in the dead of night sometime soon. He hoped not.

"I'll see that the documents are picked up," Nathan volunteered as if he'd read his mind.

Jared smiled his thanks. Right now, one thing absorbed his thoughts. The same thing that had been a constant companion for the past two years—vengeance. With the revelation of Cassie's deception, his need to track Bryan's killer had once again taken center in his world. He longed to see Will Radford brought to justice for the murder of his brother. He owed Bryan that much.

"Nathan," Jared's voice caught, and he

paused to clear his throat. "Did you get that information on Radford's activities in '62?"

The other man nodded and waved the sheaf of papers in his hands triumphantly. "Right here."

Jared pushed away from his desk and stood to his feet, fighting for control over the anticipation that suddenly erupted in him. At last, he'd have the final proof he needed.

Proof enough to ensure that Will Radford dangled at the end of a rope for Bryan's murder.

"Yes, but I don't think it's what you want to hear." Captain Evans crossed the room to stand in front of the desk.

At the warning words and intonation in the other officer's voice, Jared felt the blood in his veins cool. He forced himself to wait for the next words to come, with at least a small semblance of patience that he was far from feeling.

"I don't believe he is the man who killed your brother." The flat statement fell like rocks thrown into a pond.

"What?"

"William Radford was *not* in the city during that particular week in January in '62 that you were asking about."

A chill of denial coursed through Jared's veins, and he gripped the edge of the scarred wooden desk top.

"Are you absolutely certain of this, Nathan?"

"Absolutely. There was a White House levee that week, and our Mr. William Radford was conspicuously absent from the event. And two sources place him elsewhere at the time, as well."

"No." Jared slammed his fist onto the desk top, causing a cup to rattle with the force of his blow.

"I'm afraid it's so. There's no way around it—Will Radford was not in Washington at the time your brother was killed."

"Where was he?" Jared demanded.

"As it turns out, Radford was in Canada—meeting with several members of the Copperheads."

"Dammit," Jared swore beneath his breath.

"It's all right here in the report." Captain Evans extended the sheaf of papers.

Jared reached across the desk and took the papers. In silence, he skimmed the report, then tossed the papers down on the desk with a ragged sigh. He had thought he was so close.

"I'm sorry to bring you the news," Nathan Evans admitted.

"I know."

Jared clenched his jaw and slammed his open palm down on the papers atop the desk.

"It was all for nothing. I have been trailing an innocent man for the last two years for nothing." He ran a hand distractedly through his hair. "The liaisons I made, the relationships I pursued, all for nothing. They were worthless."

Will Radford, head of the secession plot, was the only lead he had to his brother's murderer. And that lead had just turned into a dead end.

Cassie leaned against the wall outside Jared's office, aghast at what she had overheard. The bits of conversation ran themselves over in her mind.

Jared had lost a brother to the war—no, she corrected herself—not to the war. His brother, Bryan, had been murdered. Bryan, the brother that had been "smitten" with Aunt Vangie.

Sorrow for his loss swept over her, but an even stronger emotion reached out for her. She could *feel* the need for vengeance from Jared that permeated the office on the other side of the wall.

Jared's search for his brother's killer and quest for revenge was so tangible that it practically reached out and touched her with icy cold fingers.

Suddenly, the significance of what she'd just heard swept over her.

Liaisons . . . relationships . . . worthless. That's what she'd heard Jared say.

The words repeated themselves over and over in her mind, like a chant or an awful type of incantation, bringing devastation in their wake.

A liaison? A worthless relationship? Jared's words. Was that what he called what they had shared?

Cassie bit down on her fist to keep from crying out with the agony the thought brought. With a sheer act of will she kept herself from rushing into Jared's office and confronting him with what she'd just heard from his own lips.

Her father's saying that an eavesdropper never heard anything good had never been more true. She hadn't intended to listen in on the conversation; she'd only paused outside the door to wait until the other man left. She'd intended to surprise Jared with her visit.

Oh, it had been a surprise all right, her heart chided her, digging the agony in deeper. A horrible, unforeseen, painful surprise.

Now it was crystal clear to her. He had been seeking information and revenge. He had only been using her to get close enough to learn of Will Radford's involvement in the secession plot. And then to flush Will out into the open. It had all been part of a planned search for his brother's killer.

She had been one of those "worthless liaisons" of which Jared had spoken about so callously.

With sudden clarity, she realized that his

determined search had long ago become an obsession for the man she loved. It was plain to see that his quest for revenge governed his mind, as well as his heart.

She recalled again the fact that Jared had never told her that he loved her. At last, now she understood why he hadn't declared his love for her. It had never existed. Except in her mind. And in her own heart.

Cassie felt like a broken china doll that a careless child had played with until it wasn't of any more use, then had tossed it aside into the rubbish heap. Pain cut through her like repeated slashes from the shattered china shards.

No, it couldn't be true, she fought against the certainty that was staring her in the face.

Could it?

Had Jared only been using her to get to Will Radford? Had he manipulated her to flush out the head of the secession plot?

Yes, a little voice whispered to her cracking heart. She felt the love inside her shrivel into a hard lump within her.

Damnation. Jared Montgomery was truly a blue-bellied Yankee through and through.

A sob tore at the back of her throat, and turning away from the door, she fled the building, heedless of any curious stares she might draw.

She never intended to lay eyes on Captain Jared Montgomery again, she vowed.

Eighteen

Cassie returned home to find the two-story brownstone a bustle with commotion. She halted a half a block away and stared in alarm at her home. Several horses were tethered in front of the house, and two uniformed soldiers stood in an attentive stance, positioned at either side of the closed front door.

Soldiers?

Her heart thudded in her chest as fear gripped hold of her. What had happened while she was gone?

Mama!

What trouble had her mother gotten herself into this time?

She'd only been gone a short while, but she never should have gone to see Jared and left her mama alone. Guilt rushed over Cassie in relentless waves. She should have been here when the soldiers arrived; she should have been here to protect her mother from whatever calamity her impulsive actions had catapulted her into.

Instead, she had been standing in the hall outside Jared's office, eavesdropping and hearing things she didn't want to hear.

Cassie caught up her skirts and ran the remainder of the short distance to the house, heedless of the soldiers standing guard or of drawing their full attention to herself. Her only thought was to reach her mother in time to stop only heaven knew what from happening.

Halfway up the front steps, her arm was caught by one of the sentries, and she was jerked to an abrupt halt. The sudden action almost sent her tumbling head first.

"Ma'am, you can't go in there right now," the uniformed soldier on her right announced. "You will have to wait outside with us."

"But I live here." Cassie pulled her arm quickly out of the soldier's grasp.

She started forward again, only to be detained by the second soldier.

"I have to go in," she demanded. "Let me pass."

The two soldiers looked at each other, and one raised his eyebrows. "Take her inside to Captain Evans," he ordered the other man.

The soldier led Cassie into the house and up the stairs to the second floor without breaking his stride.

"Captain Evans? Sir?" he called out when they had reached the stair landing.

"In here," a man's voice answered from Cassie's bedchamber.

The soldier ushered Cassie into the room. Her mother, Aunt Vangie, and several men stood in the crowded confines of her bedroom.

The man released her arm and turned to the officer in charge. "Sir, she claims she lives here."

"Cassie," Alicia burst out.

"Who is this?" Captain Evans demanded.

"My daughter."

"Cassie Van Dorn."

Cassie and her mother both answered at almost the same time.

"Oh, my gracious," Vangie cried, rushing across the room to her. She caught Cassie's arm with both her hands. "It's simply awful. But now that you're here, I'm sure everything will work out."

"Miss," Captain Evans nodded to Cassie.

"What is going on here?" she demanded of the officer who was obviously in command.

"I'm sorry, miss, but we've had to arrest your mother," he told her.

Cassie knew her mouth dropped open at his admission. Fear threatened to overwhelm her, and she fought it back down.

No, she wanted to scream out in denial. Instead, she forced herself to close her mouth and try to show some degree of calmness and self-assurance. The captain was not likely to listen to a half-hysterical woman. She took a step away from Aunt Vangie's clinging hands.

"What is the charge?" she demanded, her chin raised in a determined effort not to show any sign of fear or guilt to the soldiers surrounding them.

"Treason." Captain Evans brushed a hand down his uniform jacket.

The word cut through the tension-filled air of the room with the force of an explosion. It rocked Cassie to her satin-clad toes.

Treason.

The single, horrible word echoed and re-echoed in her mind, bringing with it visions of prison walls and a hangman's noose. She shut her eyes against the picture, but it only grew stronger. Instantly, she snapped her eyes back open.

"Cassie," her mother said her name with a firm insistence that was uncommon to her.

"Mama?"

"It's just a little misunderstanding. If you will let me continue, I'm certain that I can explain it all to the nice captain here."

No, Cassie knew she couldn't let her mother say another word. Heaven only knew what she'd confess to without realizing the danger.

She scarcely noticed when Aunt Vangie left her side to stand closer to the officer. In typical Vangie Maitland style, she fluttered her lashes at him, now completely ignoring both Cassie and her mother.

"Let me explain—" Alicia began.

"Captain Evans?" Cassie almost shouted his name out, in her eagerness to stop her mother from saying something that they would all regret.

He turned to her. "Yes, miss?"

"Whatever makes you think my mother is involved in anything like treason?" She attempted to put as much righteous indignation into her voice as she possibly could.

"The evidence we discovered," he stated.

"Evidence?" Cassie's voice wavered on the word.

Had her mother hidden away another shipment of morphine again?

"Yes, miss."

Captain Evans reached into his uniform jacket's breast pocket and withdrew a packet of papers. He held them out to her as proof.

Cassie's breath caught in her throat, threatening to choke her. She tried to swallow down the sudden lump that had formed, but failed. Unable to breathe or look away from the papers in the officer's hand, she stared at them as if they were a snake about to bite her.

They couldn't have been any more dangerous if they had contained a venomous snake.

Cassie recognized the packet of papers instantly. She had seen them often enough in the past. They were the defense plans for the city of Washington; she knew this without even touching the parchment. These were the same plans she had retrieved from the Admiral's bedroom. The same papers she had stolen back from Jared.

Her heart sank to her toes. There was most assuredly no way out of this situation.

For a brief instant, she wondered where the soldiers had found the missing papers. Then, she shoved the question aside. It didn't really matter now.

"Cassie, dear," her mama's voice cut into her despair. "As I was just telling the nice Captain—"

"Mama," Cassie tried to warn her.

"Cassie, dear, please stay quiet a minute." Alicia turned to her with a glance of admonition. "I can explain this myself."

"No!" Cassie didn't realize that she'd spoken the denial aloud until her mother whirled back to her.

"Cassie."

"Mama—"

"As I was about to say—"

Cassie knew she had to stop her mother from saying another word. She hadn't the slightest idea of the trouble they were all in. Her mother didn't even know what the papers were.

"Captain Evans," Cassie interrupted, catching his arm with her hand.

He turned to her with a look of inquiry.

"My mother doesn't even know what that packet of papers contains."

"Cassie—" Alicia tried to stop her.

"She doesn't. I—"

"Cassie, let me handle this. I can explain," Alicia repeated.

However, Cassie knew with absolute certainty that the only one who could "explain" was her.

"Captain Evans," Cassie challenged him. "Ask her what's in the papers, and see that what I'm saying is right."

"Ma'am?" The officer turned to Alicia.

Her mother licked her lips, then looked from the captain to each of the men around him, as if they would provide her with the correct answer.

"Ma'am?" the captain repeated.

It was obvious to Cassie and the men that Alicia didn't know what was written on the papers, however much she was frantically trying to come up with an answer.

"Those papers will contain the defense plans for the city of Washington," Cassie announced with a bold defiance she was far from feeling.

She knew with absolute certainty that her announcement would earn her a prison sentence. Or maybe worse.

Once again, the image of the hangman's noose appeared before her. But she'd had no choice. She couldn't allow her mother to go to jail for what she herself had done.

"And my mother?" she asked.

"Mrs. Van Dorn is released."

Cassie sagged with relief, then quickly stiffened herself to face what was to come.

"Miss, if you will accompany my men?" Captain Evans requested, but his tone of voice made it clear that the words were anything but a mere request.

"Where are you taking my daughter?" Alicia demanded, stepping in front of the captain to detain him if need be.

"To Old Capitol Prison."

The flat statement sounded a death knell in Cassie's ears.

The walls of her prison room seemed to close in around her, and Cassie paced the cold room. Was there nothing she could do to get herself out of this?

Damnation!

Cassie knew taking the oath would not get her out of this situation. In fact, she doubted if it would do her even one whit of good.

Fury at her predicament rolled over her in waves. She resisted the urge to kick out at the walls confining her. It would accomplish nothing, not even the lessening of her temper.

She had let her father down. Now there was no one to make certain that her too im-

pulsive mama stayed out of trouble. Aunt
Vangie would be of little or no use.

In fact, today Aunt Vangie had not been
of any assistance. She had stood there, in
typical Vangie fashion, fluttering her eyelashes at the officers, flirting with the men
and doing absolutely nothing of any use
whatsoever.

Frustration welled up in Cassie. Where on
this earth had that packet of papers come
from?

She *knew* they had been missing from her
safe when she had checked. Since that time,
she hadn't located them anywhere.

Although to be honest, she hadn't really
looked for them. She had assumed that Jared
had stolen them back from her. After all,
she'd found his black satin mask on the floor
of her bedchamber, hadn't she?

Had he planted the papers back in her
room so that she would be arrested now that
she was of no further use to him in finding
his brother's killer?

Could Jared, the man she had loved, be so
callous? Was there a darker side to him that
she had never witnessed until now?

Cassie's heart fought acceptance of this
possibility. It couldn't be true. It couldn't.

If Jared had been concealing a cold, bit-
terly calculating side of darkness, surely she
would have seen it somehow. Wouldn't she?
Wouldn't she have at least sensed that darker

nature? She knew with absolute certainty that she would have felt its presence, in her heart.

No, the answer had to lie elsewhere. She knew that for certainty. Her heart couldn't be that wrong.

Alicia Van Dorn paused outside the office door to Captain Jared Montgomery's office. Raising her chin in a gesture that was reminiscent of her daughter, she settled her small bonnet more securely on the dark hair curled atop her head and knocked on the door.

"Come in," a masculine voice ordered from the other side of the wood panel.

The harsh voice caused Alicia to almost abandon her trip as folly, but love for her daughter propelled her onward. With a shaky hand, she turned the doorknob and pushed the door in.

Apparently she had used too much force, for the door swung open and slammed against the wall.

"What the . . ."

Jared surged to his feet in one powerful move at the noise. He stared in amazement at the dainty woman standing in his open doorway. He blinked, not quite believing his eyes.

Cassie's mother? What on earth was she doing coming here to see him?

"Mrs. Van Dorn?" He nodded to her and motioned her into the room.

For an instant, facing him, Alicia regretted her impulsive action in coming here to his office. She likely as not should have arranged to meet him at his home—away from the trappings of a Union office.

However, that was water under the bridge now, she thought, dismissing the thoughts of regret. She gathered her hands tightly around her reticule as if she were also gathering up her courage in the same movement. Once again, she raised her chin.

"Please sit down," he offered her.

Alicia ignored his polite gesture, instead choosing to stand and face him directly. She studied him.

If the captain was displeased to see her, he hid his irritation well, she thought. She couldn't tell in the slightest what he was thinking or feeling. Darn, why had her daughter had to choose such a rock-hard man?

That was just like Cassie to pick the difficult path. Her daughter had always been one to attempt to take on everyone else's problems and solve them. And she'd always done a superb job of it, too, Alicia thought with a feeling of pride.

Until now.

Now, Cassie had taken on too much and landed herself in prison. Well, she wasn't going to stand by and let that go on unchallenged.

"I need your help," Alicia announced with a loud boldness that caught Jared off guard.

"Ma'am—"

"Well?" she demanded an immediate answer from him.

Jared stared at the woman before him in amazement. What did she want? And why—

"Captain, I don't have time to play coy games with you like my sister is so fond of."

Jared's gasp passed completely unnoticed by Alicia. She crossed her arms and confronted him.

"I believed you had expressed an . . ." she paused for the first time since she'd entered the office. "Interest in my daughter," she rushed on in a single breath.

"I—"

"Dammit!" Alicia stomped her foot in a sudden display of anger. "Are you going to help me or not?"

Jared feared that Cassie's mother was either becoming hysterical or demented. Following what she was saying was like trying to follow an impassable trail without a map. He stepped around his desk to stand by her side.

"Ma'am, if you'd just sit down." He eased her down into the straight-backed chair. "I'll get you something to drink, and—"

"Sit down? How can you simply expect me to sit here and share tea, or whatever, with you when my Cassie is locked in jail!" She threw her arms out in a dramatic gesture.

"Jail?" Jared took a step backward.

"Well, actually I believe it is called prison, but that is not important." She brushed off the actual facts with an airy wave of her hand.

Not important, Jared wanted to shout. Cassie was in prison and her mother considered it "not important."

Alicia stood back to her feet in a quicksilver movement. "What is important, Captain, is that you have to get her out!" she demanded of Jared, crossing her arms over her chest in a most defiant gesture.

"Tell me what happened," he ordered.

"There was a knock on the front door—actually, it was more correctly a pounding. I swear, that young man practically shook the door off its hinges."

"And?" Jared prompted, trying to keep Cassie's mother on course.

"And when I opened the door, there were the soldiers. They practically burst right into the house. They didn't want to discuss their visit. They began searching the house almost right away."

"What were they looking for?"

Alicia shrugged in an overly innocent gesture. "I couldn't say for sure," she hedged.

"How did Cassie get arrested?" He tried to steer her back to the subject of Cassie and her arrest.

"Well, they found some papers of some

sort or other in her room. That officer became quite excited about it, too. Although, I don't know why. Those papers didn't belong to Cassie or me. And Vangie simply stood in the hallway fluttering her eyelashes."

"The officer—"

"I was trying to explain those silly papers to the soldiers when Cassie rushed in." She shook her head in dismay. "If she'd only stayed out of it, I know I could have satisfied their curiosity. We had nothing to do with those government papers whatsoever."

Government papers? It felt to Jared as if a vise had just been tightened around his heart.

"She insisted on attempting to protect me. Like she always does. It's as if she doesn't think that I can take care of myself."

Listening to her, Jared feared that he agreed with Cassie on her mother's proficiency. No one would have been able to explain away possession of government papers, if in fact, that's what Mrs. Van Dorn was talking about.

"The papers," he stopped her before she could take the breath needed to go off on another tangent of confused explanation. "Did they say what papers they were?"

"Of course not. That's what I'm trying to tell you, if you'd stop interrupting me," she admonished him.

When she didn't proceed, Jared prompted her, "About the papers?"

"Oh, yes, like I was saying, the man—he was a captain just like you—only several inches shorter, I think—"

"The papers," Jared cut in, trying to hold onto his patience. It was rapidly slipping out of his grasp.

"Yes, his name was Evans, I think." Alicia tapped her index finger on her lower lip. "That's it, he said his name was Captain Evans."

The name sent a jolt through Jared. Had this been the lead that Nathan Evans had spoken to him about earlier today? If he'd had any idea that he'd been speaking of Cassie . . .

Jared drew in a ragged breath. He'd been so caught up in thoughts of revenge that he hadn't spared Cassie a thought.

"What about the papers, Mrs. Van Dorn?" he asked in a low voice.

"Yes, well, that captain didn't say what they were. Before he had the chance to, Cassie interrupted and said she knew what they contained.

"I tried to quiet her, but she was having none of it. She just blurted it out without any thought as to the consequences. She is so insistent on protecting me, ever since Thomas left."

Jared didn't even try to figure out who this "Thomas" was.

"She proceeded to tell him what those papers were. Defense plans or something, she said."

Jared drew a breath in between clenched teeth. He'd forgotten all about Cassie still possessing the faked set of defense plans.

That omission had gotten her arrested. The steel band that had formed around his chest tightened. He had to free Cassie. It was his fault that she was in prison.

Prison . . . the thought sent a chill of fear racing down his spine.

"I'll take care of everything," he assured Alicia.

"Well—"

"I promise. Cassie will be released. If you'll go on home and wait, she'll be there soon."

"But—"

"I'll have one of my men see you home."

"Oh, no, I can take care of myself just fine. I simply don't know why everyone assumes that I can't do so."

"Please, Mrs. Van Dorn, it would make me feel much better if one of my men accompanied you," Jared insisted with a hint of steel beneath his voice. "The streets aren't safe for a woman out alone."

"Oh, very well, then. If it would make you feel better, I guess I shall say yes."

"Thank you." He breathed a sigh of relief. Jared accompanied her to the door, but at the doorway she paused to glance up at him in observation.

"Do you know, I think that just maybe I see what my daughter sees in you, Captain?"

With this, she turned back to the door again.

"Oh, you won't forget about Cassie?" she prompted.

As if he could, he thought to himself.

"I'll take care of Cassie," he promised her.

And he would, he vowed.

Nineteen

A few words in the right places, and Jared had Cassie released from Old Capitol Prison within the hour on the President's orders. Once it was confirmed that the papers were fakes, the evidence against her of the charge of treason ceased to exist. And so did the reason to keep her in prison.

Jared accomplished all this from the background, never once coming within Cassie's vision. He was determined to stay as far away from the beautiful, too tempting secessionist and her deceitful heart as possible. He even ensured that one of his most trusted men drove her home—so that she'd remain safe and out of his reach.

Her mother met her at the door of their brownstone before Cassie could even turn the door latch herself. The door swung open, and her mama swept her into her embrace.

"Oh, Cassie," her mother's voice quivered. "Oh, you're home."

She returned her mother's hug, relieved beyond mere words to be safely at home again and put the horror of the prison behind her.

Her mother held her at arm's length to look her over, then satisfied that she had been well taken care of, drew her close again.

"Cassie," she sighed the word, then put her hand over her mouth. "Oh, dear, we must try and be quiet. Vangie retired with a terrible headache. In truth, I heard her crying herself to sleep over you."

Alicia lowered her hand, then wiped away an errant tear from her cheek. Sniffing, she blinked several times and sent Cassie a watery smile.

"He did it. Just like he promised me he would," she announced in awe.

Cassie stiffened at her mother's vague exclamation. What had her mama done? How had her mysterious release been arranged?

"Mother?" Cassie used the formal name that she was coming to use more and more often of late. She drew back to full arm's length to meet her mama's gaze.

She could scarce believe that her impetuous mother had been the one to make the arrangements that enabled her to be released from Old Capitol Prison. It seemed a feat beyond her mama's planning.

"Mama, how did you do it?"

"Why, I visited your Captain Montgomery. He really is . . ."

Cassie didn't hear any further than her mother's first sentence. Her mama went to see Jared?

Oh, no. She shook her head back and forth without thinking. Whatever had come over her mother?

"Oh, yes, dear. He really is quite nice."

"Mother—"

"You're right, of course. I know I didn't approve at first," Alicia continued right on, riding over Cassie's objections with her explanation. "His being a Yankee officer and all. But, he did keep his word to me," she announced in final approval.

"His word?" Cassie felt as if all she could do was to parrot what other people said to her.

"Yes, dear."

"Mama," she murmured, "just exactly what did you do?"

"Why, dear, aren't you listening to me?" Alicia sent her a disparaging look. "I told you that I visited your young captain to ask for his help. When I explained to him what had happened, and what a big misunderstanding it was, why he promised to send you home. And he did."

Jared had her released? Because her mother had told him it had all been a misunderstanding?

Not hardly. She refused to believe it. There was most assuredly something else going on with a certain Captain Jared Montgomery. And she fully intended to find out exactly what it was.

"Well, dear, I am so happy to have you back home." Alicia threw her arms around Cassie again, then drew back just as quickly. "You really should go get your rest. I'm sure that this ordeal has exhausted you."

Cassie had to agree with her that she needed to rest. She needed to rest from any more surprises. Right now, what she wanted most was a quiet place to try to think things out and find some answers. Undisturbed.

However, her wish was not to be granted. Cassie had scarcely been in her bedchamber more than a half hour, not even enough time to change from her soiled day dress, when the sound of pebbles striking her balcony windows caused the blood in her veins to freeze. She stood in place, her feet rooted to the wooden floor.

A memory of the last time this had happened, when Will Radford had visited practically in the dead of night to demand the papers, returned to haunt her. Instinctively, she took a step backwards away from the French windows and whatever lay beyond them.

Her first thought was to run as far and as fast as she possibly could in the opposite direction. Then, reason surfaced. Running away never accomplished anything, and she'd never been one to try it anyway.

Maybe it wasn't Will Radford at her window again. It could even be Jared, couldn't it?

On stiff unwilling limbs, she crossed the room in the direction of the French windows. Another handful of pebbles rattled the glass, clattering to the balcony beyond. She halted her steps.

Clenching her hands into fists, she forced her feet and legs forward again. She had to find out who was outside, before they woke the whole house. Or, worse, brought down the roving patrols on the house.

She turned the latch and opened the doors. As she looked down to the lawn below, her worst fears were confirmed.

Will Radford stood below.

"Cassie," he called out in a low voice.

"Go away," she called back.

Turning away from the window, she had taken only one step when his next words held her firmly in place.

"You leave now, and I'll see that you go back to prison."

When she didn't turn about instantly, he added, "And your mother, as well."

Cassie whirled around to face him. "You wouldn't."

"Try me."

She knew that there was no power on earth that could make her do that. Nothing was worth risking her mother's life.

"What do you want?" she demanded of him.

He motioned for her to join him, but Cassie shook her head vehemently no.

"Cassie."

Her name on his lips carried a world of threats, none of which needed to be said aloud.

"All right," she answered.

Whirling away, she shut the French doors and fled her bedchamber. Without even bothering to check to see if anyone saw her, she dashed down the wide stairs and out the front door. She didn't so much as glance back as she rounded the corner of the house and crossed to where Will awaited her.

"What do you want?" Her voice held not a whit of welcome to it.

"You don't sound happy to see me," Will accused.

"Whatever gave you that idea? After all, working for you merely got me arrested and put in prison," she answered him defiantly.

"And you think that's where they don't want me?" He grabbed her arm. "Now, if you don't want to join me there, you will do me one last favor."

"What?"

Cassie hated herself for even asking. She

wanted to tell him where he could go for all she cared, but there was her mother to consider.

"I need a pass."

"What about the ones you have—"

He held up his hand to stop her. "I need a special pass that will get me north, to Canada. And your Captain Montgomery is just the man I need to get it from."

"But—"

"And you are just the person to get it from him."

Cassie shook her head, thinking that Jared would never simply give her a pass to enable Will to escape.

Will misunderstood her action. "Oh, yes. Or have you forgotten what that prison was like?"

"Will, he'll never agree to it."

"It's up to you to see that he does. Or who knows what the Yankees might find in your house."

Cassie gasped.

"I see that we understand each other. Don't we?"

She swallowed and nodded, unable to get a single word past the knot in her throat.

"Meet me at the train station tomorrow at noon. And come alone. Understand?"

"Yes."

She understood fully. He planned on simply fleeing the country and leaving her to

face the consequences. And they would be
many when Jared learned of her deception.

Turning away, she returned to the house
and the long night ahead of her. She had
until noon tomorrow to devise a plan to get
herself and her mother out of the latest predicament that faced them.

Only, this time, she wasn't sure that there
was a solution.

If only Will Radford hadn't insisted that
she go to Jared for the necessary pass. He
would never agree to her request, which
meant that she would have to come up with
a way to deceive him into giving the pass to
her. That was more than she could do in
good conscience.

Cassie paced the floor of her room with
the aid of the faint moonlight that streamed
through the windows. She had to come up
with another plan. She had to.

Will Radford posed a real threat to her.
Was he the person who had planted the
packet of papers back in her room for the
Union soldiers to find? Or was someone else
trying to destroy her and her mother? She
had to learn the truth before any additional
"evidence" appeared in the house.

The minutes ticked by as she devised and
discarded plan after unworkable plan. She
couldn't betray Jared; after all, she owed him
for her release from that prison. Even though
she still didn't know why he had done it—she

still owed him. He would never willingly assist her in this problem.

Besides, she reasoned, assisting Will Radford in fleeing the Union could well get her arrested again. She shuddered at the possibility.

There had to be another way. There had to be a way to keep her mama safe, not to have to betray Jared, and keep Will Radford happy all at the same time. However, if there was a way, she was darned if she could figure out what it could be.

Yet.

The next morning, Cassie stood in front of the door to Jared's house and, for the hundredth time since she'd talked to Will Radford last night, she wished there was some other way.

Sometime in the wee hours of the night, she had reached her decision. She would go to Jared, like Radford had demanded, except that she would tell him everything and ask for his help. After all, he had helped her mother yesterday. Perhaps he would be in an equally generous mood this morning.

One look at Jared's set face when he opened the door, and Cassie knew that generosity was the farthest thing from his mind. He was angry through and through.

She gathered up her suddenly wavering courage in both hands and plunged onward.

"Jared, we need to talk."

"What about?" His voice was cold, reminiscent of the Potomac in the dead of winter.

"Inside," she insisted, not willing to ask to come in, just in case he refused.

She wasn't about to carry on this conversation standing on his doorstep. When he stood rock steady at the doorway, she shoved her way past him.

"Jared, I need your help," she announced in a rush.

She'd ran the words together so much that he had to strain to make them out.

"My help?" he asked with an edge of suspicion.

"To trap Will Radford."

The words landed with the force of a blow. Jared reeled back a step. What game was she playing at now? He forced himself to harden his heart to the plea he saw in her blue depths.

In spite of everything she'd done, he still longed to sweep her into his arms, and the look of need he'd seen from her almost broke down his resolve to stay away from her. Damn it all, but he still wanted her.

He could almost believe that she blinked away a sheen of tears. Almost, but not quite, he told himself. He reminded himself of the lovers' tryst he'd witnessed only two nights ago.

"Cassie, you don't need to keep lying to me," Jared cut her off with a sharpness that startled her.

"But, I—"

"I know the truth."

As Jared ran a hand distractedly through his hair, rumpling its thickness, she stared at him in confusion. He proclaimed to know the "truth," yet she hadn't told him yet.

Something was not right. Things were most assuredly not what they seemed.

A fissure of unease began to grow within her. Nervously, she nibbled on her lower lip. Her action drew Jared's gaze like a tall tree in an empty field drew lightning in a thunderstorm. His gaze held the same impact that the bolt of lightning would.

She felt her body begin to respond, a liquid warmth starting deep in her stomach and flowing throughout the rest of her body. She tried to shut the feeling out.

"The truth?" she asked in a hesitant voice, not sure that she really wanted to hear his answer.

"About you and Radford," Jared spat the words out at her.

His anger was a tangible thing in the room. It stood between them like a specter. And it cooled her traitorous body better than a splash of icy water could have done.

"About me and Radford?" Cassie parroted. A frown pulled at her lips, and she worried her lower lip again. Whatever was going on?

"Of course you know the truth, Jared," she said in bewilderment, "I told you that the night you were shot."

His harsh bark of laughter sliced through her, catching her completely unawares. A responsive burst of anger surfaced in her. What right did he have to be accusing her of anything? Much less of only heaven, and Jared, knew what.

After all, he had been the one using her. Manipulating her to flush out Will Radford. With this thought firmly in her mind, she stepped forward, raising her chin to confront him.

"Just what are you saying, Jared?" she demanded, more than willing to hear his answer this time.

"Lady, you wouldn't recognize the truth if it stood up on two legs and bit you."

Cassie's palm itched with the overwhelming desire to slap his face.

"And exactly what is this so-called truth that you're so sure you possess?"

"Cassie, I saw you with Radford that night."

Her throat tightened. What night was he talking about? Last night?

"I saw you in his arms."

"When?" she asked, then answered, "Never."

"Yes, most definitely. Two nights ago."

"What?" she shouted. "I don't know who you think you saw, but it most assuredly wasn't me."

"It's no use lying anymore."

"Jared," Cassie spoke very slowly, emphasizing each and every word, "I did not see Will two nights ago. I have never been in his arms. And, besides, I was home two nights ago."

She crossed her arms over her chest to keep from hitting him as her anger grew with each insistence she was forced to make.

"You can ask my mother if you must. She'll tell you that I was home with her on that particular night. All night."

"Then why did I see you, wearing your dark blue cloak, sneaking away from the house and meeting Will Radford? A very intimate meeting," he added in a harsh tone.

"My cloak?" she repeated.

Could Jared have witnessed Aunt Vangie meeting Will Radford secretly?

Slowly, as if speaking to herself, Cassie murmured the thought, "It could have been Aunt Vangie. She's always borrowing some item of Mama's or mine."

"Your aunt and Will Radford? Surely you can't expect me to believe something as ridiculous as that. What about—"

Cassie raised her chin to meet his upcoming question.

"I refuse to dignify any more of your insults with a response," she said.

"Cassie—"

"And what about you?" she accused.

"Me?"

"You're nothing more than a common thief."

Jared stiffened at her accusation. "I'm a loyal Union officer."

Cassie forced out the rest of what she had to say. "For sale to the highest bidder."

That was the part that bothered her the most.

"Cassie, I never sold anything that I stole. I only retrieved government papers that were in the hands of people they didn't belong to."

"What about at the Littletons' reception?" Cassie fired out the question. "Don't forget, I saw you climbing down the trellis. Sarah may have denied anything was stolen, but I know differently."

"All I took from the Littletons were secret dispatches from the French government that were bound for Jefferson Davis."

Cassie's mouth dropped open.

"And, I'll have you to know, all I was doing was my job."

If possible, her mouth opened even wider. Jared reached across, and placing his fingers beneath her chin, pushed her mouth closed for her.

"However, only a very few trusted people are aware of that fact."

At his usage of the word "trust," Cassie's anger resurfaced. She'd trusted him, and he'd used her and manipulated her. Her anger wouldn't allow her to remain silent any longer.

"You used me to get to Will Radford," she blurted out, accusal in her voice. "Admit it."

One glance at the expression that crossed Jared's face before he could school it away was all the confirmation she needed. He couldn't have said "yes" louder, if he had shouted it.

"Cassie—"

"It's true."

She turned away from him. Somehow, in her heart, she knew that she'd been hoping to hear him deny it. But that hope had been crushed.

Jared caught her shoulder and gently turned her to face him.

"It was true—at the first." He clasped her shoulders with both his hands. "But only at first. Before I got to know you."

And to love you, he said to only himself. He wasn't quite ready to put his heart on the chopping block for her again. Not yet. But he was willing to do almost anything to keep her safe.

As she remained stubbornly silent, he offered, "About that help you need?"

Cassie drew in a deep breath, trying to make up her mind whether or not to trust him. She *needed* his help. At last, the words tumbled out over each other, and she didn't pause until she had relayed everything to him.

Twenty

Arriving home, Cassie immediately drew her mother aside, thankful to find her downstairs alone. She motioned for her to follow quietly, and then led the way into the parlor.

"Cassie, what on earth is wrong with you?" Alicia demanded.

"Shh," Cassie placed a finger over her own lips at her mother's overly loud query.

Turning away, Cassie crossed to the open doorway and eased the door closed. She didn't want to chance inviting Aunt Vangie into their discussion. The less people who knew of her dangerous plan, the better.

"We're not being arrested again, are we?" her mama asked in horror.

"No," Cassie rushed to reassure her.

"Well, then, what is all this secrecy about?"

A soft thud sounded outside the door, and Cassie froze. Holding up a finger over her mouth, she gestured for her mother to wait a moment. On tiptoes, Cassie crossed to the doorway and listened, then opened the door a crack.

She peered out, but the hall outside appeared to be empty. There was no sign of whoever or whatever had made the tell-tale noise.

Closing the door, she crossed back to her mother, brushing off the sound as the result of nerves stretched too taut.

"Cassie?"

"I'm going to go meet with Will Radford—"

"Cassie, it isn't proper for you to be sneaking off and meeting with this young man. Why—"

"Don't worry. It will be fine."

Cassie inwardly cringed at her use of those hated two words. Every time the words "don't worry" arose, trouble was most assuredly not far behind. Mentally, she crossed her fingers against any misfortune that her use of the words might possibly bring.

"Now, dear—"

"Mother," Cassie caught her hand, "Jared Montgomery will be going with me."

Jared and her had spent the better part of an hour devising and completing their plan. Now all she had to do was wait until the appointed time to put the plan into action.

But, first, she had to ensure that her mother didn't accidentally interfere.

"Cassie," her mama's voice rose in frustration. "Whatever are you talking about? I swear I can't understand a bit of it."

For once her mother knew what she'd been

experiencing for the past three years, Cassie couldn't help thinking. She schooled the smile that tempted to break free.

"Mama, listen carefully. I'm afraid that you and I may be in danger—"

"Cassie, I haven't brought in any more shipments. I swear," Alicia spoke earnestly.

"Good." The word rushed past her lips before she could stop it.

Her mother frowned at her, sending her a look of admonition.

"Mama, the day I was arrested—"

"Please, let's not discuss that. It was simply dreadful." Alicia clutched her hands tightly together in front of her.

"I'll only say one thing," Cassie assured her.

"Oh, very well."

"Someone planted those papers in my room. On purpose to ensure that I'd be arrested."

"Who?" Alicia began to wring her hands together. "I knew it was all a misunderstanding."

Cassie didn't correct her mother, instead she merely reached out to still her nervous movements. "We don't know for certain. It may have been Will Radford. We'll be setting a trap for Will, and—"

"Why ever would you be setting a trap?" Dismay colored her mother's voice, causing her to speak louder.

Well aware of the minutes ticking past with seemingly increasing speed, Cassie outlined the plan she and Jared had devised, giving her mama as few details as she could get away with.

She ended with, "And I need you to promise me that you will stay here. In the house. No matter what."

"But, I could—" Alicia began in a voice laced with excitement.

"No," Cassie fired out the instinctive denial.

The last thing on this earth they needed was her mama's well-meaning assistance. Cassie shuddered to think of what could happen if her mother intervened.

"But, dear—"

Cassie caught her mother's hands in hers, silencing her.

"Please, Mama?"

When she hesitated, Cassie rushed to add, "Remember my promise to Papa? I promised to keep you safe."

"Oh, damnation!"

Cassie gasped at her mother's startling use of the swear word.

"Well, I miss out on everything," Alicia explained with innocence.

A strangled cough burst out before Cassie could restrain it. The Baltimore riots, spying for the Widow Greenhow, smuggling morphine south—to name only the things that she was aware her dainty mother had been involved in during the past three years.

Miss out on everything? Nothing could be farther from the truth, Cassie thought to herself.

"Very well," her mother sighed deeply, letting it be known that she was making a big sacrifice. "I'll stay here."

The remainder of the time before the meeting passed with agonizing slowness for Cassie. By the time Jared picked her up for the scheduled rendezvous, she felt that she was almost as tightly strained as a violin string drawn too tight.

Tension reigned on the seemingly endless carriage ride to the train station. As instructed by Will Radford, Cassie walked alone to a secluded platform that was set apart from the others.

Nervously, she waited for Will Radford to show. The special pass that Jared had given her felt heavy in her small, velvet reticule. She clasped the drawstrings tightly, twisting them around her fingers.

Even though she knew that Jared was nearby, as well as several of his men, and watching everything, she couldn't stop the icy fingers of unease that insisted on creeping up her spine.

Something was certain to go wrong, she felt it in her very being.

The uneasy sensation gradually, but insistently, grew then changed to one of apprehension. A knot of fear began to take shape in the pit of her stomach as the minutes ticked past. The smell of coal and smoke stung her nostrils, and she blinked her eyes against the glare of the noonday sun on the railroad ties.

It felt as if every one of her senses tensed to the breaking point. So intent on trying to place every sound about her, she almost didn't hear the soft thud of footsteps until Will Radford was practically upon her. The click of his heels against the wood platform alerted her a mere instant before he spoke her name aloud.

"Cassie?"

Startled, she spun around to face him, almost losing her balance. He reached out a hand to steady her, and for an instant she thought that she saw the old Will Radford—the one who had been a friend, before whatever happened that had changed him so much of late. Desperation did strange things to some people, making them cold and hard while giving others strength. Apparently Will belonged to the first group.

"Did you bring the pass?" he demanded harshly.

"I brought it," she fired back at him, anger at his weakness overcoming her caution.

Without speaking, he held out his hand.

Cassie resisted the impulse to look over her shoulder to see for certain that Jared was there waiting. Their scheduled signal for him to move in would be when she handed over the pass to Will. That was Jared's cue to step out and stop Radford.

Nibbling on her lower lip in nervousness, Cassie unwound the drawstrings of her reticule from around her icy cold fingers. She slowly drew open the bag, trying to give Jared as much time to be in position as she possibly could.

It was now or never, she thought to herself. Mentally she crossed her fingers that all would go as planned. But, somehow, she knew it wouldn't be that easy. The niggling feeling of unease had burgeoned into dogged fear.

Closing her fingers over the paper, she withdrew the pass from her velvet bag. She could practically hear the seconds ticking past on some invisible clock.

She gripped the pass in her hand protectively a moment before she extended it to Will Radford. Then, she practically held her breath, waiting for Jared's planned appearance.

As Will seized the pass from her hand, Cassie resisted the impulse to snatch the precious paper back. With it, Will Radford could escape anywhere he chose to go, and he would always be a threat to her, and more importantly, to her mother. Where was Jared?

"Don't move, Radford," a man's commanding voice ordered.

Relief almost buckled Cassie's knees as she recognized Jared's voice instantly.

Closing her eyes in relief for an instant, Cassie drew in a deep breath, then turned to watch Jared approach. The pistol in his hand was steady and unwavering—like the man. His long strides were sure and offered more reassurance than any words could have done right now. Although the pistol in his hand also admittedly gave her an additional degree of security.

As Jared drew to a stop protectively at Cassie's side, Will turned accusing eyes to her. She forced herself to ignore him and the silent reproach.

"The pass, Radford. Hand it back over," Jared ordered, his voice brooking no argument.

Will swore violently, then thrust out his arm, extending the pass to Jared with obvious aversion.

Cassie sagged weakly in relief. It was all over. Her foolish fears and premonition that something would go wrong had been just that—merely a silly, groundless fear.

Her stomach calmed, and the accompanying knot of tension began to slowly uncoil.

It was over.

She drew in a deep sigh, thankful that she'd been mistaken, and her fears had been groundless. Jared had everything completely under control.

"Drop that gun, if you don't want me to shoot," a feminine voice suddenly ordered from behind them.

Cassie couldn't believe her ears. She identified her aunt's angry voice at once, but still found it impossible to accept. There must be some mistake.

Beside her, Jared stiffened, then glanced back over his shoulder before turning around.

"Aunt Vangie?" Cassie asked, whirling about to face her.

Today, Vangie wore the same overly-young looking, sea-green day dress as once before, complete with matching ruffles and bows. Except that today, her wide ribboned sash was askew, and above it, sunlight reflected off a gleaming gun barrel.

Twenty-one

In shocked disbelief, Cassie glanced from the bright green sash tied about her aunt's waist to the glint of the pistol held in her hands. The barrel was pointed directly at her.

"Aunt Vangie," Cassie murmured in shocked disbelief, shaking her head slowly back and forth, but her gaze never left the gun.

The shiny barrel held her attention, refusing to release her. She forced her eyes away from the hypnotic power of the pistol pointing at her to look up into her aunt's face.

Vangie's lips were drawn into a tight line, and hatred narrowed her eyes. She looked almost like a stranger to Cassie.

"Aunt Vangie," she struggled to make her voice calm and soothing, "it's me—Cassie."

"I know full well who you are," Vangie shouted at her, "and what you're trying to do."

Cassie instinctively stepped back a step from the unexpected vehemence in her aunt's voice. It was a completely unfamiliar sound from her.

"Well, dear," Vangie sneered, "you won't get away with it. I'll kill you first."

"What—"

"I won't let you do it, my dear. I can't." She tossed her head, and the gun wavered in her hand.

"Do what?" Cassie asked in a voice that came out higher pitched than she'd hoped it would.

Fear edged her words, and there was no way that she could withhold the sound—no matter how hard she attempted to keep her voice level and calm. She failed miserably. This was not the Aunt Vangie that she knew. It was as if some unknown stranger had taken her place.

"Cassie—" Jared took a step forward, trying to put himself between her and the gun pointed directly at her chest.

"Stay where you are!" Vangie screamed out, turning the gun on Jared. She raised one hand and rubbed her temple with her fingertips.

The movement caused the gun to tremble in her hand, and Vangie quickly clasped her other hand tightly around the handle to steady it. The barrel steadied, and she aimed it back at Cassie's chest with a silent determination that made Cassie's very blood chill as it coursed through her veins.

Jared stopped all movement at Vangie's tell-tale action. The woman was too unstable to try and reason with, and anything he might do right now would only place Cassie in more danger. And maybe get her killed.

He stiffened, furious at the unfamiliar feeling of futility. Clenching his hands into fists, he watched and waited for his chance. He would not let any harm come to Cassie. No matter what.

Vangie hesitated a moment, moving the gun's aim from Cassie to Jared. The action brought the taste of true fear to Cassie's tongue. She had to do something before her aunt shot Jared.

"Aunt Vangie," she said, attempting to draw her attention away from Jared.

There was no way she was going to stand idly by and let her aunt or anyone kill the man she loved. When the gun didn't move, she gulped in a breath and took a step forward. It worked—Vangie turned the gun to focus it fully on Cassie now.

Cassie forced herself to swallow down her fear. What had happened to Jared's men? Or were they too far away to witness what was going on? Or unwilling to move in with Vangie holding a gun?

"Aunt Vangie," Cassie repeated in a low voice. "What is it you think I've done to you?"

"Don't play innocent with me," Vangie

spat the words out in a burst of anger. "You've been trying to steal Will from me."

"What—"

Vangie cut her off. "I won't stand by and let you take Will away the same way your mother stole Thomas from me." The hand holding the gun shook. "Why, Cassie? Why couldn't you leave Will alone? I loved him."

"Aunt Vangie—"

"I truly cared about you, Cassie," her voice softened a moment, almost sounding familiar again.

"And you betrayed me," Vangie screamed out the last words in a blaze of fury.

"Aunt Vangie, I never tried to steal Will," Cassie denied with honesty, trying desperately to reassure her aunt and make her see reason. "I—"

"Save your lies, my dear. I don't believe you. He even sent you a note, but I intercepted it," she stated with pride. "I couldn't let you meet him at that bonnet shop. So, instead, I had the soldiers take you away."

Cassie's mouth dropped open in disbelief. Her aunt had been the one who had her arrested? Out of some misplaced sense of jealousy?

"That way you couldn't meet with Will," Vangie continued. "You see, I found your papers and decided to hold onto them, in case I had need of them. And then you began to show more and more interest in Will. I saw you meeting him outside the house. I tried to discourage you, but you wouldn't listen, would you?"

Cassie recalled her aunt's sudden, unexplained determination to marry her off. So many pieces of the puzzle fell into place—Aunt Vangie's attempt to appear younger, the nights she'd sneaked out of the house, and her unexpected acceptance of a "mere captain" as a prospect for Cassie's marriage.

She opened her mouth, but her aunt stopped her. Vangie shook her head in an erratic movement, and a single mahogany curl fell over her cheek.

"You see, I *had* to stop you. It was so easy to simply put the papers on your dressing table when I heard the soldiers downstairs," Vangie explained. "Then, you almost ruined it all by coming in too late after they'd arrested Alicia." She paused to shove back the curl that had tumbled down from her stylish coiffure. "But, it all worked out. Until my fool of a sister went to see him."

Vangie gestured to Jared with the gun before retraining its deadly aim back on Cassie once more.

"Why did you have to get her released?" Without waiting for his answer, she blurted out, "You're no better than your brother. Both of you taken in by a pretty face."

Jared stiffened, carefully holding himself in check. He resisted the almost overwhelming urge to grab Vangie Maitland and force her to tell him the truth about Bryan.

"What about my brother?" he asked in a barely leashed voice.

"Bryan!" Vangie spat the name out as if it carried a bad taste. "We were lovers."

Jared's instant denial cut the air. "No."

"Oh, yes."

Vangie smiled a slow and slightly askew smile of remembrance, then it faded and she narrowed her eyes on Jared.

"Until he left me for a debutante half my age. I loved him, and when I told him that—he said it didn't matter. He loved *her* and was going to marry *her* instead."

The gun shook violently in Vangie's hand for a minute before she steadied it.

"Well, he didn't." She laughed, the sound a harsh cackle. "I saw to that."

"How did you accomplish that?" Jared asked, clenching his fists to restrain himself from lunging for her.

"Why, I shot him," Vangie announced with a flourish and a toss of her head.

Cassie gasped and felt Jared jerk beside her at her aunt's callous and crazed declaration.

"No," she whispered.

Her aunt was most assuredly insane. Why hadn't they seen it sooner? The headaches . . . the arguments . . . the unpredictable behavior. The signs had all been there, but they had ignored them, refusing to believe the worst of Aunt Vangie. But a murderer?

Jared stiffened, controlling his raging emotions. *This* was his brother's murderer. He released his breath in a ragged sigh. The phantom he'd been chasing these past years had been a scorned woman. Bryan's death had nothing to do with the secession plot; it had been the result of an unwise dalliance with an alluring older woman, who couldn't tolerate being rejected.

Now what was he to do? Have Cassie's aunt arrested and jailed, or locked away in an institution? And risk losing Cassie's love? The burning need for vengeance flickered within his breast, then died.

Vangie's next words chased all but Cassie's safety from his mind.

"So you see, Cassie dear, I'm prepared to kill you the same way. To be sure you stay away from Will."

At the mention of his name, Will Radford stepped out from behind Cassie and Jared. "Now, Vangie, I was never interested in Cassie," he denied vigorously.

Will detoured around Cassie, keeping well out of the aim of the pistol in Vangie's hands.

"You see, Cassie. Will belongs to me." A sneer marred her aunt's pretty features. "Why, we're going to be married, and—"

"Wait a minute," Will Radford interrupted, taken back, her sudden announcement stopping him in mid-stride. "I never promised you anything."

Vangie stuck out her lower lip in a pout. "Now, Will," she cajoled. "You'll make me a fine husband, just you wait and see." She fluttered her eyelashes at him in a coy gesture.

Will blanched at her words. Without thinking, he shook his head. "I would never marry a woman too old to bear my children," he blurted out in unconcealed distaste.

Vangie's shriek of madness rent the air, chilling Cassie. Her aunt faced Will, the gun in her hands wavering between him and Cassie.

"No! First, Thomas left me for Alicia. Then, Bryan left me to marry some debutante. And now, you think to leave and marry someone young—like Cassie."

Vangie fell silent, but her eyes glittered with a strange light. Her knuckles whitened from her tight grip on the gun.

"Every man I've ever loved has left me." She pounded her chest with one trembling hand. "Me! For someone else. Not again!"

With a flick of her wrist, Vangie trained the gun on Will Radford and abruptly pulled the trigger. The loud retort of the shot echoed and re-echoed in the air around them.

As if in slow motion, Cassie saw the bullet hit Will full in the chest. He staggered backwards with the impact. A red stain began to immediately seep through his pristine shirt.

Before Cassie could even move, Jared grabbed her, pulling her behind him, attempting to shield her body with his own.

The next instant, Will Radford gasped and made a desperate lunge forward towards Vangie. His movement propelled him into her arms, and Vangie screamed in rage.

Cassie watched in stunned horror as Aunt Vangie and Will struggled in a clumsy waltz of staggering steps back and forth, fighting for possession of the gun clasped between their bodies. As his lifeblood ebbed away, Will Radford seemed to sag in defeat then, with a final burst of surprising strength, he drew himself upright.

The muffled explosion of the gun firing a second time froze all movement. Vangie and Will stared at each other an instant, then fell to the ground together.

Jared pushed Cassie away and rushed to take control of the gun from Vangie, but his movement was unnecessary. The second bullet had found its mark in her heart, killing her instantly.

Jared spun away and drew Cassie into his embrace. He turned her from the view of the couple entwined on the ground in death.

"J . . . Jared?" she asked, unable to voice the question. She drew back from his hold to glance over to where her aunt lay.

"They're both dead," he answered her unspoken question. "They can't hurt us now."

He gently turned her face away from the horrible scene and cradled her against his chest.

The thud of footsteps rapidly approaching drew them apart. Three of Jared's men raced up to them.

"Sir, we didn't dare chance rushing in while she held the gun on you," a sergeant explained their delay. "And we couldn't get a clear shot at her."

Jared nodded his acceptance of the hasty explanation.

"Captain Montgomery, we'll take care of things here, if you want to take the lady away," another uniformed soldier offered in a low voice.

Cassie felt the unshed tears burn the back of her eyes, and her throat tightened. Vangie Maitland was dead. She shook her head slightly, as if to deny the truth. No matter what, she'd still been family.

"Cassie?"

She looked up at Jared and blinked back the tears. In truth, she knew the aunt she had known and loved had died long ago to be replaced by the crazed stranger, who was now at peace.

"Come on." He led her away in silence to a waiting carriage.

At the side of the carriage he stopped. Cassie stared up at him, beginning to take in everything that she'd heard. Jared had lost family, too. His brother had been killed at her aunt's crazed hands. Cassie shuddered at the memory of Vangie's callous confession.

How would Jared feel now that the truth was known? How would he feel about her?

"Jared?" Cassie said his name in a bare whisper of sound. She had to know the answer. "About your brother's death . . ." Her voice trailed off.

Jared looked down into Cassie's sweet face and knew he could answer her with absolute certainty. "It doesn't matter anymore. It's over."

"But—"

A puzzled frown drew her brows together. The Jared she knew had lived for that revenge.

"Oh, Cassie, my darling. You freed me from my consuming need for vengeance. When I knew your life was endangered, my revenge ceased to matter. All that mattered was keeping you safe." He swept her into his arms, kissing her deeply.

At long last, Jared let himself say the words that were in his heart.

"Cassie, I love you. More than my life."

She held to him tightly, hardly daring to believe the precious words she'd heard him say. His love blotted out the horror of what she'd witnessed, outshining the darkness like a brilliant burst of sunrise after a long winter night.

"Your love gave me back my life, my darling Cassie."

His breath stirred the tendrils of hair at her ear, stirring her heart as well. He drew back to gaze into her face.

"Now make my life complete," he demanded in a hoarse voice full of need. "Marry me, Cassie. Please?"

She couldn't refuse the one thing she wanted the most in the world.

"Yes! Yes! Yes!"

She threw her arms around him, and he swung her up, lifting her off her feet.

Cassie smiled a secret smile. Little did Captain Jared Montgomery know, he had swept her off her feet the first time she'd met him in the Admiral's bedroom.

"I think you're doing it again," she murmured in a soft voice overflowing with love.

"What's that?"

"Stealing, my dear thief."

"Stealing?" he asked in a velvet-soft whisper that tickled her senses.

"Umm huh. Stealing my heart," she announced.

"Forever," he whispered against her mouth.

Then Jared took her lips in a kiss to seal their love. A kiss that surely stole her very breath away.

Epilogue

Christmas, 1865

Cassie stood in the parlor doorway of her and Jared's home, watching the happy scene of her parents together. A smile tipped the corners of her lips, and she gave it free rein.

She felt her husband's approach even before she heard his booted footsteps. As always, a tingle of awareness rushed through her body in feathery strokes at his advance. It increased to a clamor in her veins as Jared nuzzled the side of her neck, raining kisses down the exposed column of her throat.

"Umm," she murmured and snuggled back into Jared's loving embrace.

Turning her head to catch a glimpse of his handsomely rugged face, she gazed at her husband with pride. He had recently earned the new rank of Major and wore it with equal pride. He still trained troops for a now-united government since the war had ended, but he was no longer the city's "masked marauder."

She smiled at the memory of her too-tempting thief, and felt a flutter of movement from the babe growing within her.

They had already chosen the name, Bryan Thomas. She had no doubt the baby would be a boy. Jared Montgomery's firstborn would be nothing else.

"I think our child agrees with you being in my arms, don't you?" he whispered, his breath stirring the fine hairs beside her ear.

A shiver of pure sensual pleasure rippled over her as he touched the tip of his tongue to the shell of her ear.

"Umm, what?" Cassie asked in a soft voice, forgetting what the question had been.

Jared's chuckle rumbled in his chest, and she felt it against her back, like a loving caress.

He slipped his hands down from beneath her breasts to let his palms rest over the swell of life within her, that was barely discernible yet. He was eagerly awaiting watching his beautiful wife as his child grew within her.

Cassie leaned her head back on his chest and savored the pleasurable feel of his rock-hard strength. She loved him even more now than the day they'd been married. And it seemed as if that love grew more each and every day.

"Well?" he lightly nipped the lobe of her ear.

Cassie giggled, causing him to tighten his loving embrace. She luxuriated in the feel of him so close against her body. It felt as if they had practically melted into one.

Well, maybe three, she added, thinking of the baby to come.

"Umm, I think maybe he does agree." She clasped her hands over Jared's. "This does seem to be the season for babies, doesn't it?"

This holiday season had brought with it the startling news of her mother's pregnancy. Even now, Cassie stared at the tell-tale swell of her mother's stomach with continued amazement.

Her father had been thrilled at the news, strutting around in a most uncharacteristic manner for him.

He'd added in a whisper to Cassie this afternoon, "Well, that should keep Alicia out of trouble. At least for a few years."

Cassie most assuredly agreed with him. A new baby should definitely keep her mama from thinking up new schemes to catapult them all into trouble. And now that her father was home and a distinguished doctor with his own practice, he could help to keep her mama occupied and loved.

Cassie thought about the two men she loved—Jared and her father. It seemed impossible to believe that scarcely a year ago they had fought on opposite sides of the war that had torn their country apart. Now, the two men worked together to heal the bodies and spirits of this new nation.

She blinked away a sheen of tears at her thoughts of the loss of the Confederacy. Now was not the time for tears; it was a time of hope and healing. The dreams and hopes inspired by the Confederacy would never truly die or be silenced, instead those very dreams would help to make this country whole again, and maybe even stronger for its separation. The future stretched before them bright and new.

"Happy?" Jared asked in a low voice that stroked her nerve endings.

"Very," she admitted with complete honesty.

So much so, that she just wanted to savor that joy a moment. Whoever would have imagined that Jared's moonlight masquerade into her bedchamber would bring about this much happiness?

Across the room, blissfully unaware that she and Jared looked on, her mama basked in her husband's attentions, while he adjusted a shawl about her shoulders and brushed a dark wisp of hair from her cheek, fussing over her hopelessly. Cassie knew that her mama loved every moment of his ministrations.

"I don't think they'd miss us if we slipped upstairs." Cassie sent Jared a daring look from lowered lashes. Her teasing smile tempted him.

He took her up on the invitation she so willing offered, and in two quick strides, he swept her into his embrace and headed for

the stairs, heedless of whether or not her
parents looked on. His lips took hers in a
kiss that packed all the potency of a bolt of
lightning. It shook her to the tips of her toes,
and she revelled in it.

Jared's kiss spoke more eloquently than
words ever could.

Unending love. Passionate desire. Forever.

Author's Note

While history records show that the plot to induce Washington to secede from the Union was squelched at its early stages, President Lincoln and his Cabinet were concerned with the possible revival of such a plot throughout the remainder of the War Between the States.

History books do not record any evidence of a second, later plot, however, I chose to base MOONLIGHT MASQUERADE on a "what if" the secession plot had been revived as a last, desperate attempt by the Confederacy.

I hope you enjoyed the possibility of "what if" with me.

Dear Reader,

I hope that you have enjoyed Cassie and Jared's story as much as I enjoyed telling it. Once again, my wish is that I have been able to bring a little love and laughter into your life. If I have succeeded, then I am happy.

My next book will be LOVING KATE and will be a change of setting for me—we will go to the wild west and a lawman every woman will dream about! However, Lucas Brannigan gets more than he bargains for the day he meets Kate Danville. Look for their rowdy and humorous story in spring 1995.

A bit about me—I was born in Missouri, south of the Mason-Dixon line. I married the man I fell in love with in high school and now live in northern California with my husband and cocker spaniel. My husband and I have lived in five states, including Hawaii where I attended college.

When not absorbed in writing, I enjoy backpacking in the Sierras with my husband or traveling together. Of course, I am also an avid reader.

I love writing romances and believe love

lasts forever. I hope my books impart the reality of love to you, my readers.

I'd love to hear from you. If you would like to write to me or to receive a bookmark, send your letter along with a stamped, self-addressed envelope to me in care of Zebra Books, 850 Third Avenue, New York, NY 10022.

Taylor—made Romance From Zebra Books

WHISPERED KISSES   (3830, $4.99/5.99)
Beautiful Texas heiress Laura Leigh Webster never imagined that her biggest worry on her African safari would be the handsome Jace Elliot, her tour guide. Laura's guardian, Lord Chadwick Hamilton, warns her of Jace's dangerous past; she simply cannot resist the lure of his strong arms and the passion of his *Whispered Kisses*.

KISS OF THE NIGHT WIND   (3831, $4.99/$5.99)
Carrie Sue Strover thought she was leaving trouble behind her when she deserted her brother's outlaw gang to live her life as schoolmarm Carolyn Starns. On her journey, her stagecoach was attacked and she was rescued by handsome T.J. Rogue. T.J. plots to have Carrie lead him to her brother's cohorts who murdered his family. T.J., however, soon succumbs to the beautiful runaway's charms and loving caresses.

FORTUNE'S FLAMES   (3825, $4.99/$5.99)
Impatient to begin her journey back home to New Orleans, beautiful Maren James was furious when Captain Hawk delayed the voyage by searching for stowaways. Impatience gave way to uncontrollable desire once the handsome captain searched *her* cabin. He was looking for illegal passengers; what he found was wild passion with a woman he knew was unlike all those he had known before!

PASSIONS WILD AND FREE   (3828, $4.99/$5.99)
After seeing her family and home destroyed by the cruel and hateful Epson gang, Randee Hollis swore revenge. She knew she found the perfect man to help her—gunslinger Marsh Logan. Not only strong and brave, Marsh had the ebony hair and light blue eyes to make Randee forget her hate and seek the love and passion that only he could give her.

Available wherever paperbacks are sold, or order direct from the Publisher. Send cover price plus 50¢ per copy for mailing and handling to Penguin USA, P.O. Box 999, c/o Dept. 17109, Bergenfield, NJ 07621. Residents of New York and Tennessee must include sales tax. DO NOT SEND CASH.